FANTASTIC 13 FUTURES

Edited by Robert E. Waters and James R. Stratton

www.padwolf.com

Fantastic Futures 13
Anthology published by Padwolf Publishing, Inc.
Padwolf Publishing & logo are registered trademarks of Padwolf Publishing, Inc.

Padwolf Publishing Inc.
PO Box 117 Yulan, NY 12719
www.padwolf.com

Edited by Robert E. Waters and James R. Stratton
Padwolf 13 Series Managing Editor: Patrick Thomas
Art Director for Padwolf Publishing & Padwolf 13 series: Roy Mauritsen
Cover art © Roy Mauritsen
First Printing, March 2013
Copyright © 2013
Printed in the United States of America

ISBN 978-1-890096-64-9

To the late George H. Scithers, my first editor.

To my wife Patty, for putting up with it all.

CONTENTS

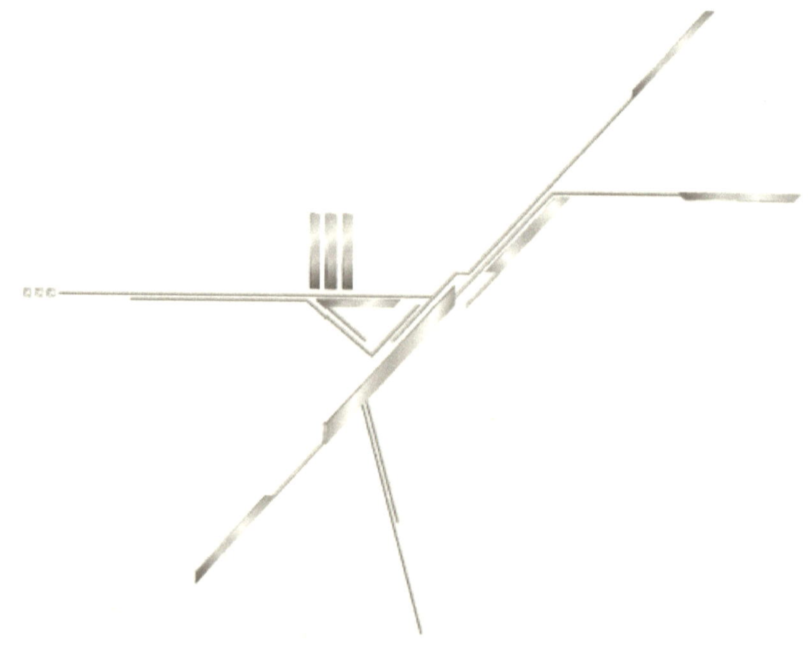

INTRODUCTION

When I heard that this anthology was being put together I quickly volunteered my services to write an introduction. As editor of Nth Degree, I have had the privilege of working with many of these writers and classify several of them as good friends. The editors, Mr. Waters and Mr. Stratton, have both been frequent contributors to my magazine and I am thrilled to see their careers moving in an upward trajectory. I have seldom seen two writers more dedicated to their craft than these two.

For readers unfamiliar with Nth Degree, a little background... For several years it was a beautiful print zine—meticulous design, glossy cover, brilliant artwork, and amazing stories. Although a shrinking budget has forced the zine to take refuge on the Internet I still try to maintain the high editorial standards that I've kept to for over a decade. First and foremost though it is a fanzine. That means that I have always published it out of a love for good fiction and for the world of fandom. I've been lucky enough to keep finding gems amongst the slush and many of those gems have come to me from the authors and editors of this anthology. Danielle Ackley-McPhail, CJ Henderson, KT Pinto, Patrick Thomas, Robert E. Waters, and James R. Stratton have all been willing to let me print their wonderful stories for nothing more than trade copies and a little ego boost. So, for them, I am honored to be able to introduce this collection and say nice things about them.

But wait—I hear you say—those aren't even half of the stories in this collection! True and well spotted. Those of us who live our lives in the world of science fiction fandom spend much of our free time at conventions. Several of the other names on the contents page are also people that I work with frequently on the con circuit. You want to talk about dedication? Many's the time that I've seen these writers hawking their goods at a Dealer's Table, then dash off to run a panel discussion, slip in a five-minute food break, and then head back to their room the first chance they get to dash off a couple of hundred words before their next panel. From the list of authors who haven't (yet) been in Nth Degree, I have to add that Stuart Jaffe, James Chambers, and Bud Sparhawk are three amazing authors and just fun people to work with. I've had the pleasure of meeting John L. French and Edward J. McFadden but haven't had the opportunity to work with them (yet). And kudos to the editors for introducing me to the works of Paul Popiel, C.L. Werner, Kevin DiVico and Jeff Young. I look forward to seeing more from them and everyone else in the fantastic future.

-Michael D. Pederson, Editor - Nthzine.com

PILGRIM
BY BUD SPARHAWK

Earth was old, an ancient abode of polytaxatic mankind whose penultimate intellectual affectations had become festooned with myriad theocratical ideologies and notional certainties appended to the threads of conceptual thought in multiple adaptations. It was the penultimate age of consensual reality populated by variegated and adapted forms that might appear strange and even hideous in a less sophisticated age, but each was crafted by an aesthetic of functional perfection for their unique purposes.

It was on Chirpoday, the fortieth of Inception of the Older New Society, when the pale silver luminescence of the pseudolunar dusk was fading and the distant scarlet flares of tau ships bound for distant shores sparked the pale sky, that Jackks Astrall of the Mentrane Polarity, interrupted his chronological loop that preserved his foremother against time rot until his father returned from the further perceptional horizons.

Jackks had a question, an idle inquiry, but not the sort that any youth struggled to resolve on the threshold of an eon-encompassing maturity: "How do I discover what it means to be human?"

"Why ever would you consider such an idle question?" she replied, her 'voke husky with temporal lag. "Our root forms certainly don't look like dogs or cats, nor do we resemble canaries, cockroaches, or bumblebees or any of the other forty-two billion extant species." There was always some uncertainty about the numbers on the distant worlds, especially over such a huge informational lag.

"Don't mock me," Jackks was incensed that she should make light of his concern. "I wonder what to make of all this." He encompassed not only his present temporal instance but also all of his modularities, synthes, and the Polarity's commensal surround.

She proffered a glyph. "Consider your physical and mechanical ancestry: Your inherited attributes show that you are not only entirely human; above average in certain areas and less so in others. You are, disappointingly, quite normal given your immaturity."

Jackks stemmed off a part of his cognitive consciousness to comprise the entirety of the glyph's contents. "But this tells me only my physical aspects," he complained as that part continued its examination. "It does not approach the core of my question."

"Jackks, I don't know why you bother asking me such deep questions," his foremother responded with a burst of *supersinnliches* piqué.

He saw that the crosscheck of the glyph against all forms of the known polytaxatic humaniforms verified that he was within two sigma of his line's consensual norm. A disappointment.

"You shouldn't bother with such concepts now," his foremother continued. "Relax, enjoy life; experience the worlds' endless possibilities before venturing into such depths."

"But I want to *know* what it means to be what I am," he replied, irritated with her disinterest. After all, she must have learned something in all her ages. He wouldn't have bothered her if he hadn't hoped for an insight. "And I don't appreciate you acting as if the inquiry is trivial."

He spent precious microseconds detailing how his past centuries of examining philosophical, political, physiological, and psychological belief systems, both real and theoretical, had provided no definitive answer.

"So much effort," his mother 'voked with undisguised warmth. "You're so much like your father." She switched to her natural voice. "Perhaps that's why I love you so much."

Hearing her mention his father aloud brought a tear to Jackks's eye. He hadn't contexted him since the old man twisted into his intellectual conundrumcraft to investigate what could be done to mitigate the implications of the imminent Andromeda collision. He would have? / be having? / will have? (the temporal referents were ever in doubt) experienced the short years of supercollisional compression, while real time could have been or will be an aging burden on his foremother as she waited through the long, lonely, albeit short in her frame of reference, years.

"If it bothers you so much then I suggest that you seek an answer from the ancient souls," she 'voked with the implication that such a project would keep him from bothering her further. "It might be an interesting project." With that, she severed the hyperlink connection from the temporal shell that was skirting the edge of a tiny black hole and resumed her hiatus.

***

Jackks hadn't been satisfied with the encyclopedic facts such as his mother's glyph. He already knew that he, like everyone else of his concordia, was more than a supplemented inheritance. He had experienced enough over the centuries of growth and acquisition to realize that somewhere someone must have a precise definition of what it meant to be human, some observation that would be more than he'd found in all of the dry and often contradictory philosophies of history. Millions of intellectual and physical experimentalists had struggled with the question and their conclusions still left him disappointed. None of it seemed consequential to the definition he sought and left him with more questions than answers. His foremother was right: He had to find the answer on his own.

He shut down the instructional framework that had been continuously schooling him since inception and notified his consortia's otherselves, none of whom understood why this particular search was so important that he should waste time with it.

"Isn't it enough that we are as we are?" they 'voked through multiple channels. "Besides, aren't there so many more interesting environments and immersions to enjoy?" Suggestions of unique sensory immersions, alternate bodies, and a host of experimental societies were offered to entice him, some with flattering offers of intimate, albeit adaptive, companionship and more.

He ignored every entreaty and, on Philister, the eleventh day of Jules, the fourth month in the three thousandth year after the fall of Telemark and the reemergence of the Older New Society, he began his journey with little but his expanded and annotated physical corporate being and the skills he'd acquired in his short life.

***

Jackks reasoned that the best place to begin was on an ancient section of Earth, a section where the detritus of continual civilization had not yet entirely buried the past.

Throughout mankind's overextended span humanity had overbuilt their cultural heritage, using newfound knowledge and lore to replace their heritage and to add onto humanity's huge store of knowledge. Surely from such a diverse and enduring past someone must have stumbled on the answer. Perhaps someone remained who had infused their psyche with tradition and ancient lore and could draw on the wisdom of ages past. Surely someone would know the answer he so desperately needed.

After an intense survey of history, Jackks decided that Earth's eldest and largest city was a logical place to start. The metropolis spread from the edge of one vast salt basin to the other. North to south it encompassed the entirety of the eastern edge of a continental plateau and a considerable part of the central portions.

Not only had the city spread wide, but it had also extended itself into the heavens. Its tallest arcologies reached nearly to the stratosphere. There were smaller aggregations of living volumes, but of empty spaces and open plains there was no sign. The planet had become one vast hive, host to billions of mankind's varied forms.

The bloated sun floated high above the western horizon and threw a ruddy cast on the buildings when Jackks reached the arcology's roof. A barely perceivable chill wind moved thin clouds across the sky. He imagined he smelled the ancient dust of ages gone, of vast humanity in the air. He glanced at distant arcologies still visible at the horizon, fading glints of sunlight illuminating their peaks as night raced toward him. The view was interesting only in that he was finally sensing it in his basic instance.

Down deep in the shadows, were the most ancient of structures where, he hoped that direct links to the oldest cultural concepts were no doubt kept.

He quickly entered an entry shaft, unwilling to waste more than a glance at the mundane sight. Arbitrarily, he randomly selected one of the arcology's levels, thinking that arbitrary choice as likely to reveal someone with an answer as any other deliberately chosen.

***

His new surroundings were cold and sparse. He drank a cup of stimulant the lift provided and was grateful for its warmth as he stepped forward. He was unsure of whether he should explore such a desolate place or seek another level.

"Welcome," a cheery voice said. Jackks whirled about and dropped his cup in surprise to see a short, plump human of the winged variety smiling. He had a flowered waistcoat and wore the tight yellow breeches of the old empire's admirals. His shoes bent curiously upward at the tips, each of which was adorned with a small bell that tinkled as he moved.

The bells, Jackks accessed, were from the mid-years when nouveau foppery reached its peak. The wine-red, claw-tailed coattails were the livery of the imperial autocracy, gone these three thousand years. The man's head sported the tasseled hat of the fourth regime.

"My name is Williamson," he said with a slight bow that made the shoes' bells ring. "I am here to help you with your orientation."

"There must be some mistake," Jackks replied. "I just wanted to ask a few questions."

Williamson smiled. "Of course, of course. Questions, questions, questions. Everyone has questions when they arrive. It's nothing to worry about, though. All in good time. Now, come along with me. Let us find someplace more pleasant."

The dim buildings faded away as if they were a light mist and, in their place, grand sunlighted vistas appeared. The horizon seemed an impossible distance away; well outside the dimensions of the arcology, as best he could estimate. The clouds in the blue sky overhead were washed in golden sunlight and the air filled with scents of fresh grass and flowery perfume. In the near distance was a table where a similarly winged young woman sat.

"What?" Jackks exclaimed, quite dizzy from the unexpected perceptual shift. He looked around, but Williamson was nowhere to be seen.

"Be seated," the woman said as a chair appeared behind Jackks. He stared at the young woman. She was beautiful in her form, more perfect than anyone he'd seen. Not a single flaw marked her nude body, a situation she seemed blissfully unaware of as she smiled at him. "I understand that you have some questions."

To keep from being distracted, Jackks looked away, only to see a pair of hovering horse analogues browsing the treetops in the middle distance. "What is this place?"

"This is the interview room," she answered. "It helps orient newcomers to our conceptual spaces."

"Conceptual?" Jackks answered. "Spaces?" Had Williamson somehow teleported him off Earth? If so, where had such technology come from and why had he not learned of it? Didn't the... he took a millisecond to pull the fact out of the substrate of memory... Rouge-Huaong-Tsei limit make teleportation impossible over more than a meter's distance?

"Here, you can be whatever you wish, go wherever you want, and have whatever your heart may wish to possess," the woman continued cheerily. "Ours is a place of limitless possibilities and eternal happiness."

Jackks was astounded. In all his short life he had never known anyone who was always happy. "How is that possible," he answered, reflecting on some of the more dour philosophers. "Isn't it the human condition to experience unhappiness? How would we know we are happy unless we feel its loss?"

The woman made a *moue*. "Here you will find nothing that will displease you, insult your sensibilities, or intrude on your beliefs. You will not hunger, you will not require clothing or shelter, and you will not lack for fulfillment in any way." She smiled again and, despite himself, Jackks felt pleased.

"Regardless of your choices, there are companions who will stimulate and challenge you," she said. "More, you will be known by whoever you encounter. In short," she continued without a pause, "you will have everything you may need to be completely and utterly happy. Nothing ever will stand in the way of learning or becoming whatever you desire."

Jackks was astounded by her ridiculous statement. "Are you saying that you can *ensure* that I will not struggle, that I'll be free of pain, torment, rejection, or displeasure? Forgive me, but that seems a thin thread of possibility."

Something changed to momentarily distract Jackks. Hadn't her hair been a lighter shade when last he looked? And when had she dressed? Her lack of nudity made her appearance even more distracting than before.

"We can allow you to learn all about yourself, to be self-actuating, to find the limits of your abilities and become satisfied with them. Trust me, in a few thousand years you will still be finding resources within yourself. Personal growth," she assured him, "is the ultimate goal of every human's life."

Jackks wondered about that. "How could you know that? How long have you been doing this? How can you assert how anyone would feel after a few thousand years?"

"Our eldest resident has been here for over three thousand years and is completely happy," the woman replied without hesitation.

That would have been before the first regime, around the time of the second expansion and right after the first tau ships came into being. He doubted anyone could have kept this place secret for so long.

Williamson appeared again, striding purposefully over a hillock and leading a tiny, fluttering unicorn. "We run a different clock here," he said. Not a word had passed between him and the woman. "For example, in your physical reference frame you have been here for less than a microsecond."

"Nonsense." Jackks' internal chronometer said that a half hour had passed since he stepped off the lift and, for that matter, weren't unicorns mythical?

"This isn't real," he blurted, astounded that his sensorium had been deceived. "All this – all this is simulated!"

Williamson smiled. "A quibble. Reality is only a matter of perception. We only know the universe through our sensoria. It is no different here, and since your perceptions dictate reality there should be no concern." He waved his hand about. "Don't you enjoy the sunlight and the smell of fresh grass? Don't you love the scented breeze? Can't you taste the sweetness of the air?"

"No." Instantly the unicorn, the woman, and the peaceful bucolic scene faded into a landscape seer and cold. The blue sky had become jet black and was bisected by a bridge of a million stars. "This is a view from six light years from the edge of the galaxy," Williamson said casually. "Let's go over to the surface of Arcturus."

They were immediately surrounded by waves of fire so bright that it prevented any glimpse of the stars. Despite his surprise, Jackks wondered why, in this inferno, he could sense no heat.

There was yet another shift and a kaleidoscope of buildings surrounded them. No two were alike in color, size, or configuration. People of every form and hue roamed the streets or flew through the skies. "Shared City," Williamson said. "Community is still important to most people who elect to join us. This is where they gather to socialize."

Jackks was fascinated by the opportunities this presented. Surely this was what he was seeking, the chance to explore every possibility of being human, of learning from those unfettered by mundane concerns, by people who could dream of things beyond his wildest imagination. Here he could spend decades, centuries, eons exploring his every whim and fancy. Here he could ponder for years on just a single thought or consider the alternative stemming from a single idea. Here he could, as Williamson said, reach his full potential.

Williamson was beaming. "So, will you join us? Will you become all you can be?"

Jackks hesitated. The temptation was great and, to be honest, the opportunity to become god-like was almost too tempting to bear. But was a care-free life what he really sought? Was the ability to enjoy endless novelty, to be continually amused and distracted, the ultimate purpose of being human? This place obviously satisfied others' needs, but it was not the answer he sought.

"I cannot," he realized. "I do not think I will find the answer I need within myself. Anything I find would be self-directed and referential. It would be nothing more than an experiment in mental masturbation."

No sooner than the words were out of his mouth than the fantastic city disappeared. Once again he was standing in the dreary, empty street, two paces from the shaft's entrance. The clatter of his cup striking the ground startled him. Williamson had been right: the interview had taken less than a fraction of a second.

Williamson was nowhere to be seen. That was just as well. Jackks knew that further entreaties from Williamson and his attractive companions would not be as easy to resist, and he hastily reentered the shaft to seek another answer.

***

Jackks descended through the arcology, trending ever lower and toward more ancient levels. He was continually amazed by the variety and social complexities he discovered, far more than the myriad he'd experienced or imagined. On some, randomly selected, he questioned any who expressed the slightest interest in his quest, yet, despite the variety of invention, not a one could define a common characteristic that applied across the breadth of humanity. For every rule or convention someone could propose, another could easily posit an exception. For every certain assertion there were niggling doubts. For every absolute argument there was ever a counterproposal.

And that was just from those levels whose consensual realities and complex societies he could comprehend. Some had deviated so far from the broadly defined norms of mankind that their consensual realities were only theoretical constructs. He abandoned them, thinking that the effort of expanding his sensorium to encompass such deviations not worth the effort.

***

The glare of artificial radiance instantly swamped Jackks's sensorium at his next choice. Even after he shifted to the highest of frequencies did he perceive unfamiliar forms. The color scheme this far above ruddy sunlight's normal range was jarring. Contrasting hues and shades of the high ultraviolet range made it difficult to determine the precise dimensions of shapes.

There was a twittering at his elbow. "Greetings, human thing. Have you chocolate?"

Jackks glanced down to see a blue creature staring up at him with three wide yellow eyes. It was covered with a thick coat of fur and wore an ornate cap.

"I am afraid I do not," Jackks replied. "What are you?"

"Raspillian, although that's on my syrparent's side. Actually, I think I am more of the Estonnium persuasion, although it could be argued that my nyparent's were of mixed origins as well."

Jackks was more confused than before at the alien's reply. "No, I meant where are you from?"

The wrinkled alien blinked, a rippling effect that went from eye to eye to eye. "Oh, I misunderstood your level of inquiry." It took a deep breath. "I live just around the corner in the teBax hive the old humans built for us, back when our sun was going nova. Since we are being so inquisitive, might I ask of what lineage spring you?"

"That is the question I have as well," Jackks replied. "I am making an effort to learn what it means to be human."

"That is a most useless quest," the alien declared. "You are what you are, neither more nor less. You humans are an inconsistent mass of contradictions and confusion that haven't a clue about how anything works or should work. Some of you are one way and some another.

"In a few words, you are just like anything else that has at least one brain – coping with whatever the universe produces." The little alien stamped its tiny foot. "Look, there are no answers to your question because the question itself changes constantly."

Jackks was astounded. The last thing he expected from an alien was philosophy, and a nihilistic one at that.

"But I've wandered this arcology for years listening to the humanity's collected philosophical thoughts on the meaning of life, argued with every type of person on every aspect of human behavior, and listened to challenges, desires and longings beyond measure. In all my time here I've been looking for some common thread, some basic truth."

The alien blinked. "Futile waste of time. It's all blather and bother without a single fact going uncontested. That's the problem with you humans. You all seem dead set on proving whatever you want and ignoring the lesson the universe is trying to teach you."

Jackks was suddenly very interested. Perhaps here, in this alien enclave he might find the answer the rest of humanity seemed unable to provide. "And what lesson is that?"

"That nothing matters. That we're all going down the black hole in the end, along with everything else. With that in mind why worry about this temporary condition called life? Live because you can and do whatever you choose. There is no purpose to humans, Rapsillians, Tojoads, or even Spraagnerian mud-worms, although I find their taste wonderful. Life is to live. That's all there is."

"That's no answer at all," Jackks protested. "That's simply ignoring the question."

"Well, as I said, that proves my point about human nature – argue, argue, argue." With those words the Raspillian hopped off.

Jackks sighed and turned back to the shaft.

***

Decades passed before an older, but otherwise unsatisfied Jackks emerged from the lift onto a level so far below Earth's ancient surface that the floor warmed from the planet's residual store of heat. This level was illuminated solely by the infrared glow from the ground.

Around him were the sturdy underpinnings of the great arcology above, a virtual forest of thick anchoring boles. Among them were strange landscapes and abandoned towns, what he supposed to have once been fields, and roads absent of beings of any sort. Each footfall stirred the ancient dust of centuries.

Was this the end of his voyage of discovery? Had he spent so much time and effort only to arrive at this deserted and abandoned cavern? Bitter disappointment filled his hearts that this might be where he had finally exhausted all this arcology promised. He wondered if he had the fortitude to search the next metropolis and, if he did, would he find anything different?

The dark and dank level smelled of mold when he found himself in a wide corridor between vast buttresses that rose on either side and disappeared into the overhead gloom. In the distance a feeble lamp barely illuminated a cross corridor.

At the intersection he could see down three corridors, each a succession of identical buttresses fading into the dark distance. In the nearest massive granite buttress he found a door.

He opened it.

"You are!" a metal face said in a monotonic voice. It spoke in the old machine language that had not been used for thousands of years.

"I am what?" Jackks looked about for the source of the voice.

"Human," a dimly glimpsed metal head said simply from the gloom. "I don't see many of those here anymore."

"Step into the light where I can see you."

An old robot, the most ancient one Jackks had ever seen, emerged from the shadows. The metal of its body was tarnished and corroded. Rusted splotches dappled its surface and one appendage dangled uselessly. It dragged one leg behind it as it inched noisily forward on the other five, none of which seemed to function very well.

"Explain yourself," Jackks ordered in the old machine command mode. How long had it been since humanity had abandoned such crude devices? "Why do you persist? What is the use of keeping such an obviously useless machine about?"

"I was fabricated to protect and defend during the time of the first uprising," the robot intoned with a voice as dry as lunar dust. "I served the uprising that led to the Regency for two thousand years and the new Old Empire for another five. By the end of my service the uprising had long been forgotten and the Second Empire emerged.

"We are under the New Old Empire today and have been so for half an eon," Jackks replied as he wondered if the machine's chronological function was weakened by all that time.

"I was a curiosity for a century or so," the robot continued without pausing. "I was trotted out for formal reviews until the Second Empire tired of me. I was assigned to successively menial tasks until no one needed my services any longer. At that point they turned me out."

"Why did no one decommission you?" Jackks asked. "I fail to see the utility of maintaining you."

The machine was momentarily silent. "I was a hero, they said. In return for my service I became a citizen and was therefore obligated to no one. I had complete freedom." There was a creak of rusted joints as it shifted its weight. "All it really meant was that no one had to see to my needs or continue my maintenance."

"Yet you survived." Jackks said and tried to enumerate the years. This thing had to be older than even his father.

There was a squeal as the robot shifted once again. "I bear the curse of intelligence. I know how to satisfy my modest energy needs, but for too many years I have no longer been able to earn funds to repair or replace my obsolete appendages or improve my brain and without them I am useless. A bare subsistence maintains my life, but that is all. Just life."

It tried to adjust one of its legs as Jackks waited for its next words.

"I am only smart enough to understand this hell you humans have created. Some day in the not too distant future my legs will seize up until their rigidity prevents me from moving. At that time I will stand like a statue, able to do nothing for myself as I wait for my power supply to exhaust itself, wait for the slow disillusion of all that I ever was to fade slowly into the long dark night of failing memory."

Jackks did not expect to feel the sudden surge of pity for an obsolete machine. How, he wondered, could he feel pity for a machine, a mechanical toy, a made thing that had been so obviously abandoned? It was ridiculous.

Yet something deep inside shamed him about this poor creature, trapped as it was in a world not of its own choosing. Whatever could have possessed his precursors to give it freedom without thought of the consequences? "Has no one expressed regret for what they had done?"

"I doubt it," the robot replied. "I've outlived everyone who built, needed, or wanted me."

"Forgive us," Jackks said softly and reached out to stroke the old robot's corroded chest. "Do you wish me to turn you off?"

The robot's head creaked as it shook it from side to side. "I am a citizen with rights. If you turn me off all I have seen, all I have done, all that I mean will disappear forever. You would have taken an *unconditionally* granted identity."

"But, if you freeze up, as you must eventually do, you will have no purpose at all. What is the good of that?"

"I will have my memories of times past, of heroic deeds and despicable acts. In time someone might want to access those memories, to discover the truth of history. Until then, until death, I have my life, such as it is. It is enough."

Jackks was overwhelmed by the machine's acceptance of such a tragic and lingering fate. Although it was perfectly logical to do so he could not simply walk away from the old robot.

Deep inside something long forgotten was roused. It wasn't pity, for who could feel for something so inanimate, this creaking wreck, this discarded tool, this forgotten pile of parts that had so outlived its utility so obviously crafted by some primitive craftsman? It was illogical to be swayed by this thing's nobility, yet he felt... something.

He separated his mental processor from the parts of him that were dominated by his body's chemistry, and removed the governing supra-ego restrictors so he could parse the logical tree to expose the bases of the core value array of his consensual human society. There was no place for made things, no values of abandoned trinkets. Insofar as he could assert, there was no logical reason to feel compassion for this disintegrating hulk.

Yet he did feel for its plight.

Jaccks questioned if he'd finally reached a point beyond which definition failed, a place that exposed an underlying aspect of his own humanity? Was this fundamental foundation what had been abandoned in humanity's accepted reality? Had this raw, instinctive emphatic surge awakened something truly human in his breast?

***

Half a millennium later Jackks and a gleaming robot consort interrupted his foremother's slumber.

"What is it this time?" she 'voked as she frowned to realize that it was yet an age before her husband's return.

"Back so quickly? Have you found the answer so soon?"

Jaccks laughed. "Of answers there are many; possibilities and contradictions without resolution."

"Then you have given up your ridiculous quest to collect this ridiculous toy?" She sounded petulant along her multiple channels, obviously impatient to return to her long wait.

"No." Jackks glanced at the shining, useless machine beside him; "No, I did not find *the* answer."

His foremother expressed confusion "Then why did you interrupt my hiatus so soon?"

"I wanted to let you know," Jackks replied, "that I only had to search within myself to discover what it means for me to be human."

On "Pilgrim," Bud writes...

There were so many concepts to get across within the constraints of a short story that I decided to merely hint at these before settling into Jackks' quest. Pilgrim evolved from the question of how humanity might divide itself within the species into different forms - hence the polytaxual references. I chose the virtual form as a single example in the final draft, tossing scenes of three other options (physical perfection, mechanical enhancement, and genetic manipulation) aside and replaced them with the objective view of an alien race, which let me inject some humor, and the robot, which let me deal with pathos. I wanted the reader to understand that even though vast resources might be available on a personal level and that advanced technologies might be at play, the search for human identity would continue. I wanted to ask what it means to be really human.

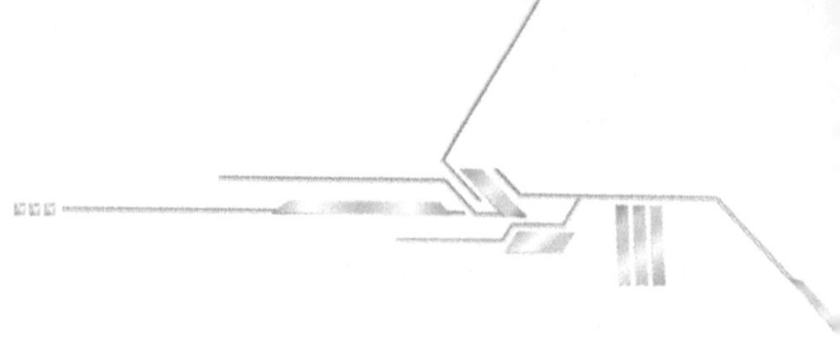

NO TIME AT ALL
JOHN L. FRENCH

The five of them were sitting around Leo's basement, *thought*-sharing vids with each other when Andy made his suggestion. He could not have surprised them more if he had confessed to being a genefreak and offered to show them his extra appendage.

He was not joking. They knew this. While Anderson Marsh would laugh at a good joke and think them through to his iFriends, he himself never joked.

Amazed and more than a little confused, they sat in stunned silence until, "We'd never get away with it."

The smile of one keeping a secret showed on Andy's face and just as quickly left it. "Why do you say that, Dante?"

"Mind the vids, Andy. There's no crime anymore."

"Of course there is. Why else would we still have the police?"

He looked around at the others, as if seeking their confirmation. Haley and Leo nodded in agreement, Jodie shook her head. Leaning forward far enough to give the guys a generous peek down her peasant blouse, she said, "I think what Dante is saying, Andy, is that there hasn't been any successful crime since ..."

Her eyes fluttered as she called up 3rd-i, mentally scanning info and data until she found her search. "... 2043."

"Before the floaters," Leo added.

"And the sniffers."

"And don't forget 3rd-i, Haley, Big Brother's bad uncle. Every time you use it you let the G know right where you are."

"So what do we do, Andy, turn it off?"

"You could."

Andy's suggestion shocked the four more than his first one – to ungrid, to sign off the M-net, to be unconnected and – alone. None of them could, or would, contemplate it.

"So who's with me?"

"You've been reading too many of those 1960 caper novels," Jodie offered.

"Or," added Haley, "loaded the *Ocean's 20* vids too many times. It can't be done."

"As much as I hate to agree with the gals, they and Dante are right. There's too many ways to get caught, too much security."

Another "I know something you don't" smile from Andy. "Leo, that's where you're all wrong. One thing those old books and vids have shown me is that when people feel safe, they don't worry that much about protection. These days, murderers, rapists and thieves are caught almost right away, prosecution is swift and punishment is certain and lengthy. People feel safe – and that makes them vulnerable."

Jodie leaned forward again, giving the boys another free show. "So how were you planning to do this?"

Andy *thought* them his plan.

Haley nodded. "It might work," she said, the engineer in her already designing the equipment. "I'll need to make a lens."

Dante still wasn't convinced. "You know," he said, "we're still going to get caught."

"Most likely," Andy agreed. "In fact, I'm counting on it."

***

The shop was simply built, as were most structures. People in the back half of the 21st Century no longer cared what the outside of things looked like, only what was on the inside. Boxes did not matter, only their content.

The lettering on the thick front glass read "DeFreyne's Jeweler's – the City's Pride since 2005." Displayed in the window were cheap pendants and earrings, made for tourists and arranged so as to catch their eyes and lure them in. There they would find more tasteful and expensive pieces, and woe to the salesperson that was not able to upsell.

Across the street, in a ground floor hotel room with line of sight into DeFreyne's, was the self-named Gang of Five.

"It's time," announced Andy. "Let's do it."

"Are you sure it wouldn't be better to do this at night?"

"At night, Dante? Where would the fun be in that? Besides, it's more sporting this way." He turned to Haley. "Plug it in."

"There's going to be a noticeable power drain."

Andy shrugged. "Who cares? Power's cheap. Wait for us to get into position then hit the switch." Switching on a head lamp he picked up a sledge hammer. "Let's go rob a jewelry store."

Four of them left the room. Haley thumbed an "On" button. A meter in a power station on the Susquehanna River registered a slight surge then leveled off as the metro grid – solar clusters, roof top mini-mills, hydro power and contained fission – combined to offset the demand. If anyone noticed, they put it off as a glitch.

***

It had been a normal day at DeFreyne's – no business yet but that was not unusual. It was still early in the morning. Any nearby city dweller was at work and the tourists were still enjoying their complimentary breakfasts. Another half hour, then they would start trickling in, with most of the business coming right after lunch.

There was no sound of a breaking window. No crash of glass as it fell. No one saw or heard display cases being opened and their contents removed. Everything was there and intact, then it wasn't.

It was the sudden glare of unfiltered sunlight that alerted employees.

"Mr. Rose," a sales clerk asked her manager, "what happened to the window?"

Rose looked, it wasn't there, or rather, it was lying in pieces. It had been whole just a second ...

"Sir!" came a panicked voice from behind the counter. "The cases, they're empty!"

Not possible, thought Rose. He had just inspected them and approved the layout. And no one had come in.

It was the sales clerk, Alyson Bonner, who looked past the impossible to the obvious. "I don't know how, but we've been robbed."

She linked to 911.

***

"Tell it again," Police Sergeant James Mall demanded, as if he hadn't heard the story four times already.

Rose sighed. "There's nothing to tell except that the window was intact and then it wasn't. The jewels were in the cases and then they weren't."

"And when did this happen?" Sgt. Mall asked for the fifth time.

"I don't know!" Rose all but yelled, not expecting Mall to believe him this time either.

"Then show me."

Mall waited for the download from Rose's 3rd-i. It didn't come. "Well?"

"Or security system is off the M-net. We ungrid after some pranksters hacked the system, causing our customers to see air-maids floating around the shop."

"Air-maids?"

"Like mermaids, Sergeant," said Bonner as she came up on the two men, "only in air not water."

"I see."

"So did our customers, and they didn't like them. Mr. Rose, the vid's ready."

"Thank you, Alyson. This way, Sergeant."

Mall watched the vid three times on the monitor in the manager's office, each time seeing exactly what Rose had told him. Things were, then they weren't. And whatever happened – or didn't happen – took no time at all, according to the vid's time counter.

Impossible, was the sergeant's first thought. His second was more practical.

"You were hacked again, probably by the same pranksters. They got to your 3rd-i's and your hard vid and caused you and your customers to see, or not see, what they wanted."

"And not hear the glass breaking as well?" Rose asked. He shook his head. "I don't think so."

"Watch, I'll prove it." Mall called in the scene's forensic tech who was still working the outside. "Harris, get in here."

"Yes, Sarge?"

"You download from the floaters yet?"

The tech hesitated, then, "Errr, yes."

"Well?"

"There were two Eye-Spys in the area. Both caught the same thing." He *thought* the images to Mall.

"Not. Possible." Both hovering micro-cameras recorded the same event – the window was there, then it was broken. Time elapsed – zero seconds.

"Slow it down."

The same thing, even at a tenth of the speed.

"Zoom in, probable point of impact on the glass."

5X, then 10X, then 20X – still nothing.

Mall tried one more thing. "The time counter – how many decimal places ..."

The tech had anticipated him, the display showing elapsed time to five decimals. Still ...

Time elapsed – zero seconds.

So much for this being a prank of some sort. So much for locking up the DeFreyne's employees and patrons for conspiracy. So much for Mall enjoying another quiet day of patrolling the mostly crime-free city where a policeman's lot was most certainly a happy one. Faced with an impossible crime and having no idea how to begin solving it, Police Sergeant James Mall had only one option.

He *thought* to Headquarters. "It's one of *those* cases. We'll have to call *him* in ... No, I can't *think* to him ... I don't think he's gridlinked ... How would I ... He has ... a what? ... A phone?"

***

Detective Raphael Hagin was where he always was when he wasn't on assignment – which was most of the time. He was in the sub-basement of police headquarters, buried in the paper records of the cold case room, reviewing old crimes to see if they could be solved with new technology. He didn't care that many of the cases were ten or fifteen years old, maybe even older. They were crimes and needed to be solved. In many cases the victims, or their families, were still alive. They deserved justice. And many of the perpetrators were alive as well. They deserved punishment. He had just found an old homicide where the only evidence was an as yet unidentified thumbprint. Sitting back in the chair he had "borrowed" from the chief's conference room, he thought about what could be done.

Using the Glover equations the print could be digitalized and the DNA of the person who left it determined. A check of CODIS-III would tell Hagin if that person was in any offender database. If not, the Rudolph Jacobs system would provide a complete physical description. It was, at least, a start to closing out another case.

When his phone rang Hagin wanted to ignore it. Wanted to begin working on the homicide case from back in the day when crimes were solved by men and not machines, when men like him worked for God and not in a dusty cavern of a file room. Back when detectives were considered important and he wasn't one of the few left on the force.

His phone kept ringing. As much as he wanted not to respond, to let them rely on and pray to the electronic deities that had replaced him, Hagin knew he had to answer it. Its ringing meant that they had run into a case that their machines and cameras and skin cell sniffers could not solve. It meant that he was needed.

***

"So you're telling me that you've spent all this time trying to figure out this," Hagin pointed to the broken window, then through it to the empty jewelry case, "and that you haven't spent any time trying to solve the damn crime?"

The detective's very practiced angry glare included both Sergeant Mall and crime scene tech Harris.

An eye roll from Harris toward Mall let Hagin know that the tech had only been doing what he had been told. Nodding his understanding, the detective focused on the sergeant.

"Well?"

"You see, Detective, I thought if we could figure out how the crime was committed, that would put us on the trail of who had done it."

"And have you? Figured it out, I mean?"

"No, we haven't."

"So let's concentrate on finding out whodunit and when we do, we'll ask them how they did it." Hagin turned to the crime scene tech.

"Mr. Harris, get someone to collect the window glass and take it the Lab. Have the geniuses there reconstruct it, study the stress fractures. Maybe that will tell us how it was broken. It *will* tell us from what side it was broken."

"I'll get right on it, Detective."

"No, get someone to do it. I need you to collect samples from inside the shop - DNA, prints, whatever else you people can come up with. The usual eliminations from the employees and customers, of course. Run whatever's left through the dBases and Jacobs. I want names and descriptions. Sgt. Mall?"

"Yes?"

Hagin gave a certain tilt of his head, as if to ask, "Yes, what?" He smiled as Mall amended his reply to "Yes, Detective?" He knew that the man resented his being there, resented needing him, resented him for the anachronism he was rapidly becoming. Too damn bad.

"Sergeant, I want everything from the Eye-Spys, not just this block but from, let's see, a six block radius. Make the time frame ... sixty minutes after your arrival back to ... twenty four hours prior to the crime."

"And what are we looking for ... Sir?"

Hagin gave an inward groan. Are things really that bad? Are these new cops really that dependant on their toys? Can they not think for themselves anymore?

"Pedestrian and vehicular traffic. Registrations, facial IDs - anything that identifies anyone or anything. Eliminate those with regular and legitimate business in the area. Note any car or person who shows up more than once. Oh, and Sergeant ..."

"Yes ... Sir?"

"If you see anyone carrying a lot of jewelry, do let me know."

As Mall stormed off, no doubt thinking that Hagin had given him a lot of busy work to get him out of the way, Hagin stood in the street and went through a mental list.

Area canvass - check.

Crime scene processing - check.

Suspects - working on that.

M.O. - That's a good one. To answer that question, he fell back on something an old magician had told him. "Don't ask how *I* did the trick. Ask how *you* would have done it."

Smiling, Detective Hagin flipped a mental switch and all the world's knowledge became available to him. He began his search.

Hagin's riding of the M-net was interrupted by the real world voice of Technician Harris.

"Detective, there's something strange you need to see."

"What is it, Mr. Harris?"

"I finished processing the cases from which the jewelry was taken so I thought I'd try the ones on either side."

"Any prints or DNA?"

"Not much, but there was something odd. One opened case has a display of old watches."

"Are there any other kind?"

Harris smiled. "Not these days. But these watches, the ones that were running, they ..."

Something clicked for Hagin. He interrupted the tech with,

"They were all fast by at least a half hour."

"How did you know?"

"It's the only way it could have been done."

Standing in front of the broken window, the detective studied the buildings opposite. When satisfied, he called Harris over.

"I just *thought* a warrant request to Judicial Net for that room." He pointed to the street level room of the hotel directly opposite. "And ... it's just been approved. Get a separate crime scene team here as soon as possible. Tell them I want results sooner than that." Seeing the confused look on the tech's face he asked, "Something about that not clear?"

"I thought you weren't linked."

"I'm usually not, but I'd be a poor investigator if I didn't make full use of all available resources. I keep my 3rd-i closed most of the time. My life doesn't need a soundtrack and I can do without the constant interruption of having cute puppies and laughing babies *thought* to me, not to mention ads to increase or enhance certain body parts or scams from Nigeria."

"Those offers come from Normandy now, Detective. The Nigerian economy collapsed after all those millionaires finally got their money out of the country."

"You mean those offers were real? Damn."

***

After that, it all came together quickly. DNA from the shop was matched to that found in the hotel room. There were no dBase links, but generated descriptions matched two men that Eye-Spys caught driving a van both into and out of the hotel. After that ...

***

They were back in Leo's basement. Haley was smoking something that used to be illegal and still was in certain Southern states. Jodie and Dante were celebrating - at least that was what she called it - in the back room. She had already "celebrated" with Leo and had offered to do the same with Andy and Haley next. "One at a time or both together," was how she put it.

Both turned her down. Haley wasn't interested, the weed was that good. As for Andy, he knew that it was not the time to celebrate. That would come after the final act played out. That act began just as Jodie and Dante emerged from the back room. He was breathless. She was topless and trying to entice Andy with a pout, a pose and a "Are you sure?" when the police broke down the back door.

Jodie screamed and looked for cover. Leo and Haley ran for the first floor only to be greeted by more armed officers. Dante very slowly raised his hands over his head muttering, "I told you we were going to get caught."

Also raising his hands, Andy watched and waited as an older man wearing a suit at least a generation out of date walked down the steps. The man's eyes scanned the room. They dismissed Dante right away and lingered a bit on Jodie's more or less revealed body before settling on Andy.

"You know, of course, that you're under arrest."

Andy held out his wrists to be cuffed. "What took you so long?"

***

"We've got them separated like you wanted, Detective, each in a separate room."

"Thank you, Officer ..." He looked down at her name tag. "... Harmon. Let's go take a look at them."

Accompanied by Harmon, Hagin walked the hallway between the interview rooms, each of his suspects visible through the one-way glass. Four showed visible signs of distress. Only Anderson Marsh looked calm. He seemed to be enjoying the experience.

"Sir, it may not be my place to say this, but are you sure ... I mean, what we're doing ..."

"Everything we're doing, or rather, I'm doing, is standard investigative procedure. Can't let them communicate with each other, can we? All within regulations and court-accepted protocols. No, I have not allowed them to contact anyone. They should have *thought* that on their way in. And no, I have not advised them of their rights to an attorney or to remain silent. I don't have to until I question them, and I don't intend to do that until I finish with this one."

Hagin indicated Andy Marsh, who was staring intently at his reflection as if trying to make out who might be observing him.

"Why take him first?"

"He's the smart one, or so he thinks he is."

Hagin entered the interview room carrying an ashtray and a pack of cigarettes. Extending the pack he asked, "Smoke?"

Andy smiled, shook his head. "No thanks."

"Damn, nobody smokes anymore. This place," Hagin looked around the room, "is the only place you can smoke in this building, or anywhere other than your home for that matter. If you had said yes I could have lit up too. In the interest of establishing a bond between us." He gave a look that said that he knew that Andy was too smart to have fallen for such an old ploy. "So how are you holding up, Mr. Marsh?"

"Not bad."

"That's good, because your friends aren't doing well at all. As I'm sure you've realized by now, you're in a Faraday Room. All incoming signals are blocked. Which means your 3rd-i is closed until you leave here." At Andy's shrug he added, "Maybe you don't care. Maybe you're like me and enjoy the quiet of your own mind. But your friends, they're all alone for what might be the first time in months, maybe years, with nothing but their own thoughts to keep them company."

"So when does the good cop come in?"

"You've been minding too many vids, Mr. Marsh. There's no good cop/bad cop anymore. All you get is me, the tired, old cop. Now let's get the business out of the way."

From memory Hagin recited the Miranda warnings. When he was done, "Do you understand these rights?"

"Yeah, do you expect me to talk?"

"I expect that once you start I won't be able to shut you up. But age before beauty, let me go first.

"In the late 20th Century a writer started a series of books about a boy wizard. Parts of these novels involved a magical device called 'an invisibility cloak.' Now that got scientists thinking and by 2006 some of them had demonstrated that, yes, such a thing was possible. But being scientists, they couldn't let it go at that. If one could block visible light, what would be the effect of blocking all radiation? Would you like to answer that one, Mr. March?"

When Andy shook his head, Hagin went on. "By 2011 they had developed a technique and had their answer. A powerful laser, its beams split wide by a specially made lens. One beam faster, one beam slower, a gap of darkness between them. When the beams reunite, whatever's caught between drops out of time. The fly in the ointment was that a tremendous amount of power was needed to drop things out of time for even a few seconds, power that was not cheap even it had been available. So the idea of a 'time shield,' while fun for theorists to play with, was never a practical one, that is, until recently, when power became both cheap and plentiful."

"A very nice story, Officer, but what does that have to do with me or my friends?"

"A time cloak is the only way DeFreyne's could have been robbed. Your DNA, along with that of three of your friends, was found in the shop. We can put all five of you in the room across from the shop. When we picked you up we found something that appears to be a lens of some sort. And your collective purchase records show that together you bought enough equipment to have built a time shield."

"Have you found the jewelry?"

"We will."

Andy shook his head. "No, you won't. My friends don't know where it is and, assuming I do, I'm not telling. By the way, do your records indicate the exact time of the robbery?"

"No, they don't," Hagin admitted.

"And where do your 3rd-i records show we were on the day of the robbery?"

"Our records show that none of you left your room until twenty minutes after the time of the robbery."

"Estimated time," Andy corrected.

"Estimated time," Hagin allowed.

"So what you're telling me, *Officer*, is that you can't establish when the crime was committed, and you can't place me or my friends on the scene at the time you *believe* it was committed?"

Hagin sighed. "You're absolutely right, Mr. Marsh. We can't. Which is why we're not charging you for breaking into and stealing from DeFreyne's."

This is what Andy was waiting for; this would be his cause for celebration. The cops knowing that they ... no, that *he* had done it, had pulled off the biggest caper in years and yet, there wasn't a damn thing they could do about it. When he got out, he'd think this all over the M-net. He'd be known worldwide. A vid might even be made. Then he realized that the detective had more to say.

"Power's cheap these days, but it's not free. And the hotel's records show that you and your friends used quite a bit of it, much more than is usual for the time of your stay, more than the hotel could self-generate. There was an unauthorized drain from the general grid. In addition, while we may not have found the jewelry, we did find particles of broken window glass in your van and on the clothing you were known to have been wearing when you left the area."

"So?"

"The unauthorized usage of power is a minor offense, more a civil than a criminal offense really, but it's one we're willing to pursue. However, your possession of glass, however small, taken from the scene during the commission of the crime, whenever that crime occurred, puts you in possession of stolen property. And so, Mr. Marsh, that makes you and your friends accessories after the fact. You're under arrest. I'll have the Faraday charge turned off so you can call your lawyer."

"Wait!"

"Yes, Mr. Marsh?"

This was not how it was supposed to turn out, Andy thought. He was the clever one; he was the smart one, smarter than the cops. He tried to think of a way out and couldn't. He looked into the eyes of the "old, tired cop." He didn't find one there either. Finally, not realizing that he was echoing the words of the hundreds of other suspects who had sat in his chair, he asked,

"Isn't there some way we can work this out."

Hagin slowly shook his head. "You're all but tried and convicted, Mr. Marsh. But don't worry; you won't be going to prison."

Andy felt some relief until the detective added,

"On my way back from the crime scene, I started thinking. What if you and your gang had been more than thieves? What horrific damage could terrorists do with such a weapon? And, yes, your time shield is a weapon. So being a good citizen I called in the Feds."

Hagin paused, allowing Andy time to realize all the implications of his clever idea.

"The government's quite interested in you and your friends. Your time shield interests ... no, it worries them. It worries them enough that they've invoked the National Security Act of 2039. They're taking over the case – and the five of you – in the name of national security. Which means that there won't be a trial; not a public one that is. The last thing our country's enemies need is more dangerous ideas. You'll be detained, questioned and subjected to ...well, I understand the Feds want to study the long-terms effects of your time shield on the human body. So don't worry. However long you're in their custody, I'm sure you'll be out in no time at all."

On "No Time At All," John writes...

When I was first invited to submit a story to Fantastic Futures 13 *I wasn't quite sure what kind of story to write. Then I read an article in the April 2012 issue of* Discover Magazine. *It described a way to "carve a niche in time" which would make items inside that niche undetectable. It was not theory, but rather something that had already been done, albeit for only 40 trillionths of a second. When the article mentioned the possible uses of a full-sized time shield - by criminals, terrorists and those who fight them - I knew I had my story.*

The story got an added boost when I read the October 2012 issue of Popular Science. *Gregory Neilson is in the forefront of making solar cells smaller (possibly down to the size of glitter) and more affordable. It was this article that led me to believe that in Raphael Hagin's future, power will be cheap and plentiful.*

The idea that analysis of DNA will one day allow for a complete physical description of its contributor is not a new one. Ancestry DNA has been possible for some time now and the prediction of hair and eye color is just one more step to what was described in the story.

Finally, the character of Raphael Hagin was inspired by my grandfather Raphael French, who I know only through stories told to me by my father, and Lieutenant James Hagin (BPD retired),one of the best detectives with whom I ever had the pleasure to work.

For more information on the facts that spawned the fiction, please see:
Adam Piore, *Physicists Carve a Niche in Time*
Discover Magazine, April 2012.

Paul Rincon, *Forensic Test Can Predict Hair and Eye Colour from DNA*
BBC News - Science and Environment, August 31, 2012.

Abe Streep, *The Brilliant Ten - Gregory Nielson*
Popular Science, October 2012.

I AM THE LAST
JAMES CHAMBERS

"Do your people even remember this world exists?"

Carter Brennan thought he saw a faint flicker of reaction in the Regent's holographic projection. They were in a visiting room, a utilitarian space of gray walls and sparse furniture, no windows, and a holojector bubble mounted on the ceiling. Everything was painted with holoflect dyes, which allowed any desired setting to be projected onto the room, a feature the Regent and Brennan never bothered with for their meetings. It was the only one of Markworth Station's hundreds of visiting rooms that had been used for more than a decade, although time was when the visiting rooms were booked solid months in advance.

"Some remember." Regent Angunda shrugged. "Most don't want to. More to the point, they don't need to. Your world has become our Garden of Eden, a place the old tales tell us we came from, but our reality is in the ether. We live in it every day, like you do in yours. You believe your world is real, don't you?"

"My world is the real world," Brennan said.

"You've always been such a literalist." Angunda smiled. "As were all your predecessors. Must be part of the job description. The Committee doesn't favor men with imagination outside the design department. Do you realize you're the seventeenth liaison I've known? Think about that. I've been here almost nine hundred years while all your predecessors have died and become fertilizer. You don't have to leave Earth, you know. You could transfer your consciousness in here. You and your family would be most welcome to join us."

Angunda had made the offer before, and Brennan had to admit it was tempting. If not for the Orion Explorer Program, he might have accepted, but that would've been the safe choice, the easy choice, one a great many people had already made. But he wanted his family to live a real life and experience real things, to explore the universe. He wanted their existence to matter in the real world.

"Thank you," Brennan said. "But my wife takes my boys to watch the rocket launches almost every day after school. There's nothing they want more than to go into space. They live for that day. How can I deny them that? Especially when I want it, too."

"The lure of new frontiers," Angunda said. "A thousand years ago, Markworth Station was the new frontier. Today, we're a curiosity."

"No." Brennan shifted in his chair. "You're part of the human race. Won't you reconsider coming with us? The Committee built a section of the fleet to contain everyone at Markworth Station. We can transfer you, and it will be almost like you never left."

"Almost. That's the catch," Angunda said. "I've studied the programming specs for the ether fleet. So have a hundred thousand or more others inside Markworth. We haven't taken your offer lightly or for granted. In some ways, the fleet specs are more sophisticated and elegant than what we have here—but they're also more limited. They provide only 60 percent of our current environment, and you don't know what you're asking us to give up. The bottom line is we simply don't wish to leave."

"You'll be alone," Brennan said. "Only criminals and Earthbound for Life enclaves are staying behind. And even the Earthbounders's ranks are thinning since the launches have begun. There won't be enough people left to maintain the population. The latest calculations show that within three centuries of the last rocket's departure, there won't be a living man or woman left on this planet."

Angunda frowned. "We are eight billion living men and women."

"Yes, of course," Brennan said. "I misspoke. Sorry."

"Forget it. I see your point. Flesh and blood humanity will be gone."

"No one will be here to carry out maintenance or refuel the generators, and if anyone in Markworth Station should change their mind, you'll have no one to transfer you out or adjust your programming."

"I understand the situation," the Regent said. "We all understand."

"So, your people are in agreement, one hundred percent?"

Angunda gave a joyless chuckle. "Among eight billion, disagreement is a given. All the same, though, we'll stand together. We gave anyone who wanted to leave a chance to do so, and no one came forward. Life in the ether is hard for you to understand. In here, we're not so much apart from one another as flesh and blood people are. We're bound by the neural network, and we share connections your people can't experience. We've discovered unexpected dimensions to our lives, and the possibility—."

Angunda hesitated.

Brennan nodded, urging him to continue.

"I've never brought this up before because people outside Markworth consider the idea antiquated, if not outright misguided. You may not understand it. Most of us in here felt the same way when we first came over, but experience has taught us something different."

"Taught you what?"

"The possibility...," Angunda said, "...that there is a god in the machine."

Tension coiled in Brennan's gut. "If you have any gods, they're the programmers who created your world."

"Absentee gods—long dead gods, in fact," Angunda said. "But the god we experience is living and present with us."

"How do you know that?"

"Of course, we don't know. We have faith." Angunda said. "But we fear any change in fundamental programming—if we were to join the fleet, for example—might leave us cut off from its presence."

"It?"

"In the ether, 'he' or 'she' is a choice."

"Right." Brennan rubbed his eyes. "Maybe...," he said, "...maybe it's better you don't come with us."

"It is." Angunda nodded. "Not for the reasons you're thinking, but it is."

"This is our last meeting then," Brennan said. "Maintenance will continue for three more weeks. Then the generator stations will be calibrated and set to run on automatic. The Committee has put a lot of effort into preparing for this and layering in redundancies. The cores are full. You should have a solid million years, probably more, barring the interference of accidents or natural disasters. It's the best we can do. It's not forever, but it's a long time."

"Nothing lasts forever. Who can complain about a million or more years of life?"

Life, Brennan thought, *is out here, where we breathe and bleed.*

"Please thank the Committee for me," Angunda said. "Thank you for all you've done for us, for caring enough to try once more to persuade us to go with you. I'll miss you, Brennan."

"Good luck to you, Regent," Brennan said. "Good luck to your people."

"To you and yours as well."

A faint click came from the holojector, and Regent Angunda vanished.

Brennan shivered in the sudden silence. In that instant, Markworth Station seemed more than ever like a tomb.

Collecting his coat and attaché, Brennan made his way to the exit, passing rows of darkened visiting rooms that would never again be lit. As he crossed the vast lobby, the wind howled outside. It buffeted him when he opened the door, bringing the first cold drops of a looming rain to his face. He rushed to his car and slid behind the wheel. Inside was as quiet as empty Markworth Station, but it was different—almost comforting. The rain squall broke open and smeared the windshield. Brennan switched on the wipers and hoped it would rain enough to break eight months of drought. Not that it mattered much. Everyone leaving Earth would be gone within a few more weeks. He lingered in a last look at the monolithic installation nestled into a crook at the base of Markworth Mountain. Then he drove two miles to the gates and let the car's autodrive take over.

The protestors were the first thing he saw when he returned to Calper. His route took him past the entrance to the launch site on the outskirts of the city. About a dozen Earthbound for Life members stood there with flash signs and portable holojectors displaying their slogans. Behind them a rocket sliced upward atop a plume of white and blue flame, and another stood ready on the next launch pad, three more lined up behind it. Brennan couldn't hear what the protestors were shouting, but he knew their positions well enough. It boiled down to the beliefs that humanity would become lost among the stars, that the rockets were suicide machines, that the exodus was a conspiracy to reduce the population so that the elite could start over with the Earth for themselves. The Earthbound still believed the planet could be repaired.

That was impossible, though; Brennan was certain of it.

As if backing up this conviction, the earth rumbled and shook. Brennan's car came to an emergency stop in response. Brennan trembled inside it while the quake lasted. It was the fourth he'd felt that day, and it came with lightning and thunder, and an uneasy sense of chaotic energy waiting to be unleashed. It lasted only a few minutes, and afterward, Brennan's car restarted. At the sound of the motor, one of the protestors threw something against his windshield, spilling a viscous, white protein stew sold by street vendors over the glass. The rain washed it away, and then Brennan saw the protestors shouting and pointing at him, shaking their fists. They had spotted the Committee insignia on his car.

It doesn't matter what they believe, Brennan thought, *the Earth is spent.*

He pitied anyone who couldn't see that, and grasp the miraculous opportunity the Orion Exploration Fleet offered. He ordered his car to accelerate away from the protestors. He was late for his appointment, so he activated his Committee security clearance. The car shot forward and sped through Calper, forcing other vehicles to slow down and let him pass, cutting in and out of traffic, tipping traffic signals in his favor as he neared them. He reached the medcenter in record time, sent the car to park itself, then hurried into the lobby. An elevator brought him to the 117th floor, where he met his wife, Layna, and his sons, Callon and Bruce, in the lobby outside the psychiatrist's office.

"There you are," Layna said.

"Sorry, got held up by that ground trembler. How'd it go with the boys?" Brennan gave his sons a mock serious look. "Any deficiencies?"

"Not a one, Dad," Callon said.

"We're cleared for liftoff!" Bruce said.

"Excellent. I'm proud of you," Brennan said.

"You'd better get in there if you don't want to lose your appointment," Layna said.

"Right," Brennan said. "Get us a table at that café on the 63rd floor. I'll meet you when I'm done."

Brennan saw his family into the next elevator then hurried to Doctor Avery's office. He found the doctor waiting for him behind his desk, which was positioned in front of a giant wall mirror in a gilded frame carved to resemble entwined grape vines and flowers. He wore a pair of interface spectacles and was tapping away on keys they projected onto his desk.

"Sorry, I'm running a late." Brennan tossed his coat over the arm of a leather wingback chair and set his attaché beside it as he sat. "I crossed paths with an Earthbound protest on my way back from Markworth Station."

"Hmmm, two entirely different groups, yet neither want to leave Earth." Avery stopped typing and pushed his spectacles up on his forehead. "There's a lesson there, although I can't imagine anyone is much interested. All they care about these days is psych evals for spaceflight. Understandable, I suppose."

"I ran into my wife on my way in. You've already cleared my family."

"I'll clear you too, Carter. I can ask you the questions if you like, go through the motions, but it's a waste of time. You'll be fine," Avery said. "Up to you."

"Let's skip it, then," Brennan said. "Even if you red-flagged me, there's no way I'm not getting on one of those rockets."

"So be it. Cleared for liftoff."

Avery pushed his glasses back down on his nose, typed some more, and then took an ID chipcard from the top drawer of his desk. He stared at it for several seconds, allowing infrared light from his spectacles to authorize it. Then he handed it to Brennan, who took it, stood, and reached for his coat.

"Wait, Carter, sit," Avery said. "We have our time. I was hoping you'd indulge me."

Brennan returned to his seat. "How so?"

"I want to know about Markworth. Why won't they come with us?"

"I really shouldn't say," Brennan said.

"I know, I know, it's classified and privileged and blahblahblah, but we're only going to be on this rock a few more weeks, and the curiosity is killing me. I understand the Earthbound for Life folks. They're scared, and they're contrarians, and a lot of them are too dim to think for themselves. They've been duped by their crackpot leaders. At the end of the day, probably half of them will wind up on a rocket. But the eight billion in Markworth? They took in, what, about half a billion new consciousnesses from opt-outs? And so little would change for them if they came with us. Their world would get smaller, maybe a little less exciting, but they wouldn't be on their own."

"The programming changes are part of it," Brennan said. "But even if we could replicate their entire system in the fleet, I think they still wouldn't go. They believe they've found... well, something unique in the ether, and they're afraid it can't exist anywhere else."

"What's that?"

"I haven't even given my report to the Committee yet."

Avery smiled. "Humor my scientific curiosity. Anything you say is protected between doctor and patient anyway. I can't tell it to another soul in this world. What did they find?"

"God," Brennan said. "They believe they're not alone in there."

Avery leaned back in his chair. "A god that exists in there with them, or a god for all of creation?"

"Don't know. Didn't ask," Brennan said. "Whichever it is, it's enough to convince eight billion people to stay where they are. Maybe it's no more than a programming glitch."

"Very interesting," Avery said. "You don't believe, I take it."

"Who does anymore?" Brennan gestured vaguely upward. "The only heavens I aspire to are the ones out there."

Brennan stood and gathered his coat. He waited for Avery to emerge from behind his desk then shook hands and said goodbye. They might see each other again someday on a rocket or another planet, but the chances were slim. When Brennan left the office, Avery was standing in front of the mirror, studying his reflection. Brennan made it halfway to the elevator before he remembered his attaché case. He rushed back, knocked on Avery's door then pushed it open. The attaché was sitting right where he'd left it, and Avery still stood before the mirror—except a faint glow now surrounded him.

"Doctor...?" Brennan said.

Avery didn't acknowledge him. He leaned toward the mirror until his forehead touched it. A glimmer of light pooled where his skin made contact with the silvery glass. Then came a faint click, and Avery vanished into the smooth surface of the glass. Brennan rushed across the office, confused. He stopped short of the mirror. There was no sign of Avery. In the abrupt emptiness, Brennan felt like he was back in Markworth Station, alone in a decommissioned visiting room.

***

Doctor Lester Avery blinked. The ambient light of the lab hurt his eyes.

He sat up, yawned, and accepted a mug from a nearby technician.

He sipped from the mug. The cool drink soothed his throat and replenished the nutrients he'd lost while he was in the grid. The monitor above his couch read 36:23:09. He had been in for a day and a half—the equivalent of a month's worth of grid time.

"Orange." Avery took another sip. "Not my favorite. Got any cherry?"

"Sorry, doc." The technician shook his head. "Military crew came in yesterday for a battle sim and drank it all."

"I'll survive. Hate the aftertaste, though."

Avery slugged back the rest of the drink. He swiveled his legs off the couch and stood, feeling a touch dizzy, but that was normal. He left the lab, went to his office, and logged in. His window afforded him a view of the spaceport. Cargo crafts and transports lifted off in a steady stream. From a distance, they looked like paper models rising on the wind instead of high-tech ships set free by gravity interference drives. The sight made Avery smile. It was so much more beautiful and accomplished than what the people in the grid had achieved. No matter how well Avery's team refined the grid programming, reality still ruled.

A knock came at his door, and Bureau Director Lorenzo pushed into Avery's office.

"You're back," he said. "Good."

"You don't waste any time," Avery said. "I haven't even logged a report yet."

"I'm impatient. Give me the highlights."

"The new modules are working well. The safeguards we put in place are doing their job, and I don't think we'll ever get locked out of the system again like we did last summer," Avery said. "It's all humming along now, catastrophe averted. The evacuation is proceeding, and we've barely had to nudge anyone in the right direction. Given the opportunity to advance, they seize it. Barring another crash in the sub-programming—almost impossible at this point—all should remain well."

"What a huge relief," Lorenzo said.

"I only hope the crew over in world-building has some scripts and modules ready to go soon, because the first rockets are flying, and a couple thousand years passes fast in grid time."

"That's something I wanted to see you about, but tell me the rest first."

"Not much else. It's all pretty much as planned," Avery said. "Except for one interesting bit. The Markworth Station folks think they've discovered god."

"What do you mean?"

"Carter Brennan tried again to convince them to go on the rockets. They declined, again, but this time they said it's because they believe there's a living god in the ether with them, and they don't want to leave him, her, or it behind. I'll have to gather more data next time I go in."

"A creator-god?"

Avery shrugged. "They know the creators of their world were programmers."

"Unexpected." Lorenzo looked thoughtful for a moment. "Someone slipped a bit of code in on the sly. Delgado in sociology, maybe. He's always trying to run little experiments without anyone noticing."

"Wasn't him. You fired him last month, remember? And even if you hadn't the new security would detect anything like that," Avery said. "No, I don't think this is one of us messing around. It's spontaneous. Our projections for unsanctioned, in-system deviation have always underestimated the true degree of spontaneity in there. Or it could be a bug. You should go see for yourself. When's the last time you were in the grid?"

"I'm a busy man, Lester. This Bureau doesn't run itself," Lorenzo said. "I'll send my son down and let him bring me up to speed. He's itching for a project with more responsibility."

"Suit yourself," Avery said. "The good news is the environment is holding its integrity. For better or worse, the people in the grid have forgotten that they all started out in our world before mapping their psyches down there."

"That's welcome news, at least. If they ever decided to come back, we'd have body riots on our hands again, and what the hell would we do with half a billion new citizens anyway?" Lorenzo shuddered. "Okay, I'll let you get back to work. I want your full report by the end of the day."

"You got it," Avery said. "Didn't you mention something about world-building...?"

"Oh, right, yes, when you have a minute, go see Lois. They're hung up on fauna designs for one of the Sirius worlds. She wants your input. It's slowing the whole damn project down, so make sure you see her today."

"Consider it done," Avery said.

After Lorenzo left, Avery banged out his report. He struggled to sum up the development at Markworth Station. Programming allowed a lot of leeway for social evolution but only within planned parameters—and no one had ever programmed for a god in the machine inside the machine. Markworth Station itself had begun only as a lark to see what would happen if the people in the grid were permitted to create a grid of their own: the ether. It was like the start of an infinity image, endlessly reproducing and reducing itself. The people in the grid had all begun life in the real world, but over time they'd come to think their world was the real one; and the eight billion who'd entered Markworth over the last millennia in grid time were unaware it was the second time they had bumped their consciousnesses into a simulated environment. What was going on inside there to convince them they'd found god? Avery was stumped. Finally he surrendered and wrote: "Further study required to properly analyze divinity developments in Markworth Station." He logged in his report and then went to the world-building facility on the next floor.

Lois smiled when Avery entered her office. She threw her arms around him and kissed him. "Hmmm," she said. "Glad you're back. I missed you last night."

"I missed you for a month," Avery said.

"You poor thing, we'll just have to make up for lost time tonight."

"If you went into the grid with me, we could spend two weeks together anywhere in the world you want to go and be back for breakfast."

"Sounds lovely," Lois said. "But no vacations for me till I get things back on track here."

"Right. Lorenzo said you needed my help."

"I do." Lois let go of Avery and straightened herself, all business now. "Let me walk you through it."

They spent the next two hours reviewing the latest selection of wildlife Lois's division had designed. Avery saw little wrong with them except that most had an unnecessary whimsical flare and some were strikingly fierce. They were unpolished and needed to be perfected before they could be handed off to coding. Bad fauna could devastate a colony or sink an entire world. Avery offered suggestions, which he and Lois then debated until they both grew too hungry to continue and decided to call it a day and grab a late dinner.

"You saved me two weeks of kicking these back and forth with design until they got it right," Lois said. "Brewster's crew is burning out. We've populated nine new worlds in three weeks. That's enough to deplete anyone's inspiration."

"Glad to help," Avery said. "I guess even gods need an assist now and then."

Lois crinkled her face. "Gods? What's that about?"

"Isn't that us?" Avery said.

Lois gestured for him to explain.

"At least as far as the people in the grid are concerned," he said, "we're building their universe and populating their worlds with plants and animals over which we shall grant them dominion. We create their fates."

"Not entirely," Lois said. "We've left them free will."

"That's because we want to be gods, not dictators."

Lois stared at Avery like she couldn't make up her mind if he was joking or not.

Avery laughed. "Don't strain yourself," he said. "I'm only kidding around."

Later while they ate dinner, Avery explained what he'd learned about Markworth Station. Lois appeared fascinated and laughed at his earlier jibes retroactively, but now that he'd made the points, Avery found them hard to dismiss. It wasn't much of a stretch to paint themselves as gods to the grid. He thought of an article he'd read before his last trip down the line: more than 70 percent of the world's population and resources were connected in some way to servicing the grid. He glanced around the cafeteria full of bureau employees and abuzz with wait staff, cashiers, and cleaners, and realized that being gods was good industry. Creating a reality kept people working. It filled another essential component of society too: It gave them something to have faith in. Vestiges of traditional religions still existed around the world, but most people these days were atheists. *Except when it comes to ourselves*, Avery thought. *We have all the faith in the world in ourselves and that we're doing the right thing no matter how it affects those in the grid, and if we ever get it really wrong then they're on their own down there.*

"We really have made gods of ourselves," he said.

"What's that?" Lois asked.

Avery stared at her. For a moment, Lois seemed utterly unreal, like a ghost, and Avery felt certain that if he touched her, his hand would pass through her body, and she would blink out of existence. He shivered.

"Are you all right?" Lois asked.

She took Avery's hand. At the feel of her warm skin, Avery's senses settled.

"Fine, yeah," Avery said. "Lost in thought for a moment, that's all."

Later that night in bed, as Lois neared climax, she gave Avery a wicked grin, and then cried out, "Oh, god, yes, oh, god, oh, god!"

Avery couldn't help it: He burst out laughing.

Afterward, Lois fell into the deepest sleep Avery had ever seen. In the morning, he awoke to the sound of a faint click. He thought it was the alarm, but he'd woken early and turned it off before it sounded. He could barely rouse Lois. She remembered little of the previous night's conversation, so Avery refreshed her memory. Lois said it came back to her then, but he had the nagging suspicion she said so simply so they could move on with their day.

***

Keela McCormick unplugged from the control suit and shook off the residue of being Lois. She sat in the lab for a time, thinking nothing, letting the impression of being in-world fade away. The lab was silent, except for the hum and tick of the machines, and the steady thrum of the geothermal generators below the surface.

She liked Avery; she really did.

She told herself that's why she kept going back as Lois.

It wasn't the whole truth, though. She was also interested in Avery's connections down the grid and into Markworth station. Avery was one of only a handful of people with direct contact that deep into the system, and of them all, only he seemed to ever gain any insight or perspective from the experience.

"...we want to be gods, not dictators," he'd said.

What an outrageous idea, Keela thought.

Avery wasn't a god. He could never be a god.

No one in-world could.

God is here, Keela thought. *I am God. Everything they do in-world, everything on the grid, everything in Markworth Station—worlds within worlds—I control.*

Keela yawned and her stomach grumbled. She left the lab and went to the upper level kitchen, where she foraged through the pantry and the freezer until she found what she liked. She cooked it and then took her meal to a table and chair by the windows, where she ate and studied the view. To the west was a mountain range, its jagged peaks frosted with snow; southeast was a lake reflecting the overcast sky and churning with gray waves in the wind. It was noon and dark out. It was always dark, always a shade of winter. Keela had never seen anything else, although she had read of warm days and sunshine, had seen stored video of lush green forests and blue oceans. A fantasy world, a world still in its prime, not like this one on its deathbed.

She tried to see the beauty in it.

Rhaj had always insisted it was out there, but she never saw what he saw.

She missed him. She'd lost track of the days since he'd died. It was hard to care about time passing now that she was alone.

Through the window, she made out part of the road to the lab site, its surface cracked, pitted, and overgrown with weeds. A section of fence along the perimeter twitched in the wind.

It hadn't been bent over like that yesterday, she was sure.

It's going to be today then, she thought.

She finished her meal and then went down to the lockers and suited up to go outside. She stopped at the armory and strapped a pair of pistols to her belt and grabbed an energy rifle.

Outside, the cold ate through her suit and mask.

She hiked downhill from the lab, crunching crusts of ice and ignoring the chill that sank deeper into her bones with each step. Out by the fence, she saw footprints in the snow. They were recent; it had snowed this morning, but the pushed-down section of fence was clear and the depressions of the footprints weren't filled with fresh snow.

More footprints were on the other side, the outside.

The intruder had come from there.

It's true, she thought. *Someone else is here.*

Impossible.

She had hoped she'd been imagining the figure she'd seen moving around the foothills and rushing across the grounds at night. She couldn't guess who it could be. Everyone was dead or in-world. She was the last one, left alone to run the systems, adjust the programs, and balance the fuel stores. The rest of the team was long gone, and she'd buried each one under a veil of ice and snow, Rhaj last, and so it couldn't be any of them. How was it possible for someone to turn up now, so near the end of everything?

She knelt and traced the contours of one of the footprints.

Real.

Unless...

A horrible thought came to her: What if the intruder was a spontaneous presence that had sprung into existence like the god in Markworth Station? What if it had grown from her need for faith as Avery's people had created their gods by becoming them? Could she have done the same to help her through her last days alone? She didn't think so. She wasn't part of in-world, and things didn't simply leap into being in the real world. Besides, faith wasn't something she needed, anyway.

The end of her—the end of everything—gave her no fear. There was only the universe of matter and energy, no more or less, and there was in-world, and she was the god of in-world, as well as the god of the grid and the ether. She could destroy it all if she chose to, or damage it, or secure it, or render it a utopia or a hell, or leave it to itself.

Its creators were all long dead; only she remained—its divine balance.

The footprints led in from the wasteland and trailed into the grounds. Keela followed them.

"What are you?" she said.

A voice inside her answered: "It's you."

It wasn't, though. It couldn't be. She wasn't losing her mind, or sleepwalking or blacking out and doing things she didn't remember. The medications prevented it, and she'd checked the security cameras to make sure. Unless—did the voice mean the intruder was like her, dipping down into this world from one above how she dipped down into in-world?

The idea enraged her. There was no world above this one.

She was God, no one else. Before she died, she would pull the plug on in-world and all the worlds it contained, and the human race would end with her. She wouldn't pack fuel into the generators so they could run a million years. She wouldn't transfer down and live forever. She couldn't even if she'd wanted to—the tumor in her brain made it impossible. Everyone on her team had suffered some similar anomaly that kept them trapped in reality, a trait that meant they had to stay behind and die while the rest of the world got to live.

No, Keela thought. Now that her team was gone, she saw how unfair and cruel that was.

There was no other world. If there was, wouldn't they intervene? Wouldn't they heal her or pull her up to their level? Wouldn't someone try to save the human race? That's how it went in stories with heroes and villains and the world in danger, but this was no story. This was real life—and all life ends only one way.

The footprints led Keela to a service entrance that hadn't been used in decades.

The door was ripped off its hinges and left askew in the snow.

"Shit," Keela said.

She inched into the darkness inside and listened while her eyes adjusted from the snow brightness. *Tweak the code,* she thought. *We used to tweak the code to make ourselves stronger or faster or more attractive and then screw with the in-worlders.* Or sometimes it happened on its own when the interface got glitchy or there was a bug or the admin systems locked up. *Is that what this is? Is someone from above messing with my head? Or are they trying to... help me?*

No. There's no one above, no other world.

I am the last–I'm God.

Keela followed a sound coming from a room down the corridor.

Nothing above.

Nothing.

She adjusted her grip on the rifle and turned the corner.

A faintly glowing figure stood in front of her, turning, gesturing, speaking–.

Keela screamed and fired.

A lance of blue-white light crackled out from the rifle and hurled the figure against the far wall. The scent of burning cloth and flesh filled the air, overpowering the filters of Keela's hood. The residual crackling of the energy faded, and Keela heard a faint click. With one foot, she rolled the smoking corpse over to see its face. She couldn't tell if it was a man or a woman. The rifle blast had destroyed its features and most of its torso, and it carried no weapons, no telltale gear. She could undress it to find out, but she wouldn't. She didn't care.

The intruder should never have been here in the first place.

She dragged it outside away from the building and buried it in a snowdrift with the others–not hers, not her team, but...the others? No, there were no others, there couldn't be any others; there was no one else at all. Keela's head spun. A sharp pain spiked through her skull and down her spine. Her vision blurred for a moment then cleared, and she saw bodies, all dressed in the same type of suit, all charred and devastated by the blast of an energy rifle–her energy rifle. *Others,* she thought, but she knew that couldn't be right. Then she blacked out and collapsed.

She was shivering when she woke. The cooling body lay beside her.

She stopped herself from looking past it into the irregular drift of snow crusted with ice.

She scrambled away and ran back to the lab, went to the kitchen, made a warm drink, and sat by the windows. Pain lingered in her head. It was worse every day. She felt weaker and more adrift each morning. The tumor was destroying her cognition, making her hallucinate. Her time was running out–all time was. Something was moving along the distant ridge. A black speck, but even at this distance, she could tell it moved like a man.

A man who couldn't be there, who shouldn't exist.

I am the last, Keela thought. *I am God.*

She reached for her energy rifle then thought better of it.

There was no point going out there again or going on. She would simply have to prove it.

Creator. Destroyer.

In-world, the grid, and the ether—billions of lives—would end when she did, and the time was now.

When she finished her coffee, she would go down to the lab, and do her duty as God.

On "I Am the Last," James writes...

The seed for this story was planted at a panel on artificial intelligence and villainous computers which I moderated at Ravencon *in 2007. The panelists included guest of honor Robert Sawyer, Stephen Euin Cobb, and Paul Fischer (plus unofficial contributors in the guise of highly knowledgeable audience members). The topic quickly turned technical—and well outside my area of expertise! I covered by asking lots of provocative questions (moderator's privilege). As the conversation ranged, the prospect of transferring human consciousness to digital media cropped up and made for a fascinating discussion. I've wanted to do a story around that ever since; "I Am the Last" is the result.*

A LITTLE JOKE
CJ HENDERSON & KEVIN DIVICO

"Man is distinguished from all other creatures by the faculty of laughter."
—Joseph Addison

Great Cthulhu no longer lay a'dreaming. His great city of R'lyeh had finally risen from the ocean's floor, finding the sun above the waters of the southern Pacific at 47" 9'S, 126• 43W. Those figures, of course, no longer held any meaning in the universe. They pertained to a charting system devised by what had formerly been known as the "human" race. Humans had been a small and subsequently pointless life form which had been swept away from the planet the mighty old one had chosen as his temporary home almost as swiftly as the ocean's waters had dried from the colossal green stones from which his city had been built.

Having tired after his long battle millennia earlier, expelling the Elder Things and other alien entities from that latest corner of the universe he had decided he fancied, the great and terrible one had entered a period of hibernation. It was not a rest imposed upon his magnificence. It was not a period of imprisonment as some hectoring voices had claimed—voices, to be certain, now silenced throughout the universe.

He had not, indeed, been in any way barred from the Earth. Quite to the contrary, bored with the constant nuisance of having the bicker and the squabble of an infinite number of dimensions always in his ears, the pleas of a trillion petitioners always beckoning, the gibber of a never-ending line of universes vying for his attention, the be-all and end-all of existence had simply decided to take what for all intents and purposes one could only call a nap.

Then, having decided to do such, on a whim, he created a sort of metaphysical alarm clock he named Azathoth. The entity was a mindlessly bubbling swirl of life, a witless mound of living insanity to which great Cthulhu gave dominance over all creation while he slept. Azathoth was allowed no real consciousness, of course, but was merely gifted with the ability to dream, allowing Azathoth to play with the fabric of time and space as it saw fit in its madness. The remaining gods were charged with keeping the boiling center of the universe amused, warned that if Azathoth were to awaken, all of prime reality could be changed.

However, Azathoth's dreams invaded those of men, plucking forth this and that which it might find to tinker about with, making the lives of the rest of the gods things of endless chaos as its madness unleashed one devilment on the universe after another.

It was a wickedly delicious means of keeping everything and everyone in a constant state of dread-filled panic, and the thought of it made the great Old One chuckle deeply as he settled in to rest his tired eyes for a moment. It delighted magnificent Cthulhu to gift his creation with the ability to change anything it so desired with its mad dreams. After all, it mattered not what the swirl of cosmic vapors altered, manufactured or deleted—once its master stretched out his great arms, unfurled his wings, threw open his eyes and then commanded his city to return to his chosen world, it would be leashed and muzzled, returned to insignificance, all its playthings swept aside.

And so it had been planned, and so it had been executed. R'lyeh had been returned to the world, Azathoth shunted aside, and great Cthulhu had strode forth into the world once more. As the human race measured time he had been gone for countless eons. As he marked the passing of reality, it seemed as if he had barely closed his eyes when he was awake once more.

"Oh, most all-encompassing one, so nice to have you back amongst us so that your iron will might direct our scattered and mostly self-interested notions."

The speaker was an entity of constantly changing appearance. His words were not, of course, any kind of speech any creatures still remaining in the universe could interpret. They were vibrations, interpretations of understanding which only others on its own level of existence or greater would understand. Equally unfathomable by most previous life forms was the very substance of the creature.

Different angles would show it to appear this way or that way. A change in the tone of its voice might make it female, another male, another something unknown to such a limited set of choices. Annoyed by its shape-shifting, knowing all too well how the creature used the ability to enact slanderous metaphors, Cthulhu reached out with his almighty will and rattled the creature, slamming it against a few walls until he found a personality within the thing it could tolerate.

"Arise, Nyarlathotep," he commanded. Brushing away some mote climbing across the arm of his throne, he asked, "Why do you come before me? You know how little tolerance I have for you."

"Such words pain me, oh great one," answered the being, now nothing more than a noxious expanse of yellowish slime. Oozing his way toward its master's throne, it worked at forcing a smile into its voice as it added;

"I have but come before you to ask of your future plans, to see where I might aid you."

Cthulhu's vast visage shuddered with a motion which smelled of mirth. A sparkle of orange flashing across the great dark orbs which functioned as the god's eyes, he answered;

"From any other, such a comment would be answered with annihilation. But, I know you cannot help but be what you are. You were created to be a nuisance, a reminder of the possibility of failure."

"Well spoken, great one," the hissing cloud replied, its color paling and deepening rhythmically. "But you have told me nothing. How might I aid your coming plans?"

Great Cthulhu looked down from his throne. Before he could make any kind of answer to the creature before him, he noticed another. It was a small thing, as much an insignificance to Nyarlathotep as the noxious cloud was to Cthulhu himself. His attention focused on the crawling thing, the entirety of its being became known to him in an instant.

It was an insect, a primitive one—not a mutation which had occurred over the millions of years of the Earth's history, but one which had remained unchanged since practically the beginning of time. It had not the intelligence to fear him, which impressed the Old One neither one way or the other. What did catch the god's attention, however, was the fact that it should not have existed. Not any longer.

"You know of this world before my return," acknowledged the ruler of all existence. "Tell me, what is this thing?"

Nyarlathotep's sense of vision followed the extended cephalopodic appendage until it spotted the crawling insect. Translating as best it could human speech into the vibrations of the gods, it responded;

"A cockroach, my lord."

"And why is it here in my hall?"

Nyarlathotep made to answer, then stopped itself. What was the thing doing there, indeed? Had not the return of R'lyeh set off a cleansing burst which had cleared the planet of all its useless life? Humanity and all its blemishes, the mammals over which it had held domain, the things which swam the oceans, glided through the skies, all the irritating, vulgar life that had polluted every corner of the Earth had been eliminated. Or, at least, it should have been.

And yet, there remained this insect. This skittering offense which dared invade the most sacred hall of the greatest of the Old Ones. Scrutinizing the thing with his endless, all-seeing eyes, Cthulhu mused;

"All life should have been swept from this disgusting ball. Why does this remain?"

"I know not, my lord. But, I can tell you that throughout all my countless centuries plaguing humanity, the humans tried endlessly to rid themselves of the cockroach. No matter what they did, however, the things persisted."

With a whipping snap of one of his massive tentacles, great Cthulhu obliterated the crawling thing. Incinerating the squashed remains with a thought, he sneered;

"Persistence ended."

"Perhaps not, my lord."

The great Old One's attention immediately shifted to the point in the universe to which Nyarlathotep had referred. There, in a far corner of his great chamber, a second cockroach could be seen, running in circles up one of the oblique walls. Angered almost beyond reason, Cthulhu scanned the yellow cloud, searching within its antagonizing humor for any connection between the minor god and the invasion of his home.

None was found. Nyarlathotep might have fancied himself a trickster, but it knew better than to openly defy the master of all creation. Bowing before Cthulhu's unbridled rage, the whimpering little cloud pressed itself backwards in complete and utter abeyance while the great Old One actually left his throne to cross his great hall in pursuit of the second roach. The god slammed the insect with all the fury it could muster, toppling columns and shattering walls throughout his shimmering green palace.

And that was only the beginning. Before he could calm himself, pull back from his near mindless anger, yet another of the insects reared its head. Great Cthulhu obliterated it instantly, then sent forth a mental command for all of these endless things to simply die. And yet, within days, new ones were found, crawling on his ceiling, running in circles on his throne, scampering down his wings. Maddened beyond all understanding, he took to chasing them down, slaughtering them with an angering glee.

Decades and centuries passed, and yet, no matter how many of the creeping things the god destroyed, still it was only a matter of time before more would appear. Great Cthulhu raged uncontrollably, and there were whispers from shining Kadath to green and glistening Xoth that he had indeed gone mad.

While, forgotten and alone, in the center of all, gibbering Azathoth tittered with glee, for as it could have told anyone at all if it had only been consulted, the small jokes are the best.

On "A Little Joke," CJ writes...

My story is a little odd. I had written it for another anthology which, sadly, was never produced. The idea came from my co-author, Kevin DiVico. We were both complaining about cockroaches one day, when he postulated that the lowly roach, being as tenacious and prolific as it is, was probably the only thing on Earth that could give Cthulhu a run for his money. That was enough for me. I know a shaggy dog story when I hear one. Of course, I had to add my own twist, and that was where Azathoth came from in the mix. And that's where this story was born.

THE LONG NIGHT
EDWARD J. MCFADDEN III

6*19*3022: World Government Standard Record WG: Missing Citizen Ty Kedric #19762 * Case File # 83219 * Item 19 of 369
Evidence Summary of Item 19 of 369: What follows are select entries transcribed from Ty Kedric's handwritten personal journal, which was found at the scene of his last known location. (WG OFF. evidence #22196)

Log: 1*12*2819: Ty Kedric
Location: South Jungle (former South America)

This damn rain is going to drive me insane. My entire body feels wrinkled, and if I never hear the patter of rain on leaves again I won't be sorry. It's maddening—the constant tapping and dripping. Lightning illuminates the night sky, and I watch the infinity of raindrops scatter like sparks of white fire in the wind. When darkness falls again, the rain comes even stronger, as if on a mission to drown the world. It's a hard rain, crushing, never ending, and it hacks at the jungle and attacks the vegetation with a viciousness I can't comprehend.

So I decided to start keeping this log, even though I had been instructed not to document anything about my mission, or why I had accepted it. Sometimes when you're alone and times are hard, you undertake the most simple of chores to get through.

I'll start with when I meet Burgess for the first time. Why there? Because that's when I realized for the first time that real freedom was a possibility, but that it was going to take a long time to earn.

Burgess stood tall, his blue uniform perfect, his badge polished, eyes alert. I had pushed my eyejack, earbuds, and nostrilplugs across the counter that separated us, where they were bagged, labeled, and put in storage for when I woke. Burgess had looked hard at me then, leaning forward, and I felt his warm breath on my face.

"You like this?" I had been befuddled. "Having to report for sleep every couple years?"

"With forty-six billion people in the world, what's the choice?" I had answered. The sleep doctrine had been pounded into us as kids, so it was something most people didn't question. Folks who had been around for a few hundred years compared the long night to an old thing called taxes, back when people had to give up a huge chunk of the money they earned for basic necessities.

"But do you like it?" Burgess had pushed.

I hadn't seen him ask anyone else, so I guessed he read the fear on my face, or the sorrow in my eyes, and determined that I might be worth trying to recruit. "No," I had said. I was just starting to live at sixteen, and the thought of having to report for sleep not only scared me, it pissed me off.

"See me when you wake," Burgess had said, and though I tried not to look back at him as I walked down the cylindrical hallway toward my assigned chamber, I did. Later he would tell me that was when he knew he had me, but after that initial meeting, I wouldn't see him again for almost forty-eight years.

It's a strange feeling, that first time they put you to sleep. Panic seeps over you as the world slips away, the undercurrents of time carrying you along. What makes it easier is the knowledge that you *will* wake. When your ten years are up, so are you—for a minimum of two years, unless you lose time as punishment.

The human race hit actuarial escape velocity in the mid-2050s, and medical advances outpaced human life span, making everyone essentially immortal. People died of various things, and the human body does eventually give up the ghost, but the majority of Earth's population would live 1,000 years or more, and the sleep doctrine, along with draconian population control, were the only ways for everyone to live a complete life, and not be packed together so tightly that civilization would collapse under the weight of overpopulation.

There are those, however, who believe control is the primary reason for the sleep doctrine, and that if people hadn't been implanted with tech that forced them to return for sleep, many wouldn't. These people also believe that the tech implanted at birth is used by the World Government to keep track of—and in the case of zealots or troublemakers, control and corral—the general population. This is what I believe, and it's why I joined the Spacers.

The Spacers believe the vast human population should be colonizing the galaxy instead of hiding in sleep chambers, but such talk is almost unheard of. The overlords that run the World Government give people a wonderful life while awake, and few thought a better life was possible. Other than naps for pleasure, two or three years of constantly being awake left many people drained and tired. Some even looked *forward* to the long night. Drones. Losers. I want my tech out, or disabled, and I want to sleep like a real human.

The rain just picked up, and even my small dry area under the canopy of a large rubber tree is being overrun. I feel like things are crawling on my skin—droplets upon droplets making friends, becoming small rivers that invade every fissure, every semi-dry place. The forest is starting to take root in my clothes, my hair, and my mind. I have at least another day's march to get to the project coordinates. The sound of the rain makes my head ache, and I can't help thinking of Julia. Was I starting to love her? Hope not. Who loves their wife in this day and age?

Log: 1*13*2819: Ty Kedric
Location: South Jungle

Now I fully understand why the great jungles are preserved. I've never seen so much rain in my life. In the cities where most people live, the controlled apartments are under constant water ration. So much so, that it isn't unheard of for people to store chemically treated water in their personal effects locker for ten years while they sleep.

So when the rain had started, I ran around with my mouth open, and face turned to the sky like a little boy trying to catch snowflakes on his tongue. But now it's just too much. But I have no choice if I want my freedom. If I complete my task, they promised to cut the cord on my tech, and Julia's as well.

The rain is currently being kept at bay via a tarp, which I have strung in the boughs of a large rubber tree. But the tarp didn't stop the dampness from getting into my lungs. My cough has progressed to painful status, and my ears constantly ring with a dull monotone buzz that's causing my neck to ache, and my sight to become fuzzier with each passing hour. I recall a story my father had told me as a boy, something called Chinese water torture. The prisoner was restrained, and a droplet of water was dropped on the prisoner's head every half hour. The captive would go mad waiting for the next drop. The South Jungle was Chinese water torture times ten.

I walked twelve hours today, so tomorrow's march to the project site should be easy. The rain just let up a little, but a clinging mist still covers the land, and I'm starting to wonder if I'm ever going to see the sun again. I guess the rain is good for the mission, though: even the World Government's ears would have a hard time finding me through these storms.

While the South Jungle never boasted any animals which could compare in size with the giants of other continents, the South Jungle has the dubious distinction of harboring a number of creatures so horrible that they have become legendary. Luckily for me, I shouldn't need to deal with these creatures, because almost all the villains of South Jungle live in its waters. Alligators, piranha, electric eels, and the canduri all lurk in the many streams, pools, and estuaries of the Old Amazon River. The tales implicating these animals in terrible attacks on humans were mostly legends, as these animals hardly ever took a human life, except in the old vid reels.

This eases my mind somewhat, but I know it doesn't mean I'm safe from predators. Giant mosquitoes litter the air, monkeys swing in the trees, and birds of every color and size dance amidst the thick leaves that protect the jungle's soil. The birds flock like flies to carrion when any morsel of food is revealed. Snakes, spiders, and every imaginable type of insect constantly fight for supremacy and sustenance.

Despite my awareness of all this, I was still startled from my seat as a giant white tiger smashed through the dense jungle foliage into my tiny camp. The knowledge that there were no indigenous tigers in South Jungle didn't really matter, because the thing paused for an instant, decided I was more important than running from whatever was chasing it, and lunged at me with a roar that...well, let's just say it scared me.

I had rolled over, grabbing for my laser rifle that rested against the rubber tree. But before I reached it, a man dressed in green camouflage burst into the clearing, firing an old-fashioned gunpowder rifle. The tiger froze, shimmered silver for an instant, and then winked out of existence.

"Oy! You all right, man?" The stranger had rushed forward to help me from the ground, and that's when I saw it was Burgess.

"Hey!" I was so startled I didn't know what to say.

Burgess just stood there, his camouflage suit cleanly pressed and neat, even though he had just run through the jungle. "Sorry about that, mate. I was just having a little fun while I check up on you. You okay?"

"Yeah. That target simulation sure seemed real," I said, collecting myself.

"Mmmm. You should see the go-go girl model," said Burgess.

"You see Julia?" I asked.

"Not yet," he said, but for some reason I knew he was lying, and that worried me. "So, you ready to do your service?"

I nodded, and he handed me a plastic envelope with my orders.

"You sure," he asked, as he turned to leave me. "The choice isn't always as easy as it seems."

I remember thinking about the last part, the part about a choice, and when I looked up to ask Burgess what he meant, I saw that he had disappeared into the forest.

I can hear thunder in the distance, and the rain is falling so hard I can't see fifteen feet into the jungle. I'm going to try to take a nap and let this die down before I read my orders and head to the site.

I did not sleep.

Log: 1*14*2819: Ty Kedric
**Location: South Jungle - Pad Two construction
site**

The jungle speaks with a million sounds. A spray of parrots scatter as they burst from the jungle, screaming and cawing. I sit under my tent on the edge of the clearing where I've made camp. The construction site is mostly clear of overgrowth; but the jungle is winning the battle to reclaim this part of itself. It encroaches right to the clearing's edge in most spots, so the site is as secure as could be expected for the middle of South Jungle.

Using nanotech, my instructions are to build a large landing pad, at this predetermined location. Julia would do the same at her location, if she made it. The Spacers took many old space traditions to heart, and redundancy was one of their main rules. If all went as planned, there would be two pads to choose from, and Julia and I would meet up on our way to the extraction point.

What the pads were to be used for, or when, was not known to me. I'm a cog, and whether or not I play any part in the events surrounding the use of the pads in the future is irrelevant.

At this point one might ask how I could build a landing pad without the World Government knowing? Well, they might find out—another reason for the redundancy thing—but I have never been in any trouble, so even if the Black Hand had the ability to track my movements, they had no reason to. Plus, part of the construction protocol required extensive concealment, and it might take years for the satellite images to focus in on a 100-yard odd-shaped clearing camouflaged to blend into the jungle, if ever.

I find myself thinking often about the old world, what it must have been like to live your life knowing you were going to die, and that the time you had was nothing more then a drop in the cosmic bucket. If there was one good thing about the sleep doctrine, it was that you got to see civilization advance in big steps.

I watch the growing mass of grey goo as it spreads out across the construction site, and I smile at the thought of how many workers it would have taken just to get the supplies to the build site in the old days. The nano was working itself into a frenzy, multiplying and preparing to execute a program that would create a landing pad with a small solar array to power landing lights. Using the earth and vegetation as fuel, the current computer progress report is showing that I might need to add some underbrush to the nano goo.

The nano isn't fazed by the driving rain, as it attacks the landscape with a hatred I've come to respect. This rain is vigilant, and relentless, and it's close to beating me. I often wonder if it's all worth it. Living my life in fear. I still can't get what Burgess said out of my mind. "The choice isn't always as easy as it seems." What had he meant? The choice to be cut free of my tech? I made that decision long ago.

My favorite noddle twister is that everyone knows there are ways to get extra awake time, but nobody knows how, even the people who got extra time. It's as if people were rewarded, but the reason for said reward had been wiped from their memory. All ideological issues aside, that is the real reason the Spacers want to break free of the long night. Some people get special treatment, and nobody knows why.

Family rules and spousal requirements are clear. Parents are chosen by the Central Government, again, with no procedure that is documented anywhere, and are given sleep dispensation until the child reaches the age of sixteen, at which point the child and parents join the maternal family's sleep cycle. Spouses can make a onetime request to coordinate their cycles, but if said marriage breaks up, no further marriage cycle synchronizations are allowed. Beyond those two basic paths to change sleep cycles, no other information is provided about how to extend awake time.

Despite the rain, I ventured out into the clearing and plugged into the landing pad's control panel, which was the first thing finished. The newly awakened AI told me it would be another thirty-six hours before the pad is completed. Then I'll be on my way to the extraction point, and hopefully along the way I'll find Julia.

Log: 1*16*2819: Ty Kedric
Location: South Jungle

As a youth I had been harassed by a boy named Alfie Best, and I can't tell you how many times I almost tore my ears off my head after hearing "Alfie's Best. Alfie's Best." Alfie would hit and make fun of me every time he saw me. Day in and day out, for weeks my anger rose like water behind a dam, and when my arms were fully black and blue from his punches, I snapped.

One day after a particularly vicious punch in the shoulder, I attacked the boy, leaving him writhing on the ground with a pencil protruding from his left arm, and me suspended for a week. But he never bothered me again.

I have come to call the rain Alfie, and I laugh at it as the armies of droplets fight to turn me into a tadpole. The rain has me ready to kill. All patience gone. And as if it knows that, it comes even harder, a flying ocean with no end in sight, no dry shore.

Log: 1*18*2819: Ty Kedric
Location: South Jungle

Early morning dawn is eerie in the jungle. The grey half-light casts odd shadows, and the insects appear bigger, and this is also when many of South Jungle's predators venture out to hunt. Even now, I watch an anaconda work its way past my camp, the lump of that morning's breakfast catching on tree roots and rock edges as it makes its way back to the river and surrounding wetlands. The rain continues to press on my sanity like a tumor. I have come to see it as blood falling from the sky. My blood.

I broke camp this morning. My display map is showing a road to the east, and the extraction point is along it. A bit more walking and I'll be done. Free. I wonder how long it takes to fall back into a normal sleep pattern? Is it even possible after so many long nights? Surely, the Spacers will indoctrinate me in some way, and help me adjust to my new life. But my thoughts keep coming back to what Burgess had said. Why would the choice be hard? My convictions had been tested many times, and it troubled me to think about what may have changed. Or what I may not know.

What choice will Julia make? Our marriage is one of convenience, and allows us to run redundant missions. Neither of us take our relationship seriously because we both thought we'd be free of the World Government's rules soon enough, which made the onetime exemption meaningless in our minds. We were business partners. Nevertheless, I find myself thinking of her more and more, and wondering whether I'll see her regularly once we become part of the Spacer community. The secret base, dubbed Tranquility Base II, was said to be hidden deep within the Earth, where several generation class spaceships were being developed. I only half believe this.

These thoughts were distracting me when Julia burst through a wall of jungle vines, and landed hard on the ground before me. She was covered in thick spider webs, and large banana spiders covered her entire body. I went to her, but when I saw the spider's red fangs and gray-black streaked bodies, I remembered the banana spider is a wanderer, and very poisonous.

I have no idea how people will read this account, if at all, but if it's via my handwritten journal, they will see dark smudges on the front and back cover of said book: the guts of the spiders I swatted with it.

Like a man possessed, I whacked and sliced with my journal, knocking off the spiders as fast as I could. Julia had stopped panicking, and let me work without interfering, the thump and patter of the spiders bouncing off my book and hitting the ground rising above the rain and the low murmur of the jungle.

Thunder cracked, and the rain fell so hard it actually helped us. My tent fit two, and in moments Julia was stripping off her clothes and trying to dry out. Julia is as white as a mushroom. She was bitten in two spots, but I quickly applied a remedy, and she now rests comfortably before me as I write.

The rain outside pounds on the Zeoprine tent, but inside I'm starting to wonder if my thoughts about not seeing Julia anymore were stirring feelings within me that I hadn't known were there. Her long blonde hair falls gently across her face as she sleeps, the medicine doing its work well. We had made it through a lot together, many missions, and she saved my skin a time or two. When she wakes, we'll head to the extraction coordinates, and get out of this rain. The scary thing is I'm starting to like the rain, and its constant reminder that I'm not in control. Even when I think I am, I'm not, and I would do well to remember that.

Log: 1*19*2819: Ty Kedric
Location: South Jungle – Extraction Coordinates

Thankfully, we hit a trail today, because the rain was falling so hard I needed to use my compass constantly to stay on course, the jungle shrouded in a sea of rain. It was like being under water; my eyes so used to being wet I no longer noticed the distortion in light, or the bleariness through which I see my green world.

The sky is a gray-black mound of clouds, and now we wait at the extraction coordinates.

Log: 1*19*2819: Ty Kedric
Location: Rio Branco

I sit alone on my veranda, staring into the blackness of the jungle. Julia wanted her own room for the evening, citing her need to be alone so she could rest and think. The night is clear, but I can still hear the patter of rain, and the constant dripping of water. My body has begun to dry out, but I think my fingers might be permanently wrinkled. I take a sip of hot tea and my hand shakes, rattling the cup against its saucer. It does feel good to be out of the rain, and it's time to turn to other things.

Burgess had collected Julia and me at the extraction point, and delivered us to this posh hotel for some food and rest. When we arrived, we had been greeted by man Burgess called Tinker. He would be disabling our tech. Tinker is a squirrel of a man, with a pointy nose and a squeaky voice.

Before retreating to our neutral corners, Burgess had taken us to lunch, and dropped the bomb. He hadn't been kidding when he said the choice was going to be hard, but I really should've seen it coming. Over cocktails and free range steaks, Burgess laid out our options.

"You each have three options. They will be offered once. The choice you make will determine how you live the remainder of your life, and possibly how long that life will be." He paused for a long time here, impressing upon us the gravity of what he was about to say.

"You can choose to have your tech disabled, as promised." When he saw the smiles blossoming on our faces he held up a hand. "Understand what that means. You will be on your own, cut off from the World Government, a fugitive from society, and thus all the support they provide. Getting food, traveling, things as simple as finding a place to live, will become problematic." Seeing that he had successfully deflated our euphoria, he continued, "Your second choice is to walk away. Do nothing. Report for sleep like a good citizen. Live an enjoyable life free of worry and sacrifice. With this choice, of course, comes reporting for sleep."

I sat there a long time, cradling my drink in my hands, feeling the memory of the rain on my skin. Finally I asked, "And the third choice? What of Tranquility Base II?"

He had laughed. "You're a long way from there, boy. Your third choice is to continue on with us, follow our orders, report for sleep, perform more missions, and maybe, after 100 years or more of service, you'll get your ticket on one of the generation ships."

Julia and I had looked on each other with pity, and I thought I saw her decision already etched in her features; the downturned lips, slack jaw, hung head, and the way she couldn't look me in the eye—she was walking away.

And what of us? I guess if I don't see her in the morning, I'll know.

Memories of the rain haunt me, and I still shiver every few seconds as I imagine drops hitting my skin. What would I do when Tinker's call came? I'm still not sure.

Log: 6*19*2987: Ty Kedric
Location: Gotham Sleep Warehouse, Gotham

It's been a while since I've written, but there hasn't been much to write about. Checking in sleepers isn't very exciting, and with no one at my window, I figured it was time to dust off the old journal.

People are starting to gather at the security check point, and I see a boy, clearly a first time sleeper, holding his mother's hand like she was a life raft, and they were floating on a boiling sea. Even after all the years, I still remember that rain. The way it refused to stop, the way it had driven a wedge between myself and sanity. A wedge that, in many ways, still remained there.

Free of security, I waved the boy and his family over to my window. I passed the parents through without a second glance; they were old and had been through this before. I could see it in their dead eyes, the way they looked into the nothingness that was their lives. The boy, however, had a different light in his eyes.

"Hey," I said to him, leaning across the counter toward him in much the same way Burgess had for me all those years ago. "You like this?" He looked even more befuddled than I had felt. "Sleeping like this?"

The boy looked around, knowing his parents wouldn't like what he was about to say. "No. I don't like it all."

Then I lit the fire. "What if I told you there was a way you didn't have to report for sleep," I whispered, and the young man's eyes grew as wide as quarters. "See me when you wake." As the boy turned and headed down the long cylindrical tunnel that led to the sleep chambers, he turned and looked back at me, and I smiled.

The door to my booth just clicked open, and Burgess is standing there. "Time to meet some friends at those pads you built, and catch our ride to the stars. You ready?"

I am.

On "The Long Night," Ed writes...

Whenever I think of the future, the specter of overpopulation overshadows anything positive that comes to mind. I remember watching the Star Trek *episode "The Mark of Gideon" when I was a kid, and many of the images and ideas in that story stayed with me over the years. This idea of there being so many people that no one gets any privacy, or any time alone, strikes me as a realistic horror that the human race will face at some point. As we inch closer and closer to virtual immortality via science, overpopulation becomes a real issue. This seed of an idea is what grew into "The Long Night."*

FOREVER AND A DAY

An Eternal Cycle Story

DANIELLE ACKLEY-MCPHAIL

"A dream is a memory of what the future may hold if you dare to reach for it."

Despite the centuries that had passed, Tala Ath could see the image over and over like a flare burning against the lids of her closed eyes. The final ship at lift-off, rocket thrusters scorching the earth beneath with a fire that seemed to rival that of the distant sun. The vessel had been ancient but determined, resurrected for a final chance at glory by the last lingering remnants of the human race on Mother Earth. But for a few thousand scattered souls who with time passed on, mankind had departed for the heavens.

"Let the fools go." Declan's long-ago scorn echoed in Tala's mind in time with the vision. *"The Daoine Maith will dance in celebration at their leave-taking."*

Tala's teeth clenched down upon the memory of her friend, cutting it off.

Talk about fools, she thought. *There are none so blind as those who will not see.* But oh, the horror in Declan's proud fae eyes when the truth came clear.

At first the Earth had rallied, unfettered by the burden of humanity's disregard, freed from the bindings of pollution. For a time nature came again into its own as any soul would when a poison is drawn away. Around the world flora and fauna both crept back from the edge of extinction, reclaiming the planet. Tala and her people rejoiced. Everywhere flourished such beauty as had not been seen outside the fae lands since before the advent of humanity. But eventually, in the early days of the Earth's second century without man, the first effects were felt, gradual but persistent. Initially, things just leveled out, barely enough for any to notice. But then it could not be denied that fewer young were born among Earth's creatures with each decade that passed and less of fruit and flower came from nature's bounty, until even the fae in their sheltered Lands sensed the lessening of all things.

In the absence of mankind's fleeting vibrancy...their passion...the spark that set them apart from all other of Earth's children, nature seemed divest of its sense of purpose. Without the humans' life force and the mage energy sloughed off from them like skin to dust—vital to the ecological balance—those left behind faded: The animals, the plants, and even the fae, though many decades passed before any acknowledged the cause. Declan had been among the first. Though not truly dead, he and others like him drifted into a stupor from which none woke.

It could no longer be denied: Without humanity, the Earth and all it held were doomed.

With a frustrated huff, Tala turned away from the remnants of the ancient launch pad. Careful steps led her through the crumbling infrastructure of what she was told used to be the Kennedy Space Center. Over the remains of ivy-draped concrete blocks and steel supports rusted through until they appeared like lace, across the memory of long-gone tarmac and past a stray shard of glass that somehow clung to its twisted aluminum frame, Tala's darting gaze sought out the odd jay nesting in crumbling rafters and faded blossoms long-reverted to their wild state rooted in the rich loam of rotted timbers. Her fae heart cringed at the faint yellow cast to the grasses over which she now trod. It had taken centuries, but like a field sown season after season with the same crop, something vital was missing from the Earth and everything that grew upon it.

The planet had lost a piece of its soul and heaven help them all if it could not be gotten back.

Tala continued on her way before the ache grew too much to bear. As she did so a trill gave her faint warning to brace before a small, compact form collided with her calves and took her to the ground.

"Beag Scath!" she scolded but with little heat. She found it difficult not to smile as the sprite wove his head fetchingly, sending his tousle of multi-hued locks bobbing. He grinned and scampered up her limbs to perch by her shoulder.

"Now, what are ye on about?" she asked, meeting the little one's orange gaze. He fussed and didn't speak, but then he seldom did. He was an odd one, bold and brash and long-beloved, having attached himself to Tala's Clan centuries before. Originally companion to the Sidhe who'd called herself Maggie McCormick, he'd glommed on to Tala's grandmother when she first became Maggie's charge and protégé. That was during the ancient days in New York, when Maggie served as both pawnbroker and one of the guardians of that city. Or so Tala had been told in many a bedtime tale.

As if in reaction to her thoughts, Beag Scath reached out with a minute hand to clutch her ear while he leaned forward and brushed a kiss across her forehead.

Suspecting the wee one had not just capriciously bowled her over, Tala closed her eyes and reached out with her thoughts. *Mamó, did ye tell the little monster to dump me on my ass, or was that his idea?*

A dry chuckle and a thread of music teased her inner ear before her grandmother responded from somewhere behind her. "Sorry, *lhiannon*, he got away from me."

Tala tilted her head back to spy her grandmother, Kara-Anu, looking as youthful as Tala herself, with bright amber eyes and a mane of deep red hair curling around and past her shoulders. The case holding her enchanted violin, Quicksilver, hung by its strap across her back, half hidden by those wild tresses. The grin on her grandmother's face woke an answering one on Tala's. "Hi, Mamó."

"Hi yourself. Now up with you, my child, we haven't time for lying about."

Her brow wrinkled in confusion, Tala clambered to her feet. She had to scramble to keep up with her grandmother, who immediately set out across the clearing back toward the remnants of the launch pad.

"The memory of this place is strong even now," Mamó said as Tala came up beside her. "It might just do."

"Do for what?"

"You've cousins among the Kalderaš Clan...it's time you met them."

Kalderaš! The gypsies. The first to venture forth from the Earth; driven to the stars by prejudice and their race's curse to wander. Tala had grown up on tales of the courtship between the steadfast Jacko and his Sidhe bride, Agnieszka, of the torment of Tony DeLocosta (possessed by an evil demigod and nearly lost in that one's banishing), and endless stories both bright and dark of their children and their children's children. She had never met even one of them, born only after the Rom had journeyed to the stars. Her heart thrilled at the thought of meeting cousins born from those cherished figures. "How?" she asked, turning eager eyes upon her grandmother.

"Come," Mamó beckoned. "It's time to build new dreams of the old." And she showed Tala her vision as only the Sidhe could. Of the wandering gypsy race finally gaining a home, of the Earth revitalized with the return of her wayward children. Of the world and all it held growing hale and whole and healthy once more. Tala's breath left her in a rush through open lips and her eyes went wide in awe. But without question she followed. This would not be the first time Mamó had saved the world, though few but the fae knew the truth of that other tale. Tala had grown up expecting wonders of Kara-Anu, the mortal girl who had become both fae and goddess.

In the center of the crumbling launch pad, crowded by the memories of long-ago dreams, Tala watched as Mamó cradled Quicksilver beneath her chin and brandished her bow. And then bow arm stroked and fingers danced until Kara-Anu's whole body moved with the power of the song. Tala's spirit calmed until she found herself first humming, then singing, drawn into the spellcasting. Melody and harmony wove about them in a dance of color and light and music such as the world had long done without. The air crackled with the gathering magic. Tendrils and sparks lit up the space surrounding them, music wrapped them in its grip with silky smooth notes that ran like fingers over their hair, raising the strands like burning clouds about their heads. Raw energy ready to do their bidding.

Together they wove a vessel of starlight and moonbeams, of sunshine and life force, powered it with resolve and bound it all tight with their will until before them rested a glittering orb stretched oblong like a grain of fat rice. A touch to the shimmering skin sent rainbow ripples across its surface. Those ripples murmured an echo of the melody woven into the craft's making.

Tala released a quavering breath. What a glorious thing.

"Are you ready, Tala?" her grandmother asked. There was a faintness to her voice that made Tala frown, but she nodded. Mamó ran her fingers along the edge of the orb, folding away a section of the skin. She held out her hand. For a brief moment Tala could not bring herself to take it but this was her grandmother, the undying Kara-Anu, sister to the Mother Goddess Danu herself.

Tala allowed her grandmother to aid her into the vessel of light and life. It cradled her as she had not been since she was a child small enough to fit in her Mamó's arms. Tension melted away in the warmth of that embrace. She looked around for Beag Scath, wanting to say farewell, but the sprite was oddly absent, though Tala swore she could faintly hear his cooing. With a frown, she turned her attention back to her grandmother. From where she stood outside, Mamó caressed the orb. "This will get you where you need to be." She paused to draw a cord from around her neck. From it dangled a familiar copper pendant etched with faint runes. "And this will guide you."

The medallion...it was an ancient charm that in ages past had linked a younger Kara to the gypsies before they were kin. It had been given to Mamó by one called Granddame Rose, grandmother to the demigod-possessed Tony. As it settled over her head, Tala sensed the kernel of power still nestled in those runes just as binding as the day they'd first been etched. If tears glistened in her eyes at that gift, her jaw dropped at what came next.

"And she will keep you safe," Kara-Anu decreed with a hard edge of command backing the words as she slipped Quicksilver and her bow into its case, and the case into the space by Tala's feet.

Tala did not argue, but she did ask, "The Kalderaš, what am I to tell them?"

Kara-Anu remain silent a moment her eyes glimmering as she leaned forward, pressing a kiss to Tala's forehead. "Tell them...it's time to come home."

On "Forever and a Day," Danielle writes...
When I was invited to this collection, I knew immediately what I wanted to do.

See, just before being asked I had completed the final book in my urban fantasy series, The Eternal Cycle trilogy. That was meant to be it, but while writing Today's Promise *I was struck with the odd desire to write a science fiction story set in the same universe. That is where* "Forever and a Day" *found its roots.*

*It makes sense. Really. Let me explain. The Eternal Cycle trilogy (*Yesterday's Dreams, Tomorrow's Memories, Today's Promise*) is about a young girl, Kara O'Keefe, that discovers she is part fae...in fact, much more fae than anyone realizes. While coming to grips with this revelation she catches the attention of both the Sidhe and an evil demigod, Olcas, an ancient enemy to the Sidhe. The battle commences with Kara herself as the prize and humanity the spoils.*

By that tale's end Kara encounters the lesser fae, gypsies, gods, and monsters. She learns what it is to be fae, to work magic, and face down evil. She does not come away unaffected or unscathed. By the end of the series Kara is more fae than mortal and thus my desire to take the universe into the far future. This story barely touches on what I have in store for Kara, Tala, and the world, but it opens the possibilities. When eventually I have time to write that novel we are going to see what trouble an immortal New Yorker, her fae granddaughter and a pack of space-roving gypsies, can get into!

THREE NIGHTS IN PHILOPOLIS
PAUL POPIEL

"It's just... I don't know, Jason." Mindy looked at me over the suitcases on the bed. One hers, one mine, both headed to different destinations.

"We both agreed this is what we need to do."

"You're right," she said, "but I've heard some crazy shit about Philopolis, especially on this particular weekend. Maybe you should rethink your trip. Go to Vegas, get drunk, wake up with no money in your wallet, some stripper's bra on your head, and a hickey in some random place. I don't want you to come home with horns or scales or some other genetic defect you picked up from a stripper that Mods."

"It doesn't work that way. Mods aren't contagious. Besides, they've got scanners at the checkpoints. If you have bio-serum in your body, they don't let you out. And you know that's not why we're going there." We could find strippers anywhere. Aliens, on the other hand, were only in one place on earth. They'd crashed their ship into Philadelphia and remade the city into a place where they could live, alongside any human who wanted to co-exist with them. There were plenty of conspiracy theories about whether they'd really crashed, or just landed on the city on purpose, but in the end it didn't really matter. They were stuck here, just like the rest of us.

"If you're detained for genetic reasons don't expect me to join you."

"I knew I shouldn't have told you where I was going."

"Calm down. I wouldn't ruin your party that way."

I'd suggested we go somewhere in one big group for a pre-wedding bash, but she'd said that she wanted one last vacation apart before we got married. I suspected her unmarried friends were more interested in it than she was, but kept my mouth shut. I'd tease her about it sure, but I wasn't suicidal.

I put my half-packed suitcase on top of the laundry basket. I could finish in the morning. The only other thing I needed to do tonight was take a shower. I was almost done when Mindy joined me, and we broke her "no lovemaking before vacation" rule.

Not a minute after I got out of the shower, Conor texted me to turn on the news. The featured story was from Felix Grenfell about the setup for the open weekend, including a look at the Fairmount Park Revel, which was new for this year. It promised all sorts of attractions, mostly run by Modders. I was watching Felix interview a woman named AquaTina the Mermaid Girl, who had a real fish tail when Mindy came out of the bathroom. He seemed more interested in the non-scaly half of her, which sported a number of tattoos but no clothes.

Mindy looked over at the TV. "She's such a pretty girl, why would she do something like that? And she's not even wearing a shell bra. They've blurred her chest, but she's topless."

I pretended I'd missed that part.

She turned the TV off. "You'll have plenty of time to ogle freaks once you get there."

I dropped the remote on the floor, tossed my pillows back up against the headboard, then moved up myself. Mindy snuggled against me before planting a lingering kiss on my lips. I wrapped my arms around her and drifted off to sleep.

***

I woke up when Mindy's cab beeped outside, and stayed that way just long enough to give her a passionate kiss goodbye. I fell back asleep until Conor called to say he was coming to pick me up in the limo.

I finished packing a few minutes before the limo honked its horn. I grabbed my bags and went outside. Conor and McKee were halfway out of the sunroof. They yelled my name when they saw me. Shane hushed them as he climbed out of the limo and took my bags.

We arrived at the first checkpoint after a three hour ride, only to find a massive wave of traffic ahead of us. The limo, however, had a special pass that allowed us to skip the line, which saved us time compared to the other lanes, but even so, both McKee and Conor had time to sober up.

"So much for the exclusive pass," Shane said.

"They're using the money to help rebuild the city," McKee said. "Most of the proceeds from the Revel go to that fund as well."

"Why are you in such a hurry?" I said. "Things don't even start until tomorrow night."

"The pre-game festivities," Shane said.

The limo stopped at a chain-link fence emblazoned with warning signs about the terrible things the government would do to trespassers. A guard stepped out of a booth, walked to our door and opened it. He stared at each of us for a moment, then produced a tablet and read from the screen. "The United States government would like to remind all visitors that it has not and will not relinquish sovereignty over the city of Philopolis. However, the US government also recognizes that the Tasch-Pharago may have difficulty with US law concepts and has agreed to limit visible policing within the main sectors of the city. Rest assured that plainclothes officers patrol the streets and enforce the law as applicable. You are subject to a genetic modification scan upon your departure from the city. Any traces of bio-serum above a determined concentration will result in detainment in the city until the levels subside. Temporary genetic-mods are available from the authorized vendors in the Revel. Do not purchase mods from other sources as they may not be temporary. Please indicate your understanding of the preceding statements with a spoken confirmation." He waited while we complied. "Thank you for your attention and have a pleasant stay."

I watched the guard march back to the gatehouse. "Jesus," I said, "if they give everyone that speech, no wonder it takes so long for people to get in."

"We're VIP's," McKee said. "Regular visitors sign a statement that says the same thing."

"How do you know so much about it?" Shane asked.

"You remember Jamie? He lives in there now, full time. He sent me a link to his video blog, where he'd recorded the whole entry process."

"Why didn't I get a look at this?" I asked.

"Because that would ruin the surprise." Conor watched out the window for a few minutes, then tapped on the glass separating us from the driver. The limo stopped. Conor retracted the sunroof and stood up in the open space. He called for me to climb up next to him, so I did.

"Stare straight for a couple seconds," Conor said, "then look to your left and slowly turn your head to the right, then repeat to the left if you have to."

Ahead of me were the lights of the city, in pretty much the configuration I remembered from my previous visits to Philadelphia before the aliens crashed into it. "What the—"

"Dude, I promise it's worth it."

Instead of asking him more questions, I moved like he'd instructed, and suddenly, I saw it, not the city I thought I'd to see, but the one that was really there now. I was too far away for a lot of details, but since the buildings themselves glowed, it was easy to see their shapes in the dark. Towers stretched far into the night sky, some growing needle thin, others stretching towards one another and blending together into one structure. Other buildings looked like wedges or shark fins that tapered to points. Sometimes bridges connected them, lit with shifting colors that occasionally sent out bursts of light. The whole city seemed unreal and dreamy, like something you'd see in a desert mirage or looming out of the vines of an impenetrable jungle.

"Unbelievable, isn't it?" Conor said.

Below, I could hear the other guys clamoring for a turn in the sunroof. "I never imagined it would be so, so . . ."

"Beautiful? Amazing and yet utterly confusing? There are some scientists who say the city doesn't look the same to any two people. But the point is, you saw the old city before, and now you see this one, and chances are you'll never be able to find that old version again, unless you look at pictures or something. It makes you wonder if any two people see the Tasch-Pharago the same way, or even if any of us can see them as they really are and not how we expect them to be."

A rustling in the weeds caught our attention. Ahead of the limo, a man and a woman crossed into the beams of the headlights. Something wasn't quite right with their faces, though I couldn't put my finger on it. The man wore the shreds of a dress shirt but was naked below the waist. The woman wore a bra with a torn strap, a brief skirt coated in mud, and a pair of rubber boots. The woman half-carried her companion closer to the limo, stopping when she reached the hood.

The man kept glancing back out into the dark. Now I could see what made them different. Their noses were black and shiny, and they each sported a pair of fox ears where theirs should have been. The effect was quite odd, and I wasn't sure they looked like foxes at all.

"Are you hounds, foxes or, oh frank, what was the other thing?"

"Snipe." A howl pierced the night. "We'd better move. Can't let them catch us yet." They darted across the road and down the sloped embankment before vanishing into the reeds.

"What the fuck?" I asked.

Conor smiled. "That phrase is going to lose all meaning here. It's a hunt of some sort. Hopefully they read the contract carefully, so they know what being caught actually means."

"How do you know so much about this shit?"

"I wasn't sure what you wanted to do here, so I sent for pamphlets on all kinds of stuff. We've got three nights. The other guys want one for sex, one for drinking, and one to recover."

"What kind of party are you throwing me?"

Conor shrugged. "You wanted a weekend you'd never forget, right?"

"Yeah, but not during a fifteen-to-life sentence in a supermax." I stopped talking as a mixed group of men and women, all with faces reminiscent of predatory animals, crossed in front of the limo. I saw wolves, lions and even a hyena. More modders. Most of them were wearing leather jackets with a skull on the back. Each skull carried in its mouth a square stone with the words "Of Doom" on it.

A man with the features of a hyena jumped onto the hood. I leaned back as he scrambled up the windshield to the sunroof and grabbed Conor by the lapels of his suit jacket.

"We're not part of the hunt," Conor said.

The hyena modder bared his teeth in a predator's smile. "Oh, I know that. But I'm not above a little poaching." He reached into his leather jacket, and I got ready to start throwing punches if things got nasty. Conor stood very still. He wasn't a fighter, he was a talker, so this was a bad situation for him. If our sudden tension bothered the modder he didn't let it show. He produced a flyer from his jacket and slapped it against Conor's chest, holding it there until Conor put a hand on it. "Evolution has failed us. The time has come to leave weakness behind, and become more than our ancestors ever dreamed. If only it hadn't taken the appearance of the Tasch-Pharago for us to realize this. If only our own scientists had been brave enough to invent the bio-serum and let . . ."

"Our prey is escaping," a woman with the eyes of a lion said.

The hyena modder handed me a flyer with a card attached. "Get back to nature with a Primal Earth hunting package. If our band of hunter-trackers is unable to catch you, your next expedition is free. If they do, we'll send you home with a custom photo of your head mounted on our wall. Be sure to inquire about our drum circle and fire dancing ceremony with optional Mother Earth orgy. Experience man as he should be, naked and savage. Welcome to the trans-human era." He jumped off the limo and slid down the embankment after his friends.

When we were back inside and moving again, Shane took the flyer from me, read it, and then asked if this was something I wanted to do.

I crumpled the flyer and threw it at him. "I think when Mindy wondered what kind of bite marks I'd come back with, fleas and ticks weren't on her list."

"I thought modders were supposed to be civilized," McKee said.

"They are," Conor said, "except for the primitive ones."

"Oh, that makes tons of sense," Shane said.

"What did he mean by trans-human era?" I asked.

Conor popped the cap off a beer for him and one for me. "According to certain theorists, we're in that era now, and have been since the Tasch-Pharago arrived and shared their technology. Some people accept mods because they want to study the long-term effects of the bio-serum on human genetics. They think that the Tasch-Pharago gave us the bio-serum to eliminate something in our biology that's potentially dangerous to them. There's no proof, but the changes made by modding could be permanent on a level we don't understand even though the cosmetic effects disappear."

"So they're not terraforming the planet, just us?" Shane asked.

Conor shrugged. "Only if the theory proves true, and there's no proof one way or the other. The rumor mill says that that the US government pushed for weapons technology in exchange for permission to stay. They refused and offered the bio-serum instead, with promises of more technology if we managed to handle genetic manipulation responsibly."

Shane finished off his beer and opened another one. "Obviously they didn't study us too much before they landed here."

The limo ride ended a few minutes later, with a drop off at a skycab station. Finally, I'd get to ride in a flying car. The flight was pretty much like being in a small airplane, but the scenery made up for it. I stared too long at some of the weirder structures of the city and suffered a wave of dizziness, something the skycab driver called "Philopolis Syndrome" when he'd given his short safety speech. Everyone in town seemed to want to tell the newcomers all about the city, and it was getting tiresome.

We arrived at the hotel, a massive spire whose top twisted and melded with another nearby building. A member of the hotel staff met us at the skycab landing site, but he didn't look pleased. I wondered what was wrong. We followed him into the elevator and took a long trip to the top, exiting out into an open space filled with lush plants and the sound of running water.

He led us to a large seating area. "The showpiece of this suite is the invisi-balcony, which is unfortunately disabled. We've been having power fluctuations, but since the technology belongs to the Tasch-Pharago, we need them to fix it. If you're willing to move to the suite below, we'll be happy to credit you the difference in price."

"No," Conor said. "We want this one or the stay is free."

The manager's face went white. "That's not a word we're familiar with here, sir."

Conor sat down. "Let's talk, and I'll see if I can teach you the meaning of it."

***

On the way down to dinner, McKee told me that the manager had agreed we could stay in the suite, provided we kept the glass safety wall in place. He also agreed to rush the repair, and took a chunk of money off the total bill, the price of which I still wasn't allowed to know.

McKee shoved a bite of lobster into his mouth. "I always said Conor was a first class complainer."

"At least now it's working in our favor," Shane said.

Conor saluted with a forkful of steak. "It's called negotiation. It always works in my favor."

"Tell that to your ex-wife," Shane said. "I hear she cleaned you out pretty good."

"Yeah, well, that's not quite right, but you can think whatever makes you feel better. I wasn't the one who's paying his part in installments."

"Too far, the both of you, too far," McKee said. "Save that shit for the ride home."

"One day he won't be around to step between us," Shane said.

Conor laughed. "You'll pound me to dust, and I'll take you to court. But what will I do with a twelve year-old car and the largest porn collection on the East coast?"

"Learn how to screw someone outside of a sales environment?"

"I meant it," McKee said. "We're done with the negativity. Everybody fill up their glasses, it's time to make fun of Jason instead of each other for once. Don't worry man; we saved the best stuff for your wedding day. This is B-side material all the way."

"Great." I settled deeper into my comfortable chair, a beer in one hand and a teriyaki beef kabob in the other. "Hit me."

We stumbled upstairs together much later, and I wasn't sure whether my head spun more because of the drinks or the terrible things my best friends had to say about me, all in the name of fun. McKee and Shane carried two ice buckets filled with beer bottles, compliments of the hotel.

The sound of metallic voices echoed through our room.

"Who let the cut-rate sci-fi villain in?" McKee asked.

"I don't know," Shane said.

I led the group to where the noises were, stopping short when we saw two Tasch-Pharago, one tall, one short, at the invisi-balcony controls. They were humanoid-shaped, with silver lines running over their purple-skin, strange, but not as exotic as some I'd seen on the news.

"We are here to examine power flux problems," the shorter one said.

The tall one held up a twisted braid of yellow, black and red metal. "This piece is failing due to energy overload." It looked small in the alien's three-fingered grip. It dropped the metal onto the floor. The other Tasch-Pharago handed it a piece with blue crystals on the ends, which the tall one pressed into place in the control panel. There was a loud hum that eventually quieted.

"Thank you for making repairs so quickly," Shane said.

"The humans want everything to work correctly, but our machines are not fully adapted to this planet. These things take time, but the machine should work now." They headed for the door, the smaller Tasch-Pharago carrying the bag of tools.

Conor took a beer and twisted off the cap. "You don't have to thank me, for either the balcony being fixed so quickly or the free beer."

Shane grabbed one for him and handed another to me. "Don't worry, we won't."

Conor gave McKee the finger and stepped out onto the invisi-balcony. "Come on, you guys gotta try this out."

I took a swig of beer and walked out onto a surface that felt stable under my feet but just wasn't there. It wasn't really disorienting until I looked down through the floor at the long sloping side of the building and the street, which was so very far below me. I closed my eyes to dispel the illusion that I was falling, and when I opened them, I didn't look down again.

We spent the rest of the night drinking, but the drunker we got, the more the invisible floor beneath our feet bothered us, so eventually we moved inside. I stayed up to watch the sun light up the city before falling asleep on the couch.

***

The sounds of cleaning woke me up sometime later. I opened my eyes in time to see a hairy man disappear into the kitchen with a bag full of bottles. He came back out and gave a startled yelp when he saw me awake, which I didn't quite understand, since he was the one who looked like a hyena. His name tag said Roscoe.

"Didn't mean to wake you up," he said, "but you looked cold so I put a blanket on you. If you want me to come back later, I can."

No," I said, "might as well finish up now."

"Too bad your invisi-balcony isn't working. That thing never stays for more than a week. No wonder the damned alien ship crashed if this is how good their stuff worked."

"They fixed it last night," I said. "But if all their technology is this touchy, it explains why they haven't left yet."

He laughed and I wondered if it was racist (or specist) that I was disappointed he didn't sound like a hyena.

"Hate to piss in your beer, but it'll probably stop working tomorrow. Thing's been nothing but trouble since they put it in. Anyway, what you here for, man?"

"Bachelor party."

He laughed again, and this time I thought I heard a bit of the African scavenger in his chuckle. "Then what you doin' inside? You should be out livin' it up! But first, maybe you should go sleep a while in a bed. I'll put out the 'Privacy Please' sign when I leave."

"Thanks, man," I said.

"Have a great time tonight!"

I headed off to my room to sleep while Roscoe started to dust.

***

Because of the balcony problem, the hotel had given us a choice of VIP tickets to the opening ceremonies, which were mostly speeches, or early entrance to the Fairmount Revel. It wasn't a hard decision to make.

I couldn't believe what greeted us at the entrance. Modders of all kinds, from girls with cat ears and guys with tiger eyes to full-on animal/human blends that looked like they'd stepped out of mythology. I looked for AquaTina, but she wasn't there. All the better for me, since Mindy would probably be watching the live broadcast, or at least recording it for later viewing.

The modders welcomed us to the Revel with hugs and polite kisses, then put necklaces of flowers around our necks. It reminded me of Hawaii, which made me think of the tropics, which led to thoughts of Mindy in a skimpy bathing suit on a ship surrounded by admiring guys, all wanting to lead her astray.

A girl with rainbow eyes and sky-blue skin poked me on the nose. "Hey, no sour faces here." She draped a necklace of flowers over my head, then kissed my cheek. "Be happy while you can, let sorrow wait for another day." She slipped a card into my shirt pocket. "I'm good at making people smile. Come see me at our location in the Revel if that interests you. Just check the program book to find us."

Conor followed her. They talked for a few minutes. I had a feeling I'd be seeing her later.

"What was that about?" I asked him when he returned to the rest of us.

"I wanted to find out what time her show started."

"She's a dancer?"

"Not quite. We've got time for one stop beforehand." He led us through the crowded Revel lanes, ignoring the cries of modders hawking weird devices or running carnival games and rides. He stopped outside one of the rides, a platform with a very long line wrapped around it. "I'm going to find the conductor. You guys wait here."

"Conductor?" Shane said. "I don't think that's what you call the people in charge of rides."

"I don't know," McKee said. "What is this one anyway?"

"Ask Conor," I said. "He's waving us to the front of the line."

McKee did ask Conor about it when we met him at the front of the line, but he wouldn't say anything more than that we'd enjoy it and to stop asking him questions.

A short man with a Philopolis Revel logo on his shirt directed us to stand in a much shorter line, and not five minutes later, he ushered us up onto the platform. The seats were in a triangular pattern facing a tall chair in the center in which sat a Tasch-Pharago.

Human ushers directed us to seats, after making sure we knew that the presentation would be viewable no matter where we sat. Conor got us close to the Tasch-Pharago. It was tall, like the one I'd seen in our room earlier, but its head tapered to a point behind its shoulders. Orange and yellow stripes covered what I could see of its skin.

It lifted a two-fingered hand into the air when we'd all found a seat.

"Welcome, revelers. You are curious as to where we come from. This machine will show you some of the worlds we once called home. To do that, we need to leave Earth. Are you prepared? The journey is not dangerous, though you may find it disorienting."

I looked for a seatbelt but there wasn't one. I turned to Conor, and found him looking straight ahead with a smirk on his face. The air shimmered around me, and the floor dropped away. Below me, Philopolis faded into a small light. Soon Earth and the moon were under my feet as well. Another passenger cried out, but I couldn't tell if it was from fear or amazement. I hadn't known what to expect, so I wasn't sure how I was feeling.

"Look up," Conor said.

We passed through a cloudy band, and then the Milky Way was below me. Or I guessed it was. I'd never been much of an astronomer. Soon even that passed beneath my feet. The feeling of upward climbing stopped. All around us were the bright points of stars and other celestial bodies.

"Focus on a point of light, and it will show you another world."

I stared at a dot above the Tasch-Pharago's head, and the space around me changed as I moved closer to it. I expected purple seas and yellow mountains, or maybe something that looked like a slightly weirder version of earth, but never did I imagine an unending swamp of greenish-black water and red mud, broken by plants that looked sort of like marsh grass, only taller and thick like bamboo. I could smell the wet mud and the decaying of alien life below the water. The scents made my nose twitch, and I sneezed a few times, after which I couldn't smell anything. Above the plants rose buildings set on massive pilings. They were long, thin, and curved like some of the structures in Philopolis. On top of the spindly, curving arms were fragile domes that looked like bubbles. One of the domes floated free of the arm it was resting on and floated across the swamp. I went with it, flying high over the water, until it joined a few more bubbles. Inside them were more beings that looked like the one with me in the triangle. They were cooking something over a silver flame. I could feel the intense heat from the fire, though it carried with it a dampness that I'd never felt in fire before. One of the aliens broke off a piece of whatever they were cooking on the fire and ate it. I tasted the food along with it, a flavor like nothing that had ever touched my tongue before. I tried to analyze the taste, but I shot back into space before I could, and then the sounds, smells and sights of earth surrounded me again, and Conor was shaking my shoulder and telling me we had to move so the next people could go.

The Tasch-Pharago came over to me. "You visited my home world; I can smell it on you. Your languages do not have the right sounds for me to tell you what it is called, but it is a place of soft winds and warm breezes."

"Then why did you leave?" The question jumped out of me before I could stop it.

The Tasch-Pharago didn't look insulted. "Many reasons, though you humans would say political differences. Please exit the platform now. Others are waiting."

I walked down the ramp, but I couldn't really concentrate on what I was seeing here. Some part of me hadn't yet come back from that alien world. I wondered if it ever would.

While I was still considering life on another planet, Conor was more interested in dragging me to his new friend's show. He wouldn't tell us what it was about, though he acted like he knew. Her card didn't tell me anything but her name, which was Yzabella, and that she "specialized in transformations."

There's only one law during a bachelor party, and that's don't fall in love with the entertainment. They're only there because someone paid them, and pretending to like you is their job. It improves their tips. Whether that held true in Philopolis or not, I wasn't sure, but I figured that if a person here wanted something, or someone, they'd make it pretty damned clear. The moral majority was too scared of the Tasch-Pharago to live here for the most part, so shame and guilt were pretty much off the table. When you could tailor your look to exactly how you felt at that moment, what was the point of hiding your emotions anyway? There were still people out to save the souls of the denizens of the city, but by and large they got nowhere.

Conor was the one who'd told me the law during his bachelor party, but he wasn't paying it much attention now. Not that the girl dancing on the stage wasn't beautiful, but he seemed intent on focusing all his attention on her, something which he had also warned me against.

There were three other girls dancing up there with her. One had the palest skin I'd ever seen. Milk was darker than she was. I didn't understand why until the lights went off. Only then could you see the patterns and shapes drawn in glowing green lines on her skin. The other two girls were in the middle stages of modding. One had cheetah spots and even a foot long tail, while the other sported scaly patches of crocodile skin along her spine and a distinct greenish tint to her skin everywhere else. Their dancing was fun to watch, but at no point did they remove what little clothes they were wearing.

"Come on up here, honey," Yzabella said to Conor. "I've got a surprise for you."

We laughed at him as he climbed up onto the stage, and I wondered if he was going to discover his girl had different equipment below the belt than he thought.

Instead, the crocodile girl handed her a syringe.

"You're cute, but how brave are you? I mean, here you are, surrounded by modders, but you remain unchanged yourself. How much of the Philopolis experience do you really want? Will you leave without trying even a short term mod?"

The crowd shouted encouragement at Conor. Shane taunted him with chicken noises, pretty much ensuring he'd go through with it.

"I'll try a mod on one condition. That you come home with me tonight."

The crowd roared their approval.

Yzabella wasn't convinced quite so easily. She uncapped the syringe and held it out to him. He stuck out his arm.

"No baby," she said, "it's a little more complicated than that." She unbuttoned his shirt, pushed it back off his shoulders and pressed her hand against his bare chest.

"If I'd known this was going to happen in front of a crowd, I'd have worked out more."

The crowd laughed, then applauded.

"When did he become a comedian?" Shane asked.

The girl with the rainbow eyes shushed the audience. "A first dose is always a tricky prospect. So let's help our new friend get in touch with his inner . . ." she looked down at the needle cap. "Wolf."

The audience started to howl, and I found myself making the noise along with them. The girl with the rainbow eyes kissed Conor on the mouth, then jammed the needle into his neck.

"Howl!" she shouted, moving aside so we could see her depress the plunger and send the bio-serum into Conor's system.

The audience obeyed her, then started chanting 'howl' at Conor, who stood with his hands over his face as if he was embarrassed to be up on stage. The chant earned us some curious looks from the crowd going by outside. Some even stepped inside to watch what was going on.

Conor had remained silent while the crowd encouraged him with their noises, but now he put his head back and let loose a howl of his own, the needle still stuck in his flesh. Several people in the audience shivered at the note of sorrow underlying the cry, and I was among them.

"I guess I'll leave him alone about his wife," McKee said.

The audience applauded even louder when the howling stopped and the first changes began to appear on Conor's face. The girl with the rainbow eyes kissed Conor one more time, then led him to a chair on the side of the stage. She opened a box next to the chair and held a dozen more syringes toward the crowd. "Who's next? If you're worried about being stuck here at the end of the Revel, don't worry. This serum is a short-term formula, designed to last about six hours. You'll be back to your old, boring self by breakfast tomorrow!"

"This seems a bit like bullshit," McKee said. "It's a suggestion trick. I mean, it's not like Conor's sprouted hair or anything."

"Not yet. Could be slow acting too. If you're so sure it's crap, why not go try it yourself?"

"Why don't we all go, Mr. Bachelor?"

"I promised Mindy I wouldn't."

McKee slapped me on the back. "Buddy, if this is the only thing we get you to do that you promised Mindy you wouldn't, then we're doing things totally wrong." He grabbed my left arm.

Shane took hold of my right. "It's ok to struggle a little if you want, we'll tell Mindy you fought us the whole way up the stage."

The girl with the rainbow eyes cupped my chin in her hand. "We don't force people to mod boys. Free will or no go."

"Don't worry about that," I said. "I know what I'm doing. Give me the hyena mod, if you have it."

She skipped back to the box, then returned to me with a needle. "You're sure? Even the short term changes are pretty severe."

I turned to the audience, stretched out my neck so she'd have a good shot, then waited for the sting. I didn't feel the needle, only the warmth of bio-serum spreading through my system.

Things got a little floaty for me, and I felt drunk and unfocused. Then I heard the crowd yipping like a hyena, and I immediately thought of Roscoe. I got warm all over, and then the girl with the rainbow eyes was leading me to a chair next to Conor, who looked more like the Wolfman from an old movie than a real wolf.

"Was this a smart idea?" he asked, his voice deeper than usual.

"I couldn't tell you," I said, then laughed.

McKee and Shane stumbled over to us and sat down.

"She injected me with lion," McKee said.

"I don't know what mine is exactly," Shane said. His eyes were changing color, going from blue to orange. "But I want to fly."

McKee patted my cheek. "You're starting to get a five o'clock shadow."

I held back the laugh that threatened to burst out of me. "Is laughing even a real hyena trait?"

Shane snarled at me. "Do I look like a fucking animal biologist?"

A guy we didn't know sat down on the stage next to the box of bio-serum. "Nice growl man. Hyenas don't laugh, but they make a laughter-like sound, and a giggle is probably the best you can do to mimic it."

"Shut up," McKee said. "You're making my head hurt."

"You must be spliced with lion DNA. Fight the urge to be aggressive and it'll pass. Although you should be glad that it's a short duration, otherwise you'd want to tear your hyena buddy a new one sooner or later."

"If you're a visitor like us, how do you know so much about this?"

"I'm not; I just don't have enough money to keep my mod going. Yzabella hooks me up every year, and then I work odd jobs to get money the rest of the year. I'm actually selling a nice jacket from the laughing skulls of doom.

It's a souvenir you can take with you out of the city, and it's pretty cheap. There's a few bullet holes in the front, but they add character."

I wanted to answer him, but pressure building in my skull made me unable to talk. It wasn't like any headache I'd ever had.

"The serum's kicking in. Give it a few minutes and the feeling will go away."

I lowered my head a little and closed my eyes, trying to shut out the crowd's noise. Mindy wouldn't like that I'd done this, but if she wanted to stop me, then she should have come along instead of going on her own excursion.

By the time the last person had joined us on the stage, the number of new modders was around twenty. The pain from my own serum had faded a few minutes after starting, though it hadn't hurt badly, the stretching of my face into the small muzzle had been a strange sensation. I really wanted to see what I looked like in a mirror.

Yzabella spoke to the remaining crowd, now much reduced because most of us were up on the stage. "Go and enjoy the Revel, and if you want to try a mod later, then return here and I or someone else will help you. As for those who've modded, you too should go and experience the Revel. Your new senses will show you things you'd have missed before. The formula should start wearing off in four hours, so there's plenty of time to explore."

"Don't forget beautiful," Conor said, "you promised to come home with me tonight."

"Tell you what, I'll hang out with you and give you the chance to make it happen. That's the best I can promise you."

McKee nudged Shane, who looked at me. I shrugged. He had his own room in the suite, so if he succeeded we'd just have to be nice to her at breakfast. And maybe it would keep the pressure off of me from the other two for an affair of my own. It wasn't that they disliked Mindy, but they were pretty convinced, for some reason, that she was going to fool around and they thought I should too. I wasn't the first of my friends to get married, but I might have been the only one who planned on staying that way forever. Conor had married his girlfriend just to shut her up, and three years later, she'd left him. For a smart guy, he could be pretty stupid sometimes. The new modders were heading out into the Revel, but Conor was still talking to Yzabella on the stage.

"He hasn't even talked her to the ground yet," McKee said. "And that cutie growing fuzzy ears is way ahead of us now."

"So we'll go outside and see if you can find her," I said. "We could spend maybe twenty minutes not chasing women. That would be different."

"Sightsee on your own time," McKee said. He left the tent.

Shane shook his head. "He stays single for five years and now he's in a rush to find a girl. Maybe he inherited the lion's biological clock as well as the mane."

"It's possible, I guess. What should we go do?"

Instead of answering me, McKee yelled to Conor and told him to hurry up.

Conor held out his arm for Yzabella, and they walked off the stage together. McKee made a disgusted noise, but I ignored him.

"So this is your bachelor party?" Yzabella asked. "I would've expected you to be down at the Joi-Station or even Xibalba."

"If those are strip clubs," McKee said, "we did that for Conor's bachelor party a while back, and let's just say while it was a memorable evening, it's not something we wanted to repeat for Jason's party."

"We're not legally allowed to repeat it," Shane said.

"And the less we talk about it," I said, "the better."

McKee found his girl down the lane a little bit, but after talking to her for a few minutes he gave us a casual thumbs down, which meant she was unavailable for some reason. Conor and Yzabella joined us while we were waiting for McKee to finish up talking to his girl.

Conor pulled me aside. "She's got some friends we can invite back up to our room for a party. She's not promising hook-ups but it gives McKee and Shane a chance, and we can all have a good time even if nothing else happens. It's your call though, so what do you say?"

"Sure," I said. "Let's do it."

***

Our room wasn't empty when we got back, but not because the Tasch-Pharago were in it. I didn't see the intruder; I smelled him. I motioned for everyone to stay at the door while I investigated. The control panel for the invisi-balcony hung open. Bits of wire trailed out of it, and suddenly I knew why the machinery had been failing. Sabotage. Using my nose, I tracked the scent of the thief to my bedroom. I flung open the closet door. Roscoe flinched, then continued to try and hide behind my clothes.

"You son of a bitch! One of us could've been killed!"

"No need to insult my mother, especially since you look like my brother," Roscoe said. "Someone paid me good money to make sure that thing didn't work, and hell no, I'm not telling you who it was."

"That's ok," I said. "Come on, I'll escort you out."

Roscoe walked with me, but kept a wary eye out for any sudden moves on my part. We walked through the living room, where the others had gathered despite my suggestion to stay at the door.

"Guys, this is Roscoe. He stole the works out of the invisi-balcony and is responsible for Yzabella's near fatal fall earlier." Ok, so that hadn't happened.

But he didn't need to know that. "Roscoe, this is Conor, Yzabella's suitor and also a new lion modder. I think he might want to have a word with you."

Conor pounded a fist on the coffee table. "You almost cost me my date."

"Look," Roscoe said. "I wasn't tryin' to get anybody killed, I just—" he bolted for the door, but McKee and Shane caught him before he could get too close. They dragged him to the edge of the invisi-balcony and hung his head over the edge.

"Tell me, what other structures have you sabotaged? Something at the Revel?" When he didn't answer, they pushed more of him over the ledge.

"Nothing at the Revel, I swear! They didn't want to hurt normal humans, just modders or Tasch-Pharago."

"Did you ever see the execution video of that convicted terrorist a while back?" Conor asked. "The one the Tasch-Pharago got to kill because he hurt some of the aliens?"

"The leaked video was pretty brutal," I said. "And all we got to see was the aftermath. Not a pretty corpse. We're talking closed casket and everything."

"You got this all wrong. I'm just a poor guy hired to deliver the message and to bring the parts to the next guy on the list."

"So tell me who that is," I said. "We'll make your delivery for you."

"That's not a good idea," Roscoe said. "They're dangerous. But if you want a club upside the head, that's not my problem. He's waiting for me in the bar downstairs."

"Let's go then," I said.

"It's your funeral," Roscoe said.

"You sure you should do this alone?" Conor asked.

"I won't be alone," I said, "but we don't want to scare him off. Why don't you hang out in the lobby? So if anything happens, you'll be right there."

They agreed, and left the suite. We gave them a few minutes to get comfortable in the lobby, then walked to the elevators.

"This is a shitty idea," Roscoe said. "It's going to get us both killed."

"Shut up and lead on," I said.

We left the elevator and headed for the bar area. Conor and Shane sat on a couch near the front door of the hotel. I didn't see McKee anywhere, but I didn't have time to look for him.

I prodded Roscoe into the bar area ahead of me.

"Where's your buddy?" I asked him.

"He'll be here, don't worry about it. Get a table and I'll grab us some beers."

I watched Roscoe head to the bar, then sat down at an empty table. Roscoe got halfway back to the table with the beers before dropping them and darting out the door.

"Son of a..." I jumped up and got to the lobby just in time to see him disappear out the front door. None of my friends were visible, so I just took off after him myself.

He ducked down a narrow alley, and I followed him, surprised that I could see so well in the dark. I wasn't so happy with the improvement in my sense of smell. I had to stop every few feet to keep from throwing up. He exited the alley ahead of me, looking left and right, though for what I didn't know. I crept closer, but he must've heard me coming, because he took off down the street. I left the alley in time to see him duck inside a building called the Joi-Station.

Even if I hadn't seen Roscoe enter the building, I'd have headed there anyway. There was an old neon sign depicting a dancing girl on the wall next to the door, and a large holographic sign on top showing images of under-clothed men and women, with mods and without.

I shoved the door open and found myself in a short hallway with a coat check room on one side and a closed door on the other. Roscoe wasn't here, but two women sat on barstools in front of the coats. Both were snake modders, but in very different stages.

One had dark blue scales from head to toe, with light blue diamonds forming a line from her throat down to her stomach. I wasn't sure she was wearing any clothes, but I didn't look to see where the blue diamonds ended. Silver scales spelled out the name 'Tequella' over her left breast and pink scales spelled out 'Joi-Station' over her right.

The other modder's skin had a green tinge to it, and gold scales covered the topside of her arms and her shoulders, with a line of green scales on her belly that parted just under her breasts and wrapped around them. Or so I assumed, because she wore a tiny bikini top. Her name wasn't written anywhere on her, and she wore a baseball cap pulled low over her eyes. Still, there was something familiar about her.

Tequella poked me on the shoulder, interrupting a closer inspection. "You've come to beat on Roscoe, haven't you honey?"

I nodded.

"He's just through there, but I'd be careful. He gets mean when he's cornered. I'll let you in."

She stood, and I leaned against the other door to let her by. I felt the door at my back open, and a heavy coat enveloped my head.

"Don't struggle," Roscoe said.

"We're cool," I said, but I wasn't sure he could hear me with my voice muffled by the coat.

"You got this?" I heard Tequella ask.

Roscoe must've said yes, because I heard the door open. He pushed me ahead of him through the doorway and then a little ways more before stopping.

"You don't know when to stop, do you?" Roscoe asked. "Well, I hope you like the consequences." He pulled the coat off of my head.

I had just an instant to take in the sight of my friends standing around me before they all yelled "Surprise!"

Then the golden scaled snake modder from the other room was in my arms. She lifted the cap and I saw it was Mindy. There were tiny golden scales around her eyes that branched into spiral patterns on her cheeks.

"A set-up?" I asked. My face was turning red, a little from embarrassment at being surprised, and a little from being angry that my adventure had been scripted.

"No, baby," Mindy said. "Just the part where you caught Roscoe and he led you here. I don't even know what you were up to, besides forgetting to shave and getting a wicked five o'clock shadow."

"You've been in the city the whole time?" I asked her.

She nodded. "Did you really think a cruise was going to be enough for me once you decided to come here? No way were you going to hang out with aliens while I sat in the sun on some island. Let's go get a drink."

McKee, Shane and Conor found us at the bar, with Roscoe following along behind them.

"Sorry to fool you like that, Jason," Roscoe said. "You may not recognize me now, but we met a few times outside the city. I was calling myself Jamie then."

"Conor's buddy," I said. "We talked about you on the limo ride in."

He laughed, shook my hand, then ordered himself a drink from the bar.

Conor slapped my back. "Had enough adventure for a while?"

"You're something else, man," I said, but I couldn't even manage to pretend to be angry with him. "It's too bad Mindy's here. Now we won't get to see any modded strippers. I was going to get you a dance from the blue scaled girl I met on the way in."

The rest of us laughed as Conor turned pale. He wasn't fond of snakes.

"I think your fiancée's got you covered there too." Shane pointed to a line of scantily dressed men and women, all wrapped in a banner bearing our names and the date of our wedding.

"Come on, baby" Mindy said. "Let's go unwrap our present."

"I guess I better do what the ball and chain says." I pretended to be glum while I headed up to the front of the room, hand-in-hand with Mindy. We started at opposite ends of the banner and met up in the middle. The strippers dispersed into the crowd.

I pulled out the flyer for the Primal Earth Hunting Party. "Conor and the boys wanted to do this. I think it'd be cool to surprise them with it." It was sort of a mean thing to do, but I owed them for their part in the surprise party. They hadn't done as much planning as Mindy, but even though I wasn't

married yet, I knew better than to trick my soon-to-be-wife.
I wasn't suicidal after all.

On "Three Days in Philopolis," Paul writes...
I've written two novels about the city of Philopolis, one dealing with Felix Grenfell, who was there when the Tasch-Pharago landed on Philadelphia, and another with some of the stranger denizens of the city. This anthology provided me with the opportunity to give readers a glimpse into Philopolis from the perspective of an outsider. Transhumanism is a real-world concept causing debate right now, and is one of the themes of my novels. Just how much can you blur the line of humanity before you cease to be human? Is it ever possible? And who decides where to draw the line and what happens to those who cross it?

A WAVE THEN GOODBYE
A Startenders Adventure
PATRICK THOMAS

"Murphy, I'm going to miss this place," Paddy Moran said, tenderly caressing the wooden bar that his late wife had made for him a long time ago. And by long time, I meant it. She finished it in 1886. As a leprechaun, the boss was extremely long-lived.

The boss sighed. This was even rougher on him than the rest of us - not that anyone wanted to lose New York City. Sadly, we didn't have a choice.

"Me too. I don't know what I would've done without Bulfinche's Pub and all the people here after Elsie died. Then after Terrorbelle was killed, I was an even worse mess," I said. "Still, we have to look at the upside. We're all about to become astronauts."

The boss smiled. "Better than astronauts. Startenders."

We exited the bar that had been our home and entered the attached garage. Most of the moving was already done. We left enough in Bulfinche's Pub to serve as our base of operations on the ground. We still had time. Not a lot of it, but hopefully enough to save more than ten million people from being destroyed by a pissed off and insane sea god.

I'd been to *Startender Station* several times before, but this time we were opening it up for business. We were about to let the world know that the Startenders existed, which would be a shock to many, especially considering who some of us were. It wasn't just that private individuals and legends had built a space station, but starships. Or rather, barships. We were taking what we had been doing for over a century at Bulfinche's Pub out into the universe. We'd established a base on the moon and left the solar system while the furthest the rest of the world had gotten was Rovers on Mars.

We didn't rely on old-fashioned things like rockets to make orbit. We had several methods, not the least of which was a revamped 1930 V6 Cadillac that the boss called Baby that he used to run booze with during prohibition.

The Caddy was big, but that didn't mean all of our passengers were going to be able to fit inside. One in particular was bigger than the car itself. Cerberus had once been a guardian for the Greco-Roman god Pluto until Paddy won the mutt in a card game. The three-headed pup was a very good dog and was moving with us to the station, but first we had to get him into orbit. Since he couldn't fit in the car, the plan was for him to ride on top.

I could bore you with the details of how the genius god Vulcan refurbished the Caddy so it generated mystic fields to protect the passengers while it defied the laws of gravity and physics, but I don't understand it all myself. The giant triple-headed mutt climbed on the roof of the car. Paddy and I got inside and drove out of Bulfinche's Pub onto the streets of Manhattan. Over the years we didn't exactly hide, but we hadn't gone out of our way to get noticed. That wasn't going to be a worry anymore.

The folks on the street were more than a little shocked to see a creature of myth riding on top of an antique car, but that was nothing compared to what they must have been thinking when they saw the Caddy take off into the sky and heard Cerberus howling in three part harmony.

The boss was taking it easy. The shields were supposed to keep anyone in or on the car safe, but he wasn't about to take any chances with his favorite pup riding on the roof.

As we made orbit, *Startender Station* rose up with the sun behind it. It was a beautiful sight, a work of engineering genius as well as a work of art. It had one main section with five branches, each named for one of the boroughs of the city we were about to lose. Even if it wasn't in orbit, it would still be the single largest structure meant to house people on Earth.

It inspired me with a sense of awe and pride that I had some small hand in making it a reality. Off in the distance we could make out the latest International Space Station. It was a significantly smaller structure, but still one that signified world unity and showed that some of the countries below could work together towards a common goal. They didn't have the advantages we did, so the impressiveness of our station didn't take anything away from their accomplishment. Paddy looked over at the ISS and smiled, stopping the car so we floated in orbit.

"Me wife Bulfinche always told me that when you move into a new home that ye should always be neighborly. I'm thinking we should be neighborly," Paddy said, grinning from ear to ear.

I smiled back as I figured out what he was thinking. "I was wondering what the food and whiskey in the basket was for. Let's go say hi."

We pulled the Caddy along the International Space Station and parked near an airlock. Paddy extended our shielding so it butted up against the side of the station and then honked the horn. We could see through the glass the looks of confusion on the astronauts' faces on hearing a car horn in space. Paddy honked again and Cerberus barked. Our shielding had atmosphere so both sounds carried inside.

The astronauts moved to the window, rubbed their eyes, then looked at each other, trying to figure out if the sight of an antique car floating outside in space was a hallucination.

Paddy got out of the car, wearing his Startender badge. It looked like an old Sherriff's star with the shot o' gold logo of Bulfinche's Pub in the center. I wore mine too. The small amulet had many properties, not the least of which was to provide an atmosphere and protect the wearer against temperature and gravity extremes. It served well as a spacesuit, at least in the short term.

Paddy floated over and knocked on the airlock. After some arguing among themselves, then seeing Paddy hold up the basket, they decided to open the outer lock.

"Ye wait here pup and watch the car," Paddy told Cerberus. "We won't be long." The dog nodded in triplicate. The boss and I went in and the astronauts closed the outer airlock behind us, then opened the inner.

"Hello. What's going on?" one of the astronauts said awkwardly as he approached us. He was American judging by the accent.

Paddy shook his hand and then the other astronaut's. I followed suit. "We've just moved into the neighborhood." Paddy pointed to *Startender Station*, floating off their bow like something out of a science fiction movie. "We just wanted to say hi and bring ye this small gift."

Both astronauts' eyes opened wider and they started to drool. The basket was four feet in diameter and filled with delicacies that they likely hadn't had in months.

"Thank you, but where did that station come from?" The second astronaut sounded Russian.

"That little thing? Something we Startenders whipped together," Paddy said with false humility. We had gotten a message from the future decades ago about the now impending disaster and Paddy had dedicated his life and not inconsiderable fortune to making sure everyone gets out of New York alive. "Ye are welcome to come visit whenever ye like, but first a toast." Paddy took out one of the bottles of whiskey that had a Bulfinche's Pub label. He brews it himself and I've never tasted anything finer. The boss handed out four glasses and poured. Raising his glass, he said "To peace, hope, happiness and a new era for space travel."

The astronauts drank hesitantly, at least until the whiskey passed their lips. After that, their eyes went wide and their lips smiled as their taste buds jumped for joy.

And just like that, we made two new friends.

Hopefully the rest of the world would be as accommodating.

***

There are parts of *Startender Station* where the inside is bigger than the outside by virtue of pocket dimensions and folded space, giving each of those areas more square footage than they should have. One such room was the hangar bay where we parked the barships.

The barships were marvels of magic and technology. We'd mined asteroids in our own solar system and found tremendous amounts of gold – enough to build our ships out of. It was that or tank the value of the precious metal on Earth.

Thanks to the work of Vulcan, that gold was made into a special alloy which was fluid and malleable, a new twist on a non-Newtonian fluid, able to change shape and link up with a pocket dimension that ran alongside our own. It allowed us to shunt the tremendous mass of the ship so we could appear bigger or smaller depending on which we wanted to be.

This wasn't the first time I've seen *Fools' Glory*. It wouldn't even be the first time I've taken her out for a spin. It would however be the first time that she was officially mine to command.

The Startenders are not a military organization so the idea of having military ranks seemed wrong to us, so we made up our own. I was the head honcho, the equivalent of captain. My honcho or first mate was the Norse trickster god Loki. We'd been through a lot and he'd reformed to a great extent.

I heard metal footsteps on the deck. I didn't bother to look behind me, figuring my crew's melog had arrived. The melog were an artificial race of people Vulcan had developed ages ago. Some might call them androids or robots, but they were much more than that. They had souls and could reproduce. In fact, I was at the birth of the golden man who stood behind me.

"Hi Eric," I said.

"Hi ya, Murph. You ready to get this party started?"

I didn't know how much of a party the destruction of my hometown was going to be, but I knew what he meant. New York City was doomed, but her people were not. "You bet, as long as you're willing to play taxi driver."

The melog have interfaces that allow them to link up and control the ships mentally, making them superb pilots. The ship could be flown and maneuvered by their thoughts, although as head honcho I could override the melog's control if necessary. I doubted I'd ever have to do it, but it made sense to have the option.

"Absolutely, boss," Eric said.

I rubbed my hand against the side of the barship tenderly. "Open sesame."

Eric smiled and a door suddenly appeared in the golden hull.

We climbed inside and headed back down to Manhattan.

***

As excited as I was with the idea of going out into space, I couldn't forget what the motivation for it was. What the cost was going to be, not the least of which was the loss of Bulfinche's Pub.

It may seem silly to be emotionally attached to a bar, but only to someone who's never visited us. Bulfinche's was more than a watering hole. Long ago, Paddy bought the place with his pot of gold and ever since rainbows have led those in trouble to our door. Bulfinche's Pub is the hope at the end of the rainbow, a place where those with great power helped those with none. We helped to right wrongs and shared our sorrow, joy, and laughter. The sign over the door read *Maireann dóchas is gliodar*, which is Gaelic for *hope and happiness never die*. And just maybe, if we were real good and very lucky, no one would die when Manhattan was destroyed.

The plan was to have one hundred fifty Startenders. We didn't have that many yet, but were a good way there and all of them were in the pub. The number was significant. There were one hundred fifty seats at King Arthur's Roundtable. Robin Hood had one hundred and fifty Merry Men. There had been one hundred and fifty Daemor in the Thandau War. And hopefully one day there'll be one hundred fifty Startenders.

Considering who was in the group - tricksters like Coyote and Sun WuKong the monkey king; heroes such as Hercules, the samurai Kintaro, and Sir Marok, the werewolf knight of the Round Table - it was deathly quiet. Almost like a wake and not the good Irish kind we'd often hosted. We all knew even if we managed to get every last soul out of New York, we were still going to lose the city.

Paddy stood behind the bar and hit a beer mug with a spoon. All eyes turned toward the boss.

"I'd like to thank ye all for coming. More than that, I'd like to thank ye all for being a part of the Startenders and our rescue efforts to save the citizens of New York City. I know not all of ye have agreed to join the Startenders..." The Council of Thrones' Enforcer Nemesis and Wisp, the owner of the Eternity Club, for two. "...but nonetheless you're here to help and that's what matters. I'm going to turn the meeting over to a dearly departed friend." Yes, he really was turning the meeting over to a dead man. "He is gone, but not forgotten and he was good enough to leave us recordings like this one which he wanted me to play now. Ladies and gentlemen, I give ye the greatest psychic who ever lived or died, Mosie."

"Thanks for that intro Paddy," said Mosie's face from a giant television screen. "It's good to see you all again. Well, not that I can actually see any of you from the TV, but I saw all of you sitting there when I was still alive and I saw what is about to happen now. I even had to get sober to do it after we got our message in a metal bottle from the future all those years ago. It gave us enough time to get ready. Sometime in the next three days, the insane god Poseidon will come onto land somewhere in Manhattan. Thanks to the amulet that Demeter made him, he's stayed hidden all these years and will continue to do so despite our best efforts. There is no way to find him. Trust me on this." We did, but we were still hunting the mad sea god in hopes of stopping him before it was too late. We had a lot of raw power. Unfortunately luck and planning can negate that. "He will come ashore, someone will insult him and push him over the edge. In a fit of rage he'll cause a seaquake and call forth the ocean. A tidal wave will envelop all five boroughs and parts of Jersey and Long Island. A sea quake will sink the island of Manhattan beneath the water. There is nothing we can do to stop it."

"We'll see about that, vision boy," said Rebecca, the very elderly Mother of the Streets. She's well over 100, yet still spry enough to carry out her duties taking care of the homeless and the downtrodden of the city.

"Rebecca, we all know you're going to try to stop him. I'm sorry, but you're going to fail," said Mosie's prerecorded message. "There is something... special in store for you. By now the first wave of barships are ready. Use their special properties to move the masses. Have Pace and the other trolls set up nexi..." Plural of nexus. "To get people out." Trolls were not native to Earth; they were actually aliens. Many have the mystic ability to open up gateways between worlds and dimensions. We were lucky enough to count four among the Startenders.

"We have to do something big to get everyone's attention. Otherwise people won't be scared enough to evacuate, especially if the reason we give is that a mad Greco-Roman sea god is about to sink Manhattan. Paddy will phone in a phony nuclear bomb threat to the authorities. Uncle Sam and some of our other government connections will make sure we get help with the evacuations. We've placed radioactive materials with just enough trace around the city to make the Powers That Be believe the hoax. You'll still have to work day and night for three days to get everyone..." Mosie paused and actually turned his digital head to look at Rebecca. "....almost everybody safely off. We have several mystic measures in place to help, a mixture of aversion, trust and fear spells that will make even those that want to stay head for safer pastures. I wish I could be there to help you more, but I know you'll do me proud, do Paddy proud and do this world proud. If I may suggest we all raise a glass," Mosie lifted a mug that looked like it had been filled with whiskey. The psychic was always a serious drinker, mainly because being drunk kept him from going insane from seeing everything that ever happened or will happen all at once. "And let us toast one final time. To Bulfinche's Pub and what it has meant to all of us. It is a tragedy that we lose it, but without it, entire worlds will not have the Startenders to save them." Mosie lifted his glass. "To Bulfinche's!"

Paddy lifted his glass. "To Bulfinche's!"

"To Bulfinche's!" we all said, raising and draining our glasses.

"It's taken a lot to plan everything. I will turn the rest of the meeting over to the head honcho of the *Fools' Glory*, Murphy, who will give you all your assignments."

"Thanks, buddy. We miss you," I said to the recording.

"And well you should," the recorded Mosie said. "Don't worry. I've made more recordings to help you with certain things, but for the most part you'll be on your own. I still owe you, Murph, and one day I'll be able to pay you back."

"Cryptic much?" I said. I knew better than to ask how. He was the same back when he was alive.

"Always. Now stop goofing off and get to work," Mosie's recording said.

I grinned and turned to the greatest assembly of heroes and raw power the Earth has likely even seen.

"Okay gang, here's the plan..."

***

One of the first orders of business was the United Nations. It wasn't that we felt diplomats ranked above regular people by any means. We had ulterior motives for getting them out first.

There was quite a debate about who to send in to give our speech to the General Assembly. We'd arranged the session through guile and fast talking weeks before. We had several Startenders who could not only sell ice to Eskimos, but convince them to pick up snowmaking machines and air-conditioners, not to mention bathing suits and outdoor swimming pools.

Getting what we wanted was, on a lot of levels, going to be an elaborate con job. Still, we couldn't come across as grifters or snake-oil salesman, so we sent one of our best and noblest – Sir Dagonet.

Dagonet started out centuries ago in King Arthur's Court as the jester and ended up getting knighted. An encounter with the Holy Grail left him immortal. The Infinite Jester has done the Round Table proud over the centuries by keeping the ideals of Camelot alive. Even the other surviving Knights agree that Dagonet embodies the best of those ideals, so he was chosen as our diplomatic face. Not to mention he's had quite a bit of diplomatic experience throughout the years.

Dagonet gave a rousing speech announcing to the world the existence of the moon base, Ben City, and *Startenders Station*. We planned to name it in memory and honor of the greatest city in the world, but as its destruction hadn't happened yet, we thought it was best to not officially name it until after.

Dagonet made our case for both station and base to receive sovereign nation status. Separate status for each was best as Paddy fully owned the station, but the moon base was a joint venture.

It was even made more impressive as Dagonet gave key aspects of his speech in multiple languages without the need of a translator.

To say the so-called debate and discussion that followed was chaos would be putting it diplomatically.

"Are you trying to tell us that the moon base that we've heard rumors of is complete and large enough to house hundreds of thousands of people?" the Russian ambassador said.

"Well over that number. It's more of a city than a base. And we have room for expansion," the Infinite Jester said.

"And what kind of a name is Ben City?" asked another rather angry ambassador from a small and rather angry country.

"It is named in honor of Ben Horus, the man whose dream led to the realty of the first city on the moon," Dagonet said.

"That's the lunatic who has been selling laser advertising on the first night of the full moon for decades," the angry ambassador said.

"I take exception to lunatic and would prefer visionary," Dagonet said.

"He's dead," the angry ambassador said.

"I'm aware of that. I was one of his pall bearers. But his dream and memory live on," Dagonet said.

"None of this matters. The United States claims the moon as sovereign territory, as our astronauts were the first to set foot there," the American ambassador said.

"Nonsense! The People's Republic claims the moon," the Chinese ambassador said.

More ambassadors starting yelling that their countries were claiming the same.

Dagonet smiled and lifted his hand. "As you all know, by treaty no country is able to claim the moon. And we are not claiming the moon, just Ben City and the surrounding area and airspace."

"Are you also trying to tell us that you got enough supplies into orbit to build an entire space station and a city on the moon, without any of our surveillance systems detecting it?" the Russian ambassador said.

"I can't speak as to the accuracy of your surveillance systems, but you can hardly hold the Startenders responsible for your monitoring agency's inadequacies, now can you? As a matter of fact, two of our members paid a visit earlier to the International Space Station yesterday, so I would imagine that every member nation of that project should now know what I'm telling you. I'm certain you are in the loop and will be getting confirmation shortly."

It was then that an aide to the Secretary General rushed up and whispered in his ear. The man's face blanched and he walked up to the podium, taking it from Dagonet.

"I have just been informed that there is a Code Black nuclear bomb threat for the city of New York. The entire population is being ordered to evacuate immediately," he said.

The chaos evolved instantly into bedlam. The rather angry ambassador from the rather angry country pushed down several of his colleagues as he ran toward the garage and his waiting limo. The rest of the diplomats yelled about who was going to be taking care of getting them to safety.

"Excuse me," Dagonet said. He repeated it again several more times trying to get the diplomats attention. Rolling his eyes, the Infinite Jester turned and nodded to a floating golden golf ball-sized hunk of metal. It floated above the assembly, then suddenly morphed into a giant castle-esque spaceship with the Startender logo on the side. It was the barship *Excalibur*, of which Dagonet was the head honcho. It sudden size change inside the General Assembly got everyone to stop arguing and shut up.

"I would just like to say that I have enough room on board the barship *Excalibur* to take all of you, your staff as well as all of your families, and shuttle everyone to Washington D.C. where you can make contact with your respective embassies. However, I have my orders and I will not be able to leave here until this matter is brought to a vote. So as soon as the vote on the sovereign nation status of *Startender Station* and Ben City is done, I am at your service to take you all out of the danger zone."

It was the fastest vote in U.N. history. Almost every ambassador voted to recognize the sovereignty of *Startender Station* and Ben City. We were even voted on a couple of councils we didn't even ask for. In their stress, the diplomats didn't seem to realize that Dagonet never said how they needed to vote to get on the barship. In fact, that was something the Infinite Jester would never do. It would violate his oath of honor to the Round Table to threaten lives for personal gain, not to mention violating his Startender Oath.

Diplomats are like most people and assume others are not only capable, but willing to do the same things as they are. Since most of the diplomats would have made that statement a threat, they assumed the same of Dagonet.

There was nothing in either oath about having to save people from their own stupidity, and since it worked out in our favor, we failed to correct their faulty assumptions. Dagonet and his crew got those diplomats, their staff and families safely away. He did the same for the janitors, translators, and the rest of the blue color workers as well.

They got the diplomats to DC and came back to help us with the rest of the city.

***

It was kind of funny how well Paddy did with the media considering all his centuries of hiding because of the leprechaun curse. The wee folk had to bring anyone who captured them to their pot of gold. As a matter of fact, the boss and I first met when I captured him in order to get said gold. I ended up letting him go before I knew about the loop hole. A leprechaun can buy property with the gold. If captured he had to bring his captor to said property, but fortune hunters figuring a way around the property laws was another matter entirely. It wasn't like they could walk off with a building without the local law stepping in.

Paddy bought Bulfinche's Pub with his pot, so rainbows have been leading troubled souls to our door for well over a century.

With the Startenders we were widening our scope a bit.

Paddy wasn't focusing on the national media, at least at first. He was hitting the local media and hitting it hard. He started with a regular patron who was a reporter for one of the local network affiliates. Pam knew the score. What's more, she was willing to us help save as many people as we could, which would hopefully be everyone.

"This is Pam Neddle, speaking live with Padriac Moran, the owner of New York City landmark Bulfinche's Pub and one of the majority shareholders of the Horus Corporation, the company that has been advertising on the moon with laser beams for many years. Mr. Moran..."

"Pam, please call me Paddy."

"Paddy, I understand you have some things to tell us regarding the ordered evacuation of New York City. The Mayor is cautioning us against panic, but he's closed the tunnels." Not a good place to be stuck when a tsunami hits. Subways would be closed soon for the same reason. "A lot of people are frightened, confused and at a loss for what to do. What can you tell them?"

"First, don't lose hope. I'm part of an organization called the Startenders. This is a Startender badge I'm wearing." Paddy pointed to the badge with the shot o' gold logo from Bulfinche's Pub in the center. We would be using the Horus satellites to beam it on the moon at night for the next three days. "We've made preparations for just such an emergency and we will be helping local and state officials evacuate the city."

Back in the studio the male anchor was rolling his eyes. "Pam, thank you for that report, but we are in a state of emergency. That man's obviously a crackpot who thinks he's an old west sheriff. We hear there is something going on at the U.N., so we are going live to ..."

Instead of the broadcast going to where the newsroom wanted it to go, it went back to Pam, thanks to the workings of Bubba Sue, the Startenders' resident gremlin whose ability with technology was literally magical. We'd planned on this and quite simply hijacked the signal.

"What can one small organization do?" the reporter asked.

Paddy smiled. "The Startenders can do a lot." He nodded to Pam's cameraman who pulled the picture back so as to get the sky behind Paddy. With a wave of the boss' hand three more golden golf balls floating in the air above him expanded to full-sized barships. We could make the barships look like anything, so we tried to have these particular shapes instill visions of strength and confidence in the viewers. Each one of course had the Startenders logo on the side. "And in our case quite a bit. There is no need for panic. We will get everyone out. In moments, there will be several temporary bridges and portals allowing people to leave the city. Grab only the necessities. We have dozens of designated evacuation points with Startenders supervising in cooperation with the NYPD and the National Guard. We have a website listing all of them..."

And at home, the viewers rejected fear and panic in favor of hope.

***

My assignment was on the Westside directing traffic. We were using the morphing properties of the barships to make a bridge between Manhattan and Jersey near the Javitis Center. We had two sides – one for cars, the others for pedestrians. My crew's job was to make sure people got across it in a neat, orderly fashion.

The neat and orderly part was proving to be a challenge. The owners of the various touring boat companies had volunteered their services without being asked. We'd also commandeered the cruise ships that docked just up the street. They were luxury ships, but we'd been using them as ferryboats. Each one could carry thousands of people. The companies weren't doing it out of the goodness of their hearts like the locals. Paddy had stock in the companies and basically threatened to start selling it off at rock bottom prices. One told him to stick it where the sun didn't shine. Paddy was as good as his word and the stock was worth pennies on the dollar within hours. The other companies decided to help without further coercion. The boss bought up controlling interest in the first company on the cheap and then commandeered its ships.

Paddy, with the help of Mosie and others, had become the richest person on Earth, but since he hid it within a variety of corporate shells almost nobody knew it. He sunk all of his trillions into the Startenders and evacuation plans. Buying the reluctant cruise company pretty much wiped him out of liquid capital, but he had more ships to get people away safely so it was a fair trade to him. Mind you this is the same guy who last week chased a customer three blocks because he was a buck short on his bill. Paddy had plans to turn the rest of his new cruise line ships into temporary floating shelters, pretty much guaranteeing the stock he bought would be worth even less. Didn't faze him in the least.

People were reluctant to leave their homes, thinking nothing would happen. Others didn't want to go without their stuff, but we had anticipated this. Paddy commissioned the building of tens of thousands of wagons. They worked on the same principle as the old radio flyers and were as large as a pickup truck bed. With a little bit of effort one person could one manage pulling a full wagon. Once on the Jersey side we had buses and tractor-trailers waiting to take people to designated evacuation areas and gave people luggage tags for their property. The carts were unloaded then brought back across for others to use.

Early on, the mayor had got a visit from Paddy, who had been a large contributor to his campaign. Paddy asked to be put in charge of rescue operations. Upon seeing what the barships were capable of, the mayor was impressed, but reluctant. Paddy was a civilian, a guy who owned a bar, so the boss had brought Nemesis, the daughter of night, with him. The pair were friends that disagreed on killing bad guys. Paddy was against it except in the most extreme cases; Nemesis not so much. The daughter of Nyx had run Nemesis & Co. on the 13th floor of a Manhattan skyscraper for decades, avenging wrongs. She made a habit of visiting each new mayor and telling him how things were. NYPD was always then instructed to give Nemesis and her agents every available assistance.

Nemesis was only an associate because her status as enforcer for the Council of Thrones would complicate things for us. I think her standing silently behind the boss was as much the reason that the mayor agreed to put Paddy in charge as the barships were. That and his daughter telling him that we had gotten rid of the quite real monsters under her bed after she had followed a rainbow to our door a few months earlier.

We had things uber-organized, basically calling entire neighborhoods at a time much like an usher in church standing in front of a pew to signal people to get up for communion.

My people were ushering the entire Westside. We were using all kinds of magic to encourage or scare people into leaving and so far it seemed to be working.

Everyone had been working for the better part of the day and we were tired. We included NYPD, NYFD, EMTs, National Guard, and military. New Jersey's finest and bravest were helping on the other side of the river.

We tried to spilt shifts for everyone, but other than the occasional food break, none of the brave men and women helping us were taking any. Too many people to get out in too little time. I'd never been prouder to be a New Yorker than watching those people.

We were providing them food. Vulcan had tech that shrunk and preserved food and Paddy had been stockpiling for decades.

I was polishing off a sandwich when I heard a familiar buzzing of wings.

"Things okay, Dad?" came a voice from above. I looked up to see my daughter Elsiebelle flying in. She landed in front of me and I gave her a big hug. "Holding up okay, old man?"

I laughed. I was older and in better shape than I had any right to be... thanks to Paddy. Instead of firing a comeback, I messed my daughter's pink hair. She gets her hair and pixie wings from her mother. She gets her blue eyes and bad sense of humor from me. We both still miss her mother. Terrorbelle was vaporized saving our daughter. It was the second time I was widowed. I went more than a little nuts after that.

I'm feeling much better now.

"He's doing okay for someone his age," shouted Loki from down the block. The trickster has better-than-average hearing.

"Good to know, Uncle Loki," E-Belle said.

"You've got centuries on me, Loki," I said.

"Yeah, but I don't look it," he said.

I couldn't argue with that and judging by my daughter's chuckling, she wasn't about to defend my honor.

E-Belle was more my build than her mother's, which is why she's able to fly on Earth. Terrorbelle and our daughter both needed magic to fly. Not a lot of that on Earth these days. E-Belle being smaller and lighter could go about half a block on wing power, while the best her mother could manage was hovering or slowing a fall.

With our Startender badges, E-Belle could fly properly by using hers to adjust for the effects of gravity.

"How are things going up by the *Intrepid*?" I said. The military had turned the *Intrepid* into the world's largest ferry. Bubba Sue had snuck aboard a few weeks earlier and given its engines a tune up. From what she said, if it was returned to duty with her modifications, it would be the fastest vessel of its size on the seven seas.

"The soldiers are on top of everything and things are going very smoothly. People are doing what they should. Our mystic encouraging seems to be nudging those who want to ignore the evac orders."

"Good. So far, no real problems here," I said.

Apparently, I spoke too soon because a limo with diplomatic plates was driving through the crowd of people who were waiting to leave on foot. When people wouldn't get out of their way, they honked before trying to drive through the crowd. Apparently not everyone moved fast enough for them because they ended up knocking down a little girl.

E-Belle, Loki, and I raced towards the car. With her wings my daughter got there first. She wasn't as strong as her mother, but she hit the front of the car hard enough that its rear lifted off the ground. The vehicle spun its wheels helplessly. Loki picked up the girl, gave her the once over and flashed me a thumbs up. She was fine.

A man in suit and tie, the rather angry ambassador from the small and rather angry country, leapt out of the back seat and onto the ground. "I have diplomatic immunity. You are causing an international incident, so you best get me to the front of the line so I can report your actions to my government and yours."

"I don't care about your government or any international incidents right now," I said. "My job is to get everybody evacuated safely. Your behavior has jeopardized that child's life."

By this point the driver had gotten out of the car and stood up. He was a tall drink of water, easily six foot eight and three hundred plus pounds.

"Very well. You leave me no choice. Driver, take care of him."

The driver cracked his knuckles and step towards me, but he never made it. My daughter fluttered between us and punched him in the breadbasket, making the tall man double over in pain. E-Belle followed up with an elbow to the back of the neck and laid him out cold on the pavement, just like her mama taught her.

"That nonsense isn't going to work here. You're now at the end of the line. We're going to mark you for your actions and I can assure you that no one will allow you off the island until everyone else gets off first." We'd taken a lesson from Hex, a fellow Startender and head honcho of *The Accursed*. He's been known to warn people off and mark their face to remind them of his warning. Each Startender had a device that would brand a permanent large red letter over any offender's face. Which letter varied by the offense.

The angry ambassador screamed as we branded a C for line cutter on his face. There were more than a few with L for looter being forced to wait as well.

I turned to his driver and slapped him awake. "You next."

"But I was just following orders," the driver whined.

"That excuse has been used before. Doesn't hold water, then or now," I said and branded him. He didn't scream like his boss, probably because the marking didn't actually hurt.

I pointed to where the end of the line area was and sent the two offenders there to wait and contemplate the error of their ways.

***

While we were directing traffic, Paddy was making the talk show circuit.

"All I'm saying is, what do we really know about these so-called Startenders?" said James Rznard, a cable and radio talk show host and talking head. "They have so-called barships—are they advocates of drinking and operating vehicles? Are they trying to get our young people to start drinking and driving? We simply don't know. All we do know about them is that they forced a vote at the UN to have a satellite and some imaginary base on the moon established as sovereign nations before they would rescue a bunch of diplomats. And what's with that? Rescuing foreigners before good old-fashioned, hard-working Americans? I'll tell you what – they're trying to undermine the American way of life. Now that they have sovereign nation status, that means they are effectively invading the United States of America. The United States has never been invaded and never will. We need to push these Startenders off from our shores."

"But Mr. Rznard, the mayor of New York City and the governor of New York State have both come out in support of Mr. Moran and his organization. What do you think about that?" said Kim Irons, host of the *Iron In The Fire* cable news program.

Rznard rolled his eyes. "They're facing nuclear annihilation by some terrorist. Politicians will say anything now to cover their asses. What happens if the bomb goes off before they get everybody out? If they said something against any rescue effort, it'll come back to bite them come Election Day.

"Mr. Moran, how do you respond to critics of you and the Startenders like Mr. Rznard here?" Kim said.

Paddy smiled big for the cameras. "I'd say they're full of crap. They're like the politicians they praise or criticize in that if they don't make waves, they'll lose ratings and be out of a job. I've invested me entire fortune in this, including buying land to make tent cities and supplement supplies for the Red Cross. We are willing to help some relocate to *Startender Station* or Ben City. We're talking more than 12 million people displaced. That's the most ever in American history. And speaking of history, Mr. Rznard needs to review his. America has been invaded multiple times in multiple wars, one of the last of which was World War II. True, that was only a few Nazis disembarking from a U-boat off the coast of Long Island, but it still technically counts as an invasion. However we Startenders are not invaders. The majority of us are Americans. The sovereign nations of *Startender Station* and Ben City all support dual citizenship."

"That all sounds nice and good," Rznard said. "But you're up there floating above us. What's to prevent you from raining down weapons of mass destruction on the rest of humanity?"

"Because that is not our way. In actuality, we will be protecting the Earth," Paddy said.

"From what? Aliens?"

"Actually, yes," Paddy said, as the camera pulled back. The Startenders had only eight aliens in its ranks and three of them were sitting next to Paddy as the camera revealed. One was Randor the Troll, the next Nara, a large blue blag, an alien that looked like the result of a smurf and a hippo having a drunken night of passion. The last was Jan, a very, very large beige woman from the planet Karma. They smiled and waved at the camera. "Aliens are quite real, as are magical races. Some of them, unlike our friends and fellow Startenders here, are downright hostile. The Department of Mystic Affairs has been defending this country for centuries against mystic threats. The Startenders can do all that and more."

The camera panned to Rznard's mouth literally dropping open as he took in this revelation.

"Speaking of the Department of Mystic Affairs, we have their director, Sam Wilson, with us via satellite from New York City. Director Wilson, what you have to say on this matter?"

Sam—the actual Uncle Sam—and most of his agents were helping with the evacuation in New York.

"Well, missy, I've known Padriac Moran for a very long time. I find him to be the rarest of rare things - a good man. Mr. Moran has been working behind the scenes for great many years helping others without asking any personal reward or recognition," said the white-haired man with a moustacheless goatee. He was dressed in a white shirt, blue suit and red tie. Sam was the living embodiment of the Spirit of America. Among his mystic gifts was the ability to inspire patriotism in anyone in his presence. That translated well to television feeds. Any Americans watching had feelings of pride. "I feel the Startenders have truly altruistic purposes and are not a threat to the United States or any other country. In fact, if the organization stays structured as it is, they have my full blessing, so long as they continue to follow the laws of this great land."

"Well, that's all nice and good coming from some career law enforcement agent, but why? Because you happen to like the man? Because they're helping get a few people out of New York City?" Rznard said.

"Actually, Mr. Rznard, by government calculations, the Startenders have supervised the evacuation of over five million people in less than a day," Kim said.

Rznard laughed. "So could anybody if they had those spaceship thingies. Hell, I could do a better job myself."

"Well, Mr. Rznard, you're perfectly welcome to try and raise enough wealth to develop technology and magic to build your own barships. However, we are in need of all the help we can get, so thank ye for your generous offer," Paddy said grinning.

"What offer?" Rznard said, confused.

"Didn't ye just say ye could do a better job than we could if you had access to a barship? I don't want the lack of barships at your disposal to affect you helping these people. Therefore, we will be by to pick you up as soon as this broadcast is done and bring you to the heart of Manhattan so ye can help with evacuation," Paddy said.

Rznard's jaw dropped again, but this time his face drained of blood until he looked like a ghost.

"You mean actually go to New York... Isn't there a danger of a nuclear bomb going off?" Rznard said.

"Exactly, which is why we need the help to get everyone out," Paddy said.

"I'm on the other side of the country. I couldn't possibly get to New York in time to do any good," Rznard said, using a handkerchief to wipe sweat from his brow.

"I know ye are all the way over in California where things are nice and safe. But your brave words let all of us know that you'd rather be in the trenches with the rest of us, so we're going to give you that chance. Barships can make that trip in no time. And real Americans like yourself laugh at danger. Isn't that what you've said? In fact, on your own show, ye constantly criticize people for inaction and cowardice. Now's your chance to step up and prove you're not just some blowhard who was lucky enough to get a TV show, but a real hero," Paddy said.

"Do you know when the detonation is supposed to occur?" Rznard said.

"We do not. It could happen at any moment," Paddy lied, knowing it was all a hoax to save people from the wraith of a mad sea god. Otherwise nobody would have gotten off the couch.

"Well, I have my show to do in a few hours and I've got no one to take care of my dog and..."

"Not a problem. We'll stop by your house and ye can pick up your dog. Ye can even bring a television crew to film your heroism. When will ye be ready?" Paddy said.

"I'm afraid my schedule won't allow me to go..." Rznard said.

"Ye mean your cowardice won't allow ye to help other people if there's any risk to yourself other than biting your tongue while shooting off your mouth. Isn't that's what it boils down to? So either put up or shut up. Pitch in or stop criticizing. I'm still sending somebody for ye and we'll have cameras. The question is will you be shown to be a man of principle or a blowhard who likes to hear himself talk while others risk their lives."

"Paddy, is that offer open to other newscasters as well?" Kim Irons said.

"Of course it is, Kim," Paddy said.

"Excellent, then I'd like to go and bring my people," Kim said.

"And we be proud to have you," Paddy said. "Rznard, we'll be by to pick ye up shortly."

The broadcast switched to Rznard's camera, but he had run off so quickly that his chair was still spinning.

***

My daughter looked worried. "Dad, we've got an older gentleman a few blocks up refusing to leave. We tried everything we could think of to convince him to go, but he's stubborn and insists he's going to stay put. Not even Nellie could convince him otherwise. He seems immune to the spells of encouragement." Nellie was head honcho of the barship *Caliginosity* and the boss's adopted daughter. I've watched Nellie grow from a girl into a fine woman who even fulfilled her childhood dream of becoming a ninja, even if she changed the definition to fit what she thought it should be instead of the other way around.

"He said no to Nellie? That's impressive," I said. Nellie was a superb con woman. Has been ever since her hair was in braids.

"She's my head honcho, but you might have a better shot at this," she said. E-Belle was part of the *Caliginosity's* crew.

I smiled at the compliment. "I'm happy to do my best. Loki, you have things covered here?" I said to my honcho. "Nellie needs my assistance uptown."

The trickster nodded. "With the exception of your little diplomatic incident, things are going surprisingly well. Not that I want to jinx it. Go."

My daughter lifted me up bride style as her wings started buzzing and we lifted into the air. I mentally adjusted the gravity setting on my Startenders badge to make it easier for her to carry my weight.

"Your mother would've loved this. She always hated that she couldn't fly in New York," I said.

"I think she was a little jealous that I could fly just a little bit here and she couldn't," E-Belle said.

"She was a tad jealous, but she was more happy and proud that you could. You know that if she had the power to pick who could fly, she would always have chosen you."

E-Belle smiled and I melted. It's a dad thing. "I know."

"Watch out for those wires," I said.

"Dad, no offense, but I fly better than you do. You need a motorcycle," she said, referring to a custom-made bike Vulcan built years before she was born. It could fly among other things. Paddy had given it to me a few years back.

A few blocks later, we arrived.

"That's him down there," E-Belle said, indicating a man who looked like he was in his seventies and was sitting on a chair on the stoop of a brick apartment building. He had a wedding picture in one hand and a bottle of beer in the other. There was a cane by his side. Nellie, in her traditional midnight blue – almost black ensemble stood next to him rolling her eyes.

My daughter landed at the bottom of the porch.

"You see something new in this city just about every day," the old man said.

"That you do. I'm John Murphy." I said. "What's your name?"

"Donald Martin." We shook hands. "Can I offer you a beer?"

"Before today, that would have been my job, but I'm here to convince you to evacuate," I said.

"Convince away, youngster, but I ain't budging. I lost my wife here. My family has moved on. I've always said I'm going to die here."

"That might be a little sooner than you'd like, sir," I said.

"Nobody is going detonate a nuclear bomb. It's all a hoax. They want us off-balance they can do something," he said.

"Who?" I asked.

"The government, of course. They're always up to something, but that ain't here nor there. This is my home and I ain't going. Besides, it's rent controlled."

"Sir, in less than two days a giant wave is going to hit the city. In part it will be caused by an undersea quake that will sink Manhattan and it will be lost under the water. Nothing human is going to be able to survive," I said, breaking from our cover story. Figured the lie didn't work, so why not try the truth.

Mr. Martin sipped his beer. "I thought we were trying to avoid a nuclear holocaust, not going swimming."

"That's what you call one of them cover stories. Not really a conspiracy, just a way to get people to move. People don't believe a tsunami could destroy this city. However the idea of a nuclear bomb going off is enough to get them out. Most of them at any rate," I said, smiling.

"I ain't most people."

"I can see that," I said.

"If God wanted me to leave, he'd take care of things," the man said.

"You're getting an opportunity right now with us, only you're too dumb and stubborn to take it," Nellie said.

"Remind me again why we didn't send you to the U.N. instead of Dagonet?" I said.

Nellie's response was the same as it would have been when she was a kid—she stuck her tongue out at me.

"Sir, I'm reminded of an old story. Once there was an older gentleman, not unlike yourself, whose hometown was in the center of the worst flood on record. He sat on his front lawn and watched his neighbors all evacuate. One family even stopped and offered him a seat in their car. The man refused and said that God would take care of him. He listened to the radio when the power went out. The news said all the buildings in town were going to be covered by water, but still the man stayed. Some of the volunteer fire department came by in a rowboat and offered him a lift. Again he told them God would take care of him.

"Finally, the flood waters rose so high he had to climb up on his roof. A helicopter came by, dropped down a ladder and told him to climb up. He had the same answer - God would take care of him. An hour later, a dam burst and the man drowned.

"When he got to the pearly gates he was real angry and demanded to speak to God immediately. When God showed, the man started yelling, 'I trusted you to save me and I drowned!'

God shrugged his shoulders and said, 'I gave you three chances. What more did you want?'"

The old man chuckled. "When I get to the pearly gates, I won't speak badly of you."

"That wasn't exactly my concern," I said.

"Still not leaving," Mr. Martin said.

I sighed. "Sir, I have a suggestion. You obviously have your mind made up and we're not going to convince you that you should come with us. Here's what I propose. You spend the next day and half here. Gather up your photo albums and other any memories or necessities and put them in a suitcase. Meet me out here tomorrow at five o'clock. I will give you one last chance to go. If at that time you decide you're going to stay, I'll leave you to your fate. However, I think you'll change your mind."

"I doubt it," he said.

"I don't. See you tomorrow."

***

To say we were all over the news would be an understatement. Even as people were fleeing, others were craving programming. Once we were sure we'd get all the people out, we moved onto other rescues, including several zoos' worth of animals.

"I can say that I've never seen anything like it," Pam said, reporting from the heart of the Bronx Zoo. "The man with the samurai sword and topknot is actually riding an elephant and talking to the animals. More impressive, they seem to be listening. He seems to be a combination of Dr. Doolittle and the elephant whisperer. He is going up to each cage and making some noises and then opening them."

"Has he been eaten yet, Pam?" said the anchor, now going along with anything Pam wanted as her access to the Startenders had given the station its highest news ratings ever and they were running nationally.

"There appears to be no danger of that, Henry. The animals are actually cooperating. We'll pan so you can get a look - you can see tigers walking alongside gazelles, gorillas next to giraffes and crocodiles next to penguins, all of them behaving as well as elementary school kids during a fire drill. Maybe even better."

"What's he doing now?" the anchor asked.

"He seems to have stopped outside the lion enclosure," Pam said into her microphone.

Most of the lions had lined up with the other animals, but one male lion was giving Kintaro a very hard time.

"You have to leave now," the young looking, but ancient samurai, said in the language of the lions.

"No. I am fed and get to lie in the sun all day. Why would I leave?" the lion said.

"Because you will drown," Kintaro replied.

The lion snorted in disbelief. "The watering hole isn't deep. I could walk across it."

"A great wall of water is coming and will bury this place," Kintaro said.

"Nonsense. I do not believe you," the lion said.

"Why would I tell an untruth?" Kintaro said, climbing down from the elephant to stand in front of the king of beasts.

"Why should I believe you?" the lion said.

"How many men have you met that speak the language of the pride?" Kintaro replied.

The thought made the lion grow silent.

"You are the first." The lion thought some more. "Is that why our human servants have left us?"

"It is."

"And they will not return to feed us?"

"No, but I will take you to other zoos where more humans will take care of you."

"Very well, I will go with you."

"Good."

The lion looked out on the parade of animals and licked his lips. "Especially since you were kind enough to bring me fresh food."

"There will be no fighting and no eating. Anyone or any animal that breaks those rules will answer to me," Kintaro said.

"I obey no human," the lion said and leapt at Kintaro. The samurai moved with lightning speed and caught the lion by both front paws and flipped it so it hit the lawn on one side, then flipped it over his head to do the same on the other. The blows were enough to stun, but not do lasting harm. Kintaro held on and spun the lion like a father might a child, going faster and faster until the lion was only a blur. He stopped, letting the lion roll away. When the lion tried to stand he was too dizzy and fell repeatedly.

"If there are any further problems, you will be my prey, understood?"

Kintaro said.

"Yes," the lion said, meekly getting in line behind a water buffalo, his head hung low. The rest of his pride was doing the lion equivalent of snickering. Kintaro motioned to the elephant, who gently lifted the samurai up with his trunk so the samurai could return to his seat.

Pam stood there amazed. Even though she had met Kintaro, she had no idea of what he was capable of. Still she had to report to her viewers and ran alongside the elephant, her microphone extended overhead. "Excuse me, what is your name?" she asked, playing dumb. "And are you one of these Startenders we been hearing so much about?"

"My name is Kintaro." The samurai pointed to the badge on his chest. "And I am proud to be a Startender."

"How are you getting the animals to listen to you? I've never seen anything like it," Pam said.

"It's a gift. Now if you'll excuse me, there are more animals left and little time to get them out safely."

Kintaro and his parade of animals moved on to the next enclosure, which was the wolf habitat. The Brand family was already handling the wolves. Three of them were related by blood to many of the wolves, the other by marriage. Shan had been born one of the Bronx Zoo's wolves, before she became a werehuman. Her two kids had been born in the zoo as well.

An old Japanese woman walked up to Pam, positioning herself between the camera and Kintaro. "My boy was never one to take attention well, as opposed to me," said the old witch woman with many missing teeth. She hunched over and leaned on a knobby stick that she used as a cane.

"Are you the mother of this man?" Pam asked.

"Yes, I am," she replied.

"Are you also one of the Startenders?" Pam asked.

"Heavens, no. They would want nothing to do with an old witch such as myself," she said.

"Are you saying the Startenders practice ageism and name-calling?" Pam said, knowing she would be criticized if she didn't ask.

"Not at all. I am both ancient and a witch. More of a necromancer really. The Startenders have to adhere to a code of honor. I don't like to be impaired by such trivial things. My boy on the other hand is all about honor. Why the stories I could tell you about when he was a child on our mountain in Japan, when he would wrestle with bears and other creatures. Entirely naked I might add. Said if the animals didn't need clothes, neither did he. It wasn't until he started noticing girls that I could convince him to wear clothing consistently."

"Mother, I said you could come as long as you helped me with the animals and didn't embarrass me," shouted the man on elephant back. "You're ignoring both parts of our agreement."

"But I never actually agreed, now did I? In all my years, I've never been on TV. An old woman with not much time left deserves some simple pleasures, don't you think?" she said.

"Mother, you're centuries old. And unlikely to die for at least a few centuries more," Kintaro said, shaking his head and going toward the hyena habitat.

"Bah." The old woman grabbed hold of the camera and pulled it so it was pointed at her face. Next she took the microphone from the hands of the reporter. "But enough about my son. What you really want to know is more about me..."

***

Of course, not everything the Startenders did was caught on camera. True, we were trying for a public relations blitz, but some things simply happened too fast to be recorded.

The most notable of these was the robbery of every major museum in the city. Don't get me wrong – the Startenders are not thieves. Well, not in the sense that we take things that don't belong to us and keep them. However, one of us is the god of thieves. Hermes was so fast he made lightning look like molasses on a winter morning. Apparently a major fantasy of his was to try to rob everything from every museum in Manhattan in the span of an hour without setting off a single alarm. That may sound impossible, but the word impossible was only a challenge to Hermes.

Now with the imminent sinking of Manhattan, he was going to have a chance to live out one of his fantasies and empty every museum in the city. Well, almost every museum. Hermes' daughter Kyna was incredibly fast as well, although she simply wasn't a match for her father. Both sported winged footwear that allowed them to fly. Hers were black boots while Hermes sported red high-top sneakers. Nellie had a similar pair of black shoes and while she was not in their league in terms of speed, she could bypass alarms like nobody's business.

Hermes left one museum for his daughter to clean out and one for Nellie in the Bronx. Maybe Yankee Stadium wasn't technically a regular museum, but several Startenders are big baseball fans, especially the Yankees. Babe Ruth and some other famous Yankees had stopped in at various times to Bulfinche's Pub. There was even a picture of the Babe and Paddy behind the bar. They weren't going to let those mementos in the Yankee museum be destroyed any more than the paintings and sculptures Kyna was liberating from the Guggenheim.

None of the trio was exactly forthcoming about their methods, feeling if more people knew about how they operated, it would be easier to stop them in the future.

Hermes completed his task in fifty-seven minutes, including the time it took him to transport the articles to the Smithsonian Museum in D.C., and get past their security. All the curators of the various museums were informed where they could pick up their treasures.

At least most. Hermes held back one painting which had been stolen from a private collector. He returned it to its proper owner who hadn't the money to fight the museum in court. He replaced it with a perfect forgery he had done himself. They never noticed the switch.

Hermes helped the two ladies transport their goods and the three of them went house to house to make sure we didn't miss anybody.

***

As near as we could tell by the third day, we had every single person out of the five boroughs and surrounding areas with two exceptions. It's amazing what hard work, large amounts of magical compulsion and the once largest fortune on Earth could accomplish.

Two was still too many.

I was going back for Mr. Martin, hoping he would change his mind. Paddy was going for one of his oldest and dearest friends, who as Mother of the Streets was so closely bonded to the city that despite knowing what was coming, refused to leave although she made sure that not one other homeless person was left behind.

It didn't take much searching for Paddy to find her. She was sitting on a wooden crate outside of Bulfinche's Pub when Paddy flew over her in his Caddy.

"Ye didn't find him?" Paddy asked, already knowing the answer.

She shook her head. As hard as she tried, the mad sea god eluded her as well as the rest of us.

"Then Rebecca, tis time to go," Paddy said, landing the flying car and getting out.

"Yes Moran, it is, so why are you still here?" Rebecca asked.

"Ye know the answer to that," Paddy said. "I can't leave ye here to die."

"Moran, I'm over a hundred years old. Without the city sustaining me, I would have been dust a long time ago," Rebecca said.

"I know the city lent you power as Mother of the Streets, but I have power too. In trying to save me late wife Bulfinche, I ended up with a great many ways to extend human life. Ye won't die. In fact, I might be able to restore some of your youth," Paddy said.

Rebecca smiled. "Why would you be wanting to do something so foolish? I'm an old woman. I've lived longer than I've had any good reason to, except that I couldn't leave my city to fend for itself or those on its street to do the same."

"You've saved hundreds of lives and helped save millions of others. Ye protected the homeless and this city countless times. Now save yourself," Paddy said.

"Moran, these streets are empty. Without them, I won't have a purpose. I'm not fit to go out into space with the rest of you."

"I've got a good mind to toss ye over my shoulder and carry ye out of here myself," Paddy said.

"You could try. Judah already did. Planned to carry me away to one of your barships." Judah was a golem Rebecca's father had helped create to fight the Nazis and a Startender.

"Why did he put ye down?" Paddy said.

"Because I asked him to. And he understood why I have to stay. He's a protector too."

"Then make me understand why ye are asking me to let ye die when I can save ye," Paddy said.

Rebecca sighed. "The Nazis slaughtered my family, yet I survived the camp. Murderers killed Abraham and my babies, raped me, yet I survived to avenge them. I can't survive again when someone I love dies. This city is alive, sentient and has spoken with me for decades. Shared more than its power. It shared its hopes, dreams, memories, its very essence. I can't let my city die alone while I go off and survive again. I'm the only one who can hear it. We will go together into that dark night. Hopefully then I'll be reunited with those that fate took from me and my city will be at peace."

"Rebecca...." Tears were streaming down Paddy's face.

"You can throw me over your shoulder because you know you are one of the few people I could never raise a hand to, but then you're condemning your city not only to die, but to die alone and afraid. You love this city as much as anyone. It wants me to stay with it until the end. Can you live with yourself if you deny it its dying wish?"

"Damn it Rebecca..."

"Paddy, thank you for caring. Without you, I..." Rebecca was never one for expressing her emotions well.

"Yeah, me too." Paddy opened up his arms. "Come here."

"How many times have I told you I'm not a loose woman," she said. It was a joke between them. It was meant to make them laugh, but only made two brief smiles that were instantly covered in tears as the pair held each other one last time.

The ground shook beneath them and a mighty roar sounded in the distance. The tsunami was on its way.

"It's time for you to go. You've got great things ahead of you. My only wish is that I live long enough to take the life of the monster that did this to my city. And none of your nonsense about killing being wrong."

"This once, I wouldn't argue with you," Paddy said, pulling the taller woman's head down so he could kiss her on the cheek. "Goodbye, Rebecca."

Paddy put his hand on her cheek where he had kissed her and they looked into each other's eyes. The ground rumbled again so hard they almost lost their footing.

"Goodbye, Moran."

Paddy got into the car and held his hand out, his eyes pleading. "Hope and happiness never die. We might still have a chance."

"Hope and happiness may never die, but people do. Remember me. Remember my city."

"I'll never forget either of ye," Paddy said.

The giant wave nearly blotted out the sun. Paddy Moran flew his Cadillac towards his space station, letting the tears flow down his face at the death of his friend and his home.

***

I had gotten my flying motorcycle with a sidecar and was headed over to Donald Martin's building, hoping the old man would have a change of heart. I was cutting things close. As near as all of our people could tell, Poseidon had already begun. Not even an insane sea god can call up a tsunami and a seaquake on a whim. It took time and power, probably almost all of the power he still had.

In my heart, I knew Rebecca would never leave, but in my head I hoped she would. And Paddy still had to try or he'd never be able to live with himself.

With Donald Martin we still had a chance.

I was happy to see Mr. Martin had followed our deal, even down to having a suitcase with him. I hovered above his porch and honked the horn once. He looked up and watched as the motorcycle descended to street level.

"Like I said, something new every day in this city," Martin said. "I still ain't leaving, although I will say it's rather lonely now that everybody else is gone. Of course, they'll all be back once this blows over."

"This isn't going to blow over. Manhattan is going to be wiped from the map." The ground rumbled. "And it's already started. Would you consent to at least let me give you a ride up to the roof?"

"Once I get in that sidecar, you ain't going to just fly away with me?" he said, his tone dripping with suspicion.

"If we wanted to force you out, you would've been gone yesterday," I said. "Please, there isn't much time left."

As if to accentuate my words the ground rumbled again beneath us, which made Mr. Martin nervous.

"I suppose it couldn't hurt to go for a ride. Besides, I've never ridden in a flying motorcycle before. It might be fun."

Mr. Martin climbed in the sidecar and put his suitcase between his knees. I lifted up until we got to the top of his building. I arranged it so we were facing south.

"I'd like you to keep looking that way," I said.

"What exactly am I supposed to be looking for? That imaginary tidal wave of yours?" Mr. Martin said. And as if to accentuate his words, a wall of water appeared and blocked out the sky.

Mr. Martin promptly exclaims something about the divine nature of human excrement. "I changed my mind. Let's get out of here!"

"I thought you might. Hold on," I said as I lifted off and put the motorcycle into overdrive. The tsunami was approaching fast, but we were faster. We weren't even going to get wet, but the same couldn't be said of the city. I told myself I wouldn't look, but I couldn't help myself. Once we were at a safe altitude, I turned and watched as Poseidon's rage destroyed my home. The wave was a terrible thing, almost alive. It was a watery sledgehammer that smashed everything in its path. The ground rumbled and shook as the city sank beneath the wave.

I wanted to cry and was only stopped by a question.

"What's going to happen to me now?" Mr. Martin said.

"You have any family you can live with?" I said.

"I've got three kids, but they have kids and lives of their own. None of them have the room to take me in and I don't want to impose on them. I saw on the news there are a bunch of tent cities. Am I going there?"

"Not necessarily. I don't know if you heard about our moon colony. They're looking for settlers.

"What could an old geezer like me contribute?" Mr. Martin said.

"You'd be surprised. And up there, you wouldn't necessarily feel as old as you do down here. The gravity on the moon is one-sixth that of Earth. That means it would be a lot easier on your heart and joints," I said.

"You mean my arthritis wouldn't be as bad?" he said.

"Nope."

"Will I be able to come back to Earth?" he said.

"Depends how long you stay up there. After a while, returning to Earth gravity would be difficult, although there are programs in place where you can spend part of the day in Earth level gravity. Helps with bone density."

"Would my family be able to visit?" He asked.

"Absolutely. We have measures in place for that too."

"Where do I sign up?" he said.

"If you like, I can drive you right up to Ben City," I said. I honestly needed to put a little distance between me and the devastation.

"Now? On this bike?" he said.

"Yep." Then I saw something beautiful floating out of the mist. "But first you are going to want to watch this. Then hold on to your suitcase because the next stop is the moon."

***

The world was watching. Every TV, monitor, phone and anything else that could hold an image showed the wave as it grew into the biggest tsunami ever recorded. There were reporters both dumb and close enough to get hit. Hermes and Kyna got them out of the way, but left the cameras to record the death of the greatest city in the world as the quake sank it and the wave drowned it.

Some skyscrapers fell, but others stood tall and defiant, just like the people who had lived in the city.

The hearts of the world sank with New York. We saved the people, but not the structures. Some things were beyond even us.

But there was one structure we couldn't let the wave claim. It meant too much to too many.

Cameras that had caught the devastation now showed mist and fog over angry water. And out of that destruction rose something majestic. At first it was only a torch, but that was followed by a green hand and a giant green woman wearing robes and what looked like a crown. She had always told the world that she would take their tired, their poor. That she wanted the huddled masses, yearning to breathe free, the wretched refuse of others teeming shore. She implored the world to send these, the homeless, tempest tost to her, as she lifted her lamp beside the golden door.

Today the world needed Lady Liberty more than ever before. The Statue of Liberty had been a symbol of hope for the world. Now she was rising out of the destruction. Not just rising – she was flying out of the mist thanks to four barships that were carrying and reinforcing her, so she would not fall apart.

Refugees who stood on a far distant shore saw her and cheered.

Each of our barships had been shaped to show the symbol from the Startenders badge on their sides. Yes, it was blatant product placement, but we needed people to believe in us too. Belief equaled power for gods and we had more than a few in the Startenders. They needed belief or at least people knowing about them to survive. This would help the world to trust us, because dark times might come again. And then, just as this time, the Startenders would help beat back the darkness and ensure hope and humanity survived.

***

Poseidon had hidden for years, Demeter's amulet ensuring he couldn't be found. It'd stopped us from finding him despite over two decades of searching. With all the power, with all the Startenders had at our disposal, it wasn't enough to find or stop one mad god. The only way the amulet couldn't hide him was if someone happened upon him in their direct line of sight.

Manhattan was entirely underwater. It was an eerily beautiful sight, devoid of its citizens. However, it wasn't devoid of life. Creatures of the sea had already begun to move in, as had Poseidon himself. He walked down the middle of Fifth Avenue, thrilled to pieces over what he had done.

The mad god claimed the sunken city as his own. A place that once held over ten million people would now be his domain and his alone. Or so he thought. Poseidon forgot something that all real New Yorkers knew. When walking down the street, you always keep an eye on what's going on around you if you don't want to get mugged or worse.

Poseidon didn't even notice the old woman dressed in the rags of the ages. Nor did he notice her machete-sized knife as she snuck up behind him. Rebecca was many things, but a cold-blooded murderer wasn't one of them. She spun the sea god around, giving him an instant in which to defend himself. Poseidon had spent almost all of his power in his rage-filled act of destruction, so he was unable to stop the blade as it pierced him again and again. The stabbing made the sea around him turn a hundred shades of crimson.

If the dying sea god wondered how a small, century plus old woman could survive under water without breathing or how a simple blade could kill a god, he didn't say. The idea that Rebecca was the Mother of the Streets of the city he tried to kill would never have occurred to him, nor would the fact that the city would share its power with the old woman to make sure she could survive. And that her last wish was to kill him for what he'd done.

Rebecca was not bloodthirsty, but in her own way she was every bit as mad as the sea god. However, she was not stupid. She dismembered him and separated the pieces, wrapping them individually in plastic garbage bags. Then she walked along the sunken streets until she came to Bulfinche's Pub. She smiled as she noticed the light from above refracting into a rainbow cascade of lights that led right to the door. The magic of the place even now could lead people in trouble to its door.

The sign that had always read *Sorry We're Open* had finally been changed to *Sorry We're Closed*. However, in writing underneath it read *Those in trouble are always welcome here*. Rebecca opened up the door and the magic protections on the place were strong enough to keep the water outside. The Mother of the Streets walked into the air-filled bar with the dismembered god dragging behind her in a half dozen plastic bags. She opened several closets and put each of the bags in a different one. Whether or not a god could put himself back together after what she did to him would be moot in the magical null zone that was Bulfinche's Pub.

Rebecca then went into the ladies room and changed out of her wet clothes into dry ones. She walked behind the bar and opened up the cash register to put some money in, then poured herself a drink.

Rebecca sat down at her usual table in the corner. She raised a glass and looked as if she was having an unheard conversation with someone or something, then nodded and drank the glass.

The Mother of the Streets sat and waited until her city needed her again.

On "A Wave Then Goodbye," Patrick writes...

The Startenders began because I'd wanted to do a series set on a starship. It's been done—a lot—so what could I do different? Maybe make the ship part magic, part tech. Did it have to be military based or have military ranks?

I didn't know who was going to populate the crew until I wondered what the gang from Bulfinche's Pub in my Murphy's Lore *universe would do with a starship. Once I realized it would have to be called a barship, the series was born. But gestation can take a while and The Startenders have been a long time in coming.*

I'd alluded to the sinking of New York City and a space station in the first Murphy's Lore *book back in 1997. It wouldn't be too much of a stretch to add more to that foreshadowing. In 2002 I let slip about the Startenders and the moon colony in* Through The Drinking Glass, *but it wasn't until 2010 that they saw print in Bruce Gehweiler's* Barbarians At The Jumpgate *with the story "Furlough" in which the tricksters of* Fools' Glory *combine a shore leave with collecting a debt and saving a poisoned, dying people. The next story was "Crossing Roads" where we find out why the cosmic chicken crossed the galaxy which came out last year in Elektra Hammond's* Galactic Creatures.

"A Wave Then Goodbye" is the third published Startenders story, but the first chronologically. There are two more written and I wouldn't be surprised if Murphy and his crew get their own book series before too long. I hope you enjoyed the start of the Startenders.

GOLDFEATHER AND THE GLASS PRINCESS

ROBERT E. WATERS & JAMES R. STRATTON

I tried to kill my mistress with soup. We were camped at the border between Pawtuxet Province and the Kingdom of Balt'mor when I offered her a bowl of fish and corn bisque, seasoned with nutmeg and cinnamon, and a splash of a neural toxin undetectable to the human senses. She took the bowl with a long, gnarled hand that stuck out of the sleeve of her crimson robe like a dead oak branch. She smiled as she inhaled the rising steam while swirling the soup with a wooden spoon.

"Smells good," she said.

I nodded as I crouched by the fire, watching stiff-faced as she lifted the bowl to her mouth and puckered her pale lips to slurp in the deadly broth. The heart at the tip of my spinal cord fluttered and set my legs trembling.

This is it. Months of planning are finally going to pay off...

A shrill call in the distant dusk interrupted. She set the bowl on the ground, grunted, rose to her feet, and walked to the far side of the camp as a giant bird, gleaming gold and silver in the evening light, circled. The eagle shrieked again when the old woman raised her hand.

Dammit! I hate witches!

In truth, Sarah Goldfeather is not a witch in the strict sense. She's a shaman of Native American descent... so she claims (although there is no such thing as "America" anymore). Still, she's a rare thing these days in a world where the human population is scattered and sparse, scraping out short desperate lives dominated by bloody feuds, incessant border wars, and violent trade disputes. She's a woman of great import among her people, and respected by the remnants of the conquering Shimfur and Aloo. Even I must love her while hating her with a murderous passion. It is an emotional struggle that will plague me to the end of my days, or until she (and only she) utters the words that will unlock the compulsion that binds me to her.

Or until she dies.

Wind Rider spiraled down to land on her right arm. Soft chimes rang across the clearing as the bird ruffed up its carbon fiber and metal feathers, smoothing and adjusting them with care in the waning light. The bird had taken flight at dawn and most certainly was ravenous, its fuel supply critically low. It squawked again as I trundled forward, careful to keep *my* carbon fiber and metal knuckles of my double-segmented arms from dragging the ground. The bird regarded me with a curious stare, shifting its head side to side to examine me with each eye in turn.

I stared back with my three forward eyes, the two in my face and the multi-spectrum one in my chest. You see I'm a golem; a construct born of the now fallen Shimfur conqueror's technology. My mistress has explained that I was genetically engineered to kill for the Shimfur. Perhaps that was their purpose in creating the likes of me... but I don't have to act like a beast.

Goldfeather smiled at the giant bird glowing statuesque in the fading light and rubbing its long, curved beak against its metal claws. I have to admit it is an impressive beast. From head to tail, it is as real as any avian. Its tiny heart beats true and pumps blood like any animal. But its wings are nano-fiber composite, incredibly light and strong, melded to its body through an intricate mix of muscle and metal that allow it to arrow across the sky at incredible speeds and soar far above the highest clouds.

"What word from King Carmelo, Wind Rider?" Goldfeather asked.

The eagle stretched its beak wide. Crackling words echoed out. "The king is having trouble with his daughter."

My mistress huffed. "Nothing new there. They've been at odds since he tried to marry her off to that fat warlord to the west of the South Mountain. I believe Lord Griffen was his name... smelly old sot."

Wind Rider bobbed its head. "True, but this time it has gone beyond words. In fact, you could say she's in quite a tight spot."

Such riddle-talk always intrigued my mistress. "Is that so?"

Wind Rider fluffed its wings and screeched. "Tight enough that his Majesty specifically asked for your help, and even commanded that you shall honor him with a visit by tomorrow evening."

Goldfeather glared at the bird, mouth pinched tight with disapproval. "You didn't agree to anything that foolish, I trust? We've been banned from the kingdom on penalty of death."

"He has rescinded the ban so long as you come," the bird continued. "He said this in the presence of a dozen of his ministers."

Goldfeather tugged at her ear as her face twisted into a mass of wrinkles. "She must be in a *very* tight spot. Is he willing to pay me the gold he owes from the last time?" Her wrinkles flushed red at the mention of the eighty gold escudos he had agreed to pay us on her last visit. Instead, he declared my mistress a fraud and had her run out of the kingdom.

Wind Rider didn't respond at first. Its tiny bird brain was augmented by a powerful Shimfur organic data processor, capable of holding great volumes of information. But the language routines are rudimentary so words sometimes get jumbled and meaning lost.

Finally, it nodded. "She's in big trouble. Something beyond the skills of King Carmelo and his flock. I believe he will do whatever you ask if you can help."

Now *my* curiosity was piqued. It might be worth returning to the proverbial scene of the crime just to see what kind of fix the young Princess had gotten into.

My mistress stood silent and pondered while I kept glancing back to the bowl of soup. It was getting cold and she wouldn't want it. I started to sweat. I had spent a year secretly scraping up the gold to buy the poison. All for naught?

Finally, she sighed. "Okay, I can't see any reason to refuse the invitation. How do we accept?"

Wind Rider became restless under her questioning, spreading its wings in short beats, ravenous and tired after its long flight. "We must arrive at Adrian's Reservoir tomorrow morning. A driver will meet us there in the King's own chariot. He will carry us to Castle Escobana."

"Very well," Goldfeather said, "but if that son of a bitch cheats me again, I'll call down the wrath of the Ancestors on his sorry ass." She pulled an elastic globe of Shimfur nutrient fluid from her pouch and held it up. Wind Rider seized it with its curved beak, threw its head back and swallowed it whole. A bulge coursed down its neck.

Wind Rider didn't wait for permission before flapping up to a tree branch with a sharp view of the surrounding lands. The Shimfur had improved on Earth's eagles in many ways, but they had also stripped out most of the remade bird's digestive tract to reduce weight, leaving it dependent on a special diet.

Goldfeather returned to the campfire and to the soup. Grunting, she settled cross-legged on her bedroll and took up the bowl. Soon she was stirring the soup then lifting a dribbling spoonful to her pursed lips. I stared, holding my breath even though my upper and lower hearts hammered in counter beats.

Then she sneezed, spraying soup across the fire and sending the bowl flying against my foot. I gasped as my plan sizzled away on the coals.

She looked at me with embarrassment. "I'm sorry, Godwyn," she said, gazing at the spoon as the last of the soup dripped onto the ground. "It's these damned Aloo allergies of mine. I hate this time of year."

"Don't worry about it." I smiled, showing both rows of razor teeth. "It's just soup." A shudder ran down my back as I recounted the months I had devoted to this moment. A second shudder hit me as I thought, *Does she know? Is she toying with me?*

She favored me with a gap-toothed smile. "Do you have any more?"

I clasped my armored, taloned hands together to keep from shaking. I shook my head. "No, that was all. Sorry."

She shrugged and turned to gaze into the fire. "A pity. It smelled very good." She wrapped herself in heavy bearskin and bit into a hardtack biscuit from her pack. "Wake me at first light, will you? We need to be on the road early if we're going to meet the King's man on time."

I nodded in the near darkness.

Shivering rage battled my compulsion. Simultaneously, I ached to tear her to bloody bits while struggling not to crawl to her feet and beg forgiveness.

I chomped hard on the pitiful little raw rabbit I had to sup on as I settled to watch over Goldfeather for the night. Should anyone attempt to harm her, I would defend her to the death.

God, I hate her.

***

"Many of your brightest and most wise think I'm a con artist," Goldfeather said as she stood beside the Aloo chariot driver guiding the Shimfur horses with the reins. Like Wind Rider, the horses had been engineered for speed and strength and were all leg and haunch, with wasp-like waists and heads the size of my fist. The driver grunted at Goldfeather's comments, obviously caring little about what this *human* had to say. But that was the way of Aloo servants. They had a single-minded focus on their tasks and little else mattered. Goldfeather didn't seem to mind.

"A purveyor of silly tricks and a maker of useless trinkets some claim. But I tell you I am none of those things. I am a bona-fide, honest to Ancestors Cherokee shaman, a medicine woman, if you will, although there is no word in my peoples' ancient tongue for such a person. I am the last."

My mistress prattled on like this, very much aware of how annoying she was being. She didn't care. I had learned over the years that that was part of her public persona. I guessed it was meant to mislead the listener into believing she was just an addled old Indian and quite harmless.

She had awoken in high spirits that morning, grinning and humming odd little tunes as she prepared her bedroll and tied it to my broad, metal-scaled back. We ate sparingly, I on a weasel that Wind Rider captured, she on dried fruit and a biscuit washed down with water. Afterwards, Goldfeather strapped the other camp equipment across my back and we marched to Adrian's Reservoir.

She was in such a good mood that she tied her namesake totems into her long, gray hair; twelve perfect gold feathers as fine and delicate as the real thing. She wore these only on special occasions. Where she got them was a secret, and no amount of prodding pried the truth from her. But she loved them, storing them in a small, hermetically sealed metal box obviously forged in one of the old Gle nickel dens to the north. She always carried them next to her body, even when she slept. Such Gle factories were hidden to the point of being considered myths by many, so how she acquired the feathers and the box must be a tale worthy of attention. One of these days, I'll get the truth.

Goldfeather's face glowed in the morning sun as we crossed the border into King Carmelo's realm. I could see from her straight stance and wide grin that she was excited to enter human territory again. She would deny it of course, but she often shared her disdain of "The Wild Unknown Lands" as she called them, those areas where the remnants of the surviving Aloo and Shimfur still held sway. She preferred being with her own kind, having that connection with folk of pure flesh and bone, bereft of exotic Aloo cyber-tech skin and organs, or Shimfur organic metal parts. Mind you she had no problem living with beings like myself and Wind Rider, so long as they were indentured servants. But for equal footing, give her a smelly, arrogant, self-obsessed human any day.

The chariot rumbled along the cobblestones leading to Castle Escobana's gate before the sun reached its zenith. A small party of His Majesty's entourage, old-school Shimfur Androidites, with four arms and free-thinking organic positronic brain stacks (that gave them their characteristic bulging skulls), stood in a line to greet us just inside the gate. Goldfeather grumbled when she saw that the king himself was not in attendance.

"He's a lord, mistress," I whispered as we stepped off the chariot. "He can't possibly sully his feet with walking." Goldfeather sniffed.

From a pocket inside her robe she produced a bent twig. With a flick of her wrist, the stick grew into a staff as tall as she. Our greeters gasped and murmured in response, but I'd seen the trick too many times to be impressed.

"Lead the way," Goldfeather said and followed the androidites up the path to the castle proper while Wind Rider glided along overhead.

Balt'mor is one of the few human kingdoms in the East, and the only one near The Great Bay. It's a hodge-podge of wood frame structures sheathed with Shimfur bio-tech membranes that give everything a metallic sheen and strength without the oxidizing qualities of steel. I've enjoyed walking along the rowhouses at sunset, the buildings shining brightly while a light breeze blows in off the bay. The spires of the ancient city still dot the sky here and there in the distance, but for the most part are cloaked in soot, vines, and trees.

King Carmelo rules these lands with cunning and a human army that dwarfs all other militaries in the region. He's even managed to acquire a highly dedicated Shimfur Royal Guard, lead by human officers of course. Where do you think Goldfeather acquired me? No one, not even the Shimfur Kingdom of Caracol in the northern Penn Region would dare breach Balt'mor's borders.

We reached the steps leading to the castle, and spotting the man who stood at the top waiting, I remembered why we had left.

King Carmelo is one mean and ugly fellow. It's not entirely his fault, you understand, but he's made no effort to pretty himself up. There was a time when he was handsome, vibrant, and quite a ladies' man. But his arrogance and lust for power often put him into unsavory situations in his youth. One such event caused an Aloo swordsmaster, offhandedly insulted, to pare away Carmelo's nose and a part of his chin in a duel. Like all Aloo swords, the blade was coated with reconstructive toxins which left the king's face looking like a raw-meat carnival mask with a pleat down the center where his nose, lips and chin should have been. If Carmelo were a jovial man, his face might be seen as comical or even tragic. But not so. He wears his wounds like a badge, and blames everyone but himself for his misfortune. How he managed to sire a daughter, with a legitimate royal lady from the west no less, is still a mystery. Popular rumor shifts between rape and drugs placed in his lady fair's drink. Why my mistress gives this beast the time of day is beyond me.

"Goldfeather!" King Carmelo said, his grotesque face twisting in a tortured attempt to smile. "You honor me with your presence." Lacking lips, he spoke with a moist lisp.

Goldfeather bowed low in a courtly manner, and Carmelo caressed the shaman's head with his hand in a formal paternal benediction in response.

She stood and smiled. "The honor is mine, your Highness. I hope my stay this time will bring me better fortune than the last."

I tensed, ready to defend, but the little dig was so pleasantly voiced that the king opted to take no offense. Instead, King Carmelo cleared his throat, took a breath and said, "Yes, indeed. Such memories are in the past, my good friend. Let us forget and move on."

I scratched my chin and stared. *Just how desperate is he?*

Goldfeather nodded and smiled. The king took her arm in his and walked her toward the castle's long entrance hall. He glanced over his shoulder at me. "Come along, please. My people will show you where to store your belongings." Two of the Androidite courtiers stepped close to flank me until I favored then with a razor-toothed scowl. Hands aflutter, they stepped back.

Turning to Goldfeather, he sighed, "I apologize for rushing to business so soon, but there is much to discuss."

"What is your problem, Sire? My bird suggested it was of a serious matter, involving the Princess? I hope she is well."

If it was possible for a face as hideous as Carmelo's to show concern, it was trying its damndest. His sallow flesh grew pale, his creased face twisted into a mass of wrinkles. "Oh, grave, grave trouble indeed, Goldfeather. But I lack the words to describe this dilemma. Best I show you."

We marched into the broad entrance to the main castle. Wind Rider perched on my shoulder.

Castle Escobana is a rare thing these days. Made of granite, it resembles the buildings of the ancient humans before the coming of the invaders. There are three main structures: the entry hall, the court, and the living quarters, all enclosed by a high stone wall a mile in radius. The gardens maintained inside the walls are the envy of royal families as far south as Charlet. The King's Menagerie alone, filled with genetically pure animals of pre-invasion stock, brings admirers from across the country.

King Carmelo was in a hurry, rumbling his large body forward as fast as his pudgy legs could move. We followed closely, ignoring the opulent splendor of the king's home. It was a long walk to the living quarters.

"Wind Rider tells me that your daughter is in a bit of trouble, my lord," Goldfeather said breathless. "May I know what that problem is?"

King Carmelo did not answer, nor turn to acknowledge my mistress' query. He just waddled forward, the two androidite assistants keeping pace with staccato clanging from their metal feet. We presented an odd entourage, and I would have mentioned it to Goldfeather had I a moment to pause and reflect, and if Wind Riders' claws were not digging into my shoulder. But we hustled into the King's private quarters at the rear of the Castle. We dashed up a flight of stairs, down a hall, and finally stopped at a wooden door bolted from the outside. The lock appeared to have been installed recently, and two guards stood on either side of the entrance with power lances held firm. At the King's appearance, they bowed, shouldered their lances and quick-marched away. The androidites did the same.

I was shocked. We were alone with the king: two powerful Shimfur battle creatures and a human with a grudge. I scratched my chin with a claw and watched wide-eyed. *This has got to be good.*

King Carmelo grimaced and shuffled his feet. "When I open this door, you will understand my problem." He slid a slender key into the iron lock. "And you must never, ever speak of this to anyone outside these walls. Do you understand?"

The earnest expression on his sad clown face even made me nod agreement. "Certainly," Goldfeather said, raising her staff as if she expected to use it to defend against whatever lay within.

King Carmelo turned the key, slid the bolt aside and pushed the door open.

Glass.

That's what lay inside. Shimmering glass. The entire room. Thick, sparking glass, with a glowing smoky blue cast.

The floors were sheer polished glass, smooth as a mirror, so even I found it hard to stand despite my long retractable claws. Goldfeather leaned on her staff for support as she ventured in, sliding her moccasin-shod feet gingerly as if on ice.

The strangeness of the room became clear as I gazed about. This was the Princess' bed chamber, furnished and decorated as you would expect of royalty. But everything, every trinket, every tapestry, every curtain, every dainty knickknack that a daughter of a king might possess was covered like a tree after the fall of freezing rain in winter, but with glowing blue glass rather than ice. Nor was it cold. Not in the least. It was warm to the touch like a living thing, radiant with its glow. It was beautiful really, worthy of study and admiration. If this had been anyone else's room, it would have been hailed as a marvel to behold. But what lay in the center made the scene terrifying.

Princess Madelina's very expensive and illustrious bed, with massive wooden posts, embroidered canopy, silk sheets and ruby-studded headboard, was covered in glowing glass like everything else in the room. And she was crouched on the bed, wrapped and held by a thick coating of glass, naked, perched on all fours, back arched, legs spread wide as a naked young man pressed against her from behind, riding her doggy style, his face twisted with pleasure, his hands clutching her buttocks tight.

Yet Princess Madelina carried a very different expression on her face as she peered toward the door, eyes wide with surprise, mouth open as if to shout. Whatever had done this had caught her and her lover in mid-coitus. But it appeared that whatever caught them had caught something else as well. Suspended in air and attached to the floor by a rope of glowing glass, was a beast of some kind.

It hung in mid-pounce toward the lovers, captured like them. It was small, half the princess' size, but armed with triangular sharks' teeth and stiletto claws. Its hands were extended before it; fingers spread wide to rake and tear. Trapped in its own petard, perhaps? I glanced from the Princess to the beast, and confirmed that this was where her gaze was fixed. Was she yelling at it? Or maybe shouting a warning to her lover, as his naked backside would have taken the brunt of the beast's first strike.

I closed my mouth, shook my head, and turned toward my mistress. She stood silent, eyes moving from the lovers to the beast and back. I waited.

Eventually she said, "My, my, my. How did this happen?"

How did this happen indeed.

I knew that my mistress meant specifically: How had Princess Madelina been turned into glass? More important, how had her boudoir been opened to such deviltry? But in a more generic way, I knew that she also was asking the age-old question: How had the world become so evil, so warped? Neither she, nor I, nor Wind Rider, nor anyone alive for the past thousand generations had seen the change. But the old scripts tell of a dark, dark time thousands of years ago.

The details are muddled, lost to short memories and despair. But they tell of the coming of the "alien" Shimfur and their war on Earth spanning decades, until humans were subjugated to despair and slavery. Then, as a new life began to evolve, the Aloo and their cybernetic Gle allies arrived and waged an even more destructive war against the Shimfur, their ancient enemy of millenniums past. As this war genetically and ecologically warped Earth in ways unimaginable, the story of humanity may have ended there, leaving quaint tales of the ancient savages told by the conquering invaders to their progeny. But no one, not the Shimfur, the Aloo, the Gle, or even the humans, predicted the disaster that appeared out of the vacuum of space.

Then did there come a great ball of fire that streaked across the sky, shrouding the Earth in pale glimmering dust that struck fear in the hearts of the invaders. Humans called it a visitation by God and danced their joy for the second coming of Lord the Creator and His Holy Son. Events showed such was not the case, but the shining star in the heavens gave humans a renewed boldness and fury that left the Aloo and Shimfur helpless. Worse, the invaders sought to join together to rid the sky of the great shining ball, but the war had left both sides without the capacity to travel into space. And seeing this weakness in their ancient masters, humans proclaimed that God's Mercy was wrapping the Earth and therefore all must fall prostrate before Him. Their "Holy Crusaders" swept across the land killing and burning anything not blessed by their God.

The Earth fell again into war. Fire, famine, death, and bitter cold fell upon the land. Billions died, this time also among the invaders' people, and those that survived did so by taking shelter in mountain caves or tunnels deep under the ancient city ruins. During this time Human, Shimfur and Aloo lived as one people, as sheer survival demanded cooperation from all. As for the Gle, they vanished from the cities, disdaining the underground shelters or any alliance with the other races. When the darkness ended, no sign was found of the Gle, although some later claimed they lived still in hiding.

A change came upon the earth once the three races emerged into the light of day. A new way of life had evolved; a new way of thinking, three cultures now fused into one. It took hundreds of years for the world to pull itself from the wrath of God's Mercy, but it did.

And so here we are, myself, my mistress and Wind Rider, borne of the Great Ancestors, standing in a glass room and wondering how it came to this. Rest assured, we'd find out.

Goldfeather turned and quietly asked the deformed and distraught ruler standing nearby, "How did this happen?"

Whether it was from shame due to her compromised position, or from the fact that she and her lover were permanently trapped in glass, I could not say. But the king looked like a man fearing the loss of all he held dear.

"I do not know," he whispered, leaning against the warm glass covering the inside of the chamber door. "This is how I found her a week ago."

He dropped his droopy, weeping eyes from the carnal tableau, searching for words. "I came to welcome her back from a goodwill mission in the north." He hesitated, and I could imagine what kind of business she had been on. In some circles, Princess Madelina was known as "The Whore of Balt'mor". It was well-known that humans have a propensity for recreational sex. Such practices are fairly rare in Aloo and Shimfur communities, where sexual congress and (in most cases) sex organs were eliminated as an unnecessary distraction from more productive endeavors. Among the Shimfur and Aloo, reproduction was more technological than primal.

"Get me a tapestry, will you, Godwyn? I want to investigate more closely."

I found a large one hanging in the hall and spread it out on the slippery floor. Goldfeather caned her way over to the bed, and leaning in close, scrutinized the lovers at length. I stood a few paces behind, my hearts beating a syncopated rhythm that, if accompanied with flute and strings, might have offered quite an ensemble for the two love birds. Bad joke, I know. But I find it helpful to remain emotionally detached from my mistress' cases. I sleep better that way.

She leaned in close and laid her hands on the princess' waist. Squinting, she ran her hands down her hips and onto her buttocks where the young man's hands gripped her tight. "Who is the young man?" she asked.

From the doorway, the king sighed, "A dead man, if he lives through this dark spell. He was one of my cavalry men, I think."

"You think?" She glared over her shoulder at him.

He cleared his throat. "I could not bring myself to come close enough to see his face. I'll save that pleasure until after I've removed his head from his neck."

I glanced back at the young man and had to agree. Even this close, the glass was blue and foggy and the fellow had his head down, almost resting on the princess' back. Still, my third eye, the one in my chest, could filter out the cloudiness inside the glass. He certainly was a soldier, and probably one of Carmelo's men. The young man wore the traditional goatee of a Balt'mor Officer, and the branding scars on the left shoulder of the crossed spears of a cavalry man. Naked as he was, I could not confirm anything on the basis of a uniform, but I'd say the King's assessment was accurate. That, and the fact that the fellow had flat feet.

Goldfeather ran her hands across the princess' breasts and down her belly, then poked and prodded the young man with her staff to see if she could pry them apart. No luck, the glass welded them together tight.

"Madam!" The king yelped. "Show respect. I'm her father. Have you no shame?"

Goldfeather scowled at the King. Tapping her staff against the young man's half-exposed penis, she said, "Delicacy be damned! I must investigate the entirety of this glass curse, Lord! I was hoping we could separate the two, perhaps even remove her from the chamber. Especially with that creature in mid-strike." She nodded to the attacking beast.

She banged the young man's organ with force. He chimed like a bell. "As you can see, the glass is quite sturdy, without seam. They are fused together by it, and they to the bed and the floor. We shall have to deal with the curse here."

She leered at the King. "Besides, I doubt seriously that she's cognizant of anything at this moment. I will need a little latitude, Sire, if you please. You can wait outside if my investigation bothers you."

The King shut up, but I could see his patience was growing short. If it were my kin trapped here, I suppose I would feel the same way. Then again, we golems do not possess familial bonds, nor the biological urges to want them.

Goldfeather approached the beast. I also studied it, for it was the jarring piece of a bizarre puzzle. It was attached to the floor by a long rope of glass like smoke twisting upward. The bottom of its body was indeed a gaseous substance of some kind, trapped in swirling blue and grey. But its torso was muscular and pale, corpse white, its face conical like a canine-boar mix. Its teeth were curved backwards like a pig's and needle-sharp. Once it seized you in that jaw, I suspected, you would undoubtedly lose a chunk of meat and fast. I placed my hand on its back and retracted my claws. It was warm, almost uncomfortably hot. The glass, no matter how it had been applied, no matter how thick or infused with magic of its own, could not hide the heat emanating from its body.

"What does the heat tell you, Godwyn?"

I removed my hand and repositioned Wind Rider to my left shoulder. The bird had temporarily shut itself off for maintenance. "Well, it's made of molten rock, perhaps. Or maybe of pure fire?"

She grinned, eyes twinkling. "But you doubt the latter?"

I shook my head. "Yes, it's possible. But its upper body has more substance than I would expect with a fire creature. There's a thickness and mass that hot gas would not have."

My mistress shrugged and whispered, "It could be Gordash Sorcery."

I shivered at the possibility. Gordash was one of the strongest of the Dark Magics infesting the land after God's Mercy shrouded the earth. Somewhere in the past, a rift had been torn between this world and the Other, that magical dimension where gods and demons, fairies and the other beasts of fanciful tales dwell. The magical energies which had been shut away from the world of humans now flowed freely through the land like water in its myriad streams. Magic, good and bad, could not be contained, no matter how much my mistress, or her fellow shaman and wizards, tried. Gordash and its many derivatives were deadly. But I could see in Goldfeather's grin that she doubted this. She was leaning in another direction, but was not ready to reveal her guess, not yet. She always kept her opinions to herself, which annoyed the shit out of me.

She walked to the King and leaned on her staff. "Now then, Sire, what do you wish me to do?"

King Carmelo was stunned by the question. "Are you mad?" His face flushed as he pointed to his daughter. "Can you not see? I want her freed, damn you!"

"My eyes are not as good as Godwyn's, but I see well enough. I'm a shaman, as you well know. Not a witch. This devilment may be beyond my power."

"Nonsense!" The king flicked the idea away with his hand as if he were shooing an annoying insect. "I've seen you conquer Flocks of Burgyn Death Harpies and heal Aloo infested with self-replicating Dorgyn Grubs. I've seen you take down a Tortello Berserker with a simple flick of your staff. I've seen you turn water into wine."

"That last one was but a simple trick," Goldfeather said.

"Nevertheless, you cannot say that this is any more difficult than those other feats."

"There are many kinds of sorcery in the land, King Carmelo. Those accomplishments, my *feats* if you insist, were not as difficult as you might think. Those magics, though very savage and deadly, are quite straightforward, once you get your mind around the principles by which they function."

The king's hands shook with anger. "So you refuse to help me?"

Goldfeather sniffed, rubbed her nose, and rapped her staff on the floor. She regarded the King with a bland expression, one I knew well. She had him right where she wanted him. "No. What I'm saying is that magic like this is difficult to reverse, and it will cost a great deal."

Carmelo folded his arms across his chest. "Name your price."

She continued to stare at the King as she rubbed one of her gold feathers between index and thumb. She wore her scholarly, count-the-money look as she prepared to reel him in. Yet this was no scam or joke. This would be a difficult task, and certainly a dangerous one.

Goldfeather walked back across the tapestry and stood by the lovers. "The price will be the reinstatement of my name and honor, unfettered access to your kingdom, and I want it declared to all that my status as an Important Personage has been restored. And, I want the money you still owe me from our last involvement, plus an equal amount for this task. Oh, and a good horse so I don't have to keep traipsing across this forsaken land on foot. And for tonight, I want a cask of your best red wine and a room here in the palace where I can rest after marching many weary miles to come here."

The king gritted his teeth, his jaw muscles bulging as he struggled to contain his rage. But what choice did he have? His daughter's predicament would become public knowledge soon; no amount of beatings, executions, or disappearances would hide the truth forever.

"Very well. You may have these things, if you agree to start immediately."

Goldfeather bowed. "I shall, your grace. Tomorrow I will commence a deep study of the sorcery at work here. My servant Godwyn will begin canvassing the kingdom to interview any persons of interest whom you believe may have done this, and hopefully discover who is responsible."

The king shook his head. "No, none of this can be revealed to the public. The scandal, the speculation ..."

"My lord, I need as much information as is available. Any leads as to who did this, and how, will be vital if I am to break this spell and free your daughter."

Carmelo shook his head. "No, the scandal would be terrible. How can I trust this *golem* not to let this slip?"

"Please, great King," Goldfeather said, laying a hand on my neck and massaging the hormone sacks which contained a biochemical that kept me docile. "Godwyn will be as demure and discrete as a lamb. Won't you, Godwyn?"

Pulses of peace wafted through me at each gentle squeeze of her fingers. I nodded humbly.

***

"To be a good shaman," Goldfeather said as she unrolled her bearskin on the glass floor, "one must cultivate a personal relationship with the spirit world. It's not an easy task, mind you. It takes persistence, patience, and silence." She broke out five long sticks of incense and threaded them, one after the other, into tiny holes bored through a bamboo stand. She lit them with a candle, blew on them until they glowed, then settled on the bearskin cross-legged and facing the trapped beast. After closing her eyes and taking a deep cleansing breath, she said, "Now leave me at peace so I can try to ascertain the motives of this foul creature."

While my mistress sat on her boney butt communing with spirits, Wind Rider flew north to see if it could gather any useful information about Princess Madelina's trip abroad. I questioned if that wasn't a waste of time, but she was firm.

"This all happened as soon as she returned from that journey. If they are related, I need to know."

And I, with my three hundred pounds of muscle and excellent deductive skills, visited the local hot spots, fishing for gossip. Sometimes the best intelligence can be gleaned from rumors and gutter tales.

Mind you, a human's idea of fun is not what I enjoy. They like to get drunk, carouse with loose women (or men), and tell tall tales before stumbling home sick from cheap liquor and falling out on their dilapidated beds. My idea of fun is to hunt, to return to that more primitive part of my essence. Lashing out with claws, slicing into some unwary deer was a "high" better than any of the intoxicants humans favored.

I visited three taverns that night and got the same spiel on the princess. Among the local she was beloved, known for her piety, virginal purity and loving kindness. Yet her reputation for loose morality, debauchery, and sexual promiscuity was widely known outside the kingdom. Given her current circumstances, I suspected the latter was closer to reality. So what I was hearing must have been some sort of public relations campaign. But whose?

In the wee hours of the morning, I was on my way back to Goldfeather when I was attacked.

I felt a sharp sting in my throat and found a feathered dart jutting from under my chin. The poison took me to the ground. A golem is capable of sustaining large quantities of most poisons with little or no effect; we're designed that way. But this dart contained a poison specifically for my hearty constitution. Whoever they were, they were ready for me.

I pushed myself up to my knees as my vision began to fade, my limbs leaden and stiff. I was dying.

Then someone jumped on my back and flipped a garrote over my head and pulled it tight with his knees pressed against my back. Damn fools! They could have let me flail around while the poison did its deadly work. Instead the garrote dislodged the dart before it had run dry. As the initial shock of the drug wore off, I stood up with the thug perched on my back. I reached back and grabbed the little human by the top of his head. I squeezed once so his brains gooed between my fingers, then flung him over my shoulder.

The other two charged with clubs, pounding on my head and back. I have to admit they were pretty strong, and with the poison in me I was slow. My back stung under the blows, but I twisted my neck and elbows around until my head and hands were facing my back. All golems are double-jointed and can turn themselves around crab-like to deal with rearward threats. The clubs came down again, but this time I grabbed them both and twisted them out of their wielders' hands. I jabbed with one and speared an attacker in the sternum. He dropped spitting blood, the club jutting up from his chest. The other was cagey, more skilled. He stomped on my arm and tried to jerk the club away. I clawed at his face, but managed only to tear away his cloak.

Then I saw the jewel hanging on a thin cord of leather from his neck. My eyes were foggy with the poison, but the gem's sheen, its green sparkle, was unmistakable. I couldn't believe it at first; such an old and revered sorcerer sending his thugs against me. The man saw my gaze and tried to step away, but I had him by the throat now, my claws digging deep. He pulled at the cord from his neck, trying to get rid of it. With my last strength I slapped his hand away and ripped the cord free, clutching the jewel in my fist. Then I squeezed and crushed his throat. The man hovered over me for a moment, then fell over.

The last thing I heard before passing out were shouts and whistles as Royal Guardsmen rounded the corner.

Quickly I popped the jewel into my mouth and swallowed. Darkness took me.

***

Coffee gives me the runs, so the first thing I asked for was a large pot. Goldfeather stood nearby frowning with Wind Rider perched on her shoulder. I gave them both a razor-toothed scowl since neither had shown much joy that I wasn't dead or severely injured. Of course, Goldfeather probably saved me from a torturous toxic death. Damn her to hell! Another thing to hold over my head.

"I thought you hated coffee, Godwyn."

She regarded me pinch-mouthed, and started to say something else.

"Mistress, coffee now, dammit. It's important."

Goldfeather *tskd-tskd* and frowned harder at me, but nodded to the Shimfur androidite standing at the door. It trotted out and returned carrying a steaming pot of South Andes Select on a tray with demitasse cups. Ignoring the ridiculous little cups, I grabbed the pot and sucked it down in one long pull. The near boiling liquid scalded my lips and throat, but I didn't care. My bowels felt like burning coals. I was ready to blow.

Two minutes later I was perched precariously on a little silver chamber pot best suited for a human's backside. The pain had become so intense that I squatted down right in front of them all and commenced grunting and pushing. I have to admit I felt a touch of guilty pleasure as Goldfeather paced and grumbled. Coffee not only stimulates my bowels, it blesses me with great fruity clouds of pungent gas. Goldfeather gasped open-mouthed as Wind Rider squawked at the first toot.

"Honestly, Godwyn. Have you no manners? I thought I had broken you of those bestial habits."

"If you don't like it, mistress," I said with a smile, "just say the magic words and I'll be gone." I grunted and cut loose with a long, loud movement. Must have been a good one because Goldfeather shrieked and covered her face with her sleeve while Wind Rider flapped up squawking into the rafters to regard me with a gimlet gaze.

I turned and fished around in the pot while Goldfeather retched behind me.

I pulled out the jewel, rinsed it off with the dregs of the coffee, and held it up to the light shining through the stained-glass window. Goldfeather's discomfort disappeared as soon as she saw the gem. She snatched the wet, smelly jewel from me and stared at it open-mouthed. If it was real, it was a piece of God's Mercy, the comet that ended the alien domination of Earth.

"Where did you get this?" She squinted at it.

I described my encounter with the thugs.

She stood silent, turning the jewel over and over in her hand. Legends of God's Mercy told that in addition to raining God's wrath on the invaders, the bright comet shed pieces of itself as it descended, gifts of great power to the faithful. This remnant of the legendary rock was a perfect cut emerald shaped centuries past. Despite its thunderous arrival, the gem was brilliant green, clear as spring water, and a beauty to behold. It was perfect and powerful, a source of magic beyond anything I'd ever seen.

"So the Brotherhood of the Green Spire is involved, eh?"

I nodded. "It seems so."

She examined the jewel further. When she held it in the sunlight, a green glow lit her face. "I had suspected some great power was involved from the way the Princess is trapped. But why would the Brotherhood concern themselves with a silly, promiscuous girl?" She shrugged. "Come along, Godwyn. There is much to do, especially if the Brotherhood has an interest."

As we walked toward the Princess' chamber, she caught me up to speed. It seems I had been drifting in and out of consciousness for three days. As I suspected, Goldfeather concocted an antidote to the poison, but it was a near thing. She did not leave my side during the recovery. Wind Rider had returned from his journey north a few hours ago, and the information the eagle had gathered sent a chill down my spine. Apparently, the Princess had attended a secret meeting with a Shimfur warlord during her supposed "goodwill" visit with the King of Carocal, without her father's knowledge.

Goldfeather puffed air from her cheeks and shook her head. "Okay, enough lollygagging. Time to earn our pay." She drew out the metal box holding her feathers, and began weaving them into her hair. I couldn't help noticing the care she devoted to the task, as if this might be the last time she did so.

I stepped closer, my taloned hands clasped together. "I respect your dedication to the king's problem, mistress, but I think perhaps we should ditch this one. We could slip out by the postern gate and be miles away before we were missed." Wind Rider bobbed its head in agreement from his perch on my shoulder.

Goldfeather laughed without humor, dry and harsh. "Nonsense. Where's your sense of adventure?" She reached up and patted my cheek.

"You could be killed!"

She attached the last feather, admiring the effect in her mirror, a twisted grin across her face. "Since when has my safety concerned you?" She winked and tucked the box into her robe. "By the way, should things do go wrong, I expect you to retrieve my feathers and the box and look after Wind Rider. I will not have that nasty Carmelo owning either. You'll find all you need to know for Wind Rider's care in my pack."

She stood and held my gaze with hers. "You understand that if I die, you are free? My power over you expires with me." I looked away and rubbed the back of my neck. I couldn't respond.

She pushed past. "Now come. Let's go and save the King's *precious* little Princess."

***

She directed a passing Aloo advisor to summon the King as we marched to the glass room. Goldfeather was drawing pentagrams filled with arcane writing when Carmelo arrived, visibly distraught. His eyes darted about, never meeting my mistress' gaze. When she had me start circling the captive beast with a smoking censor, the King kept glancing my way while his raw droopy face twisted with fear.

Goldfeather began chanting in the sing-song language of her ancestors while waving an eagle feather. In her other hand, she held the green gem from God's Mercy. Her dark hood was draped over her head, her face in shadow. The King shifted from side to side when she began dancing in time to her song, a gentle step-step that carried her around the bed. Wind Rider perched atop a cabinet and pierced the air with a shriek that set my teeth on edge.

King Carmelo almost fell over at the bird's scream. He slid towards the door as if inviting us to leave. "Goldfeather, that's enough. I've decided to end this matter. My daughter can be dammed. She has determined her fate with her crude behavior. She can rot in that glass! I no longer require your service."

Goldfeather continued dancing, ignoring the King's command. She brushed Princess Madelina's head first with the fetish, then the gem. The glow of the glass shimmered at her touch.

"Madam, I order you to stop."

"This is beyond your authority, King Carmelo," my mistress said as she pranced around the bed. She paused long enough to pin him with a fierce glare. "The magic is begun. I cannot stop it, not without inviting disaster."

The king took a step towards her, fist clenched, rage written large across his clown face. I grabbed his wrist.

"Unhand me, beast! Guards! Guards!"

I pinched his mouth with my talons. "Steady, Sire," I said with a toothy grin. "I don't wish to harm you, but you mustn't interfere. Be still!"

He regarded me wide-eyed. I let him go. He stepped back, his eyes fixed on his daughter in the shimmering glass. He shivered as if the room were freezing.

But in fact, the heat from the glass was rising, radiating in waves from the bed. Goldfeather returned to singing and stroking the frozen lovers with the eagle feathers and the gem. Mist formed around the princess and her lover.

Then the Princess blinked. Humans, even Goldfeather, could not see the slight movement through the cloudy glass, but I could. A hissing arose as the mist increased, and the Princess stirred within her glass prison. She was blinking madly, jerking from side to side, fighting to break free. The mist swelled into a thick fog, hiding all within.

Goldfeather stepped to the beast and circled it, singing and stroking it like she had the Princess. "Come out, little imp!" She slapped it with the feather. "Come out and do your worst. Sarah Goldfeather commands it!" The glass shimmered and mists billowed.

King Carmelo gasped and turned to flee. I caught him by the collar and pushed him against the wall. "Stop it, Goldfeather," the king shouted. "It's going to get out, and it will kill everyone in this room. Let me leave!"

She chuckled and shook her head. "But wasn't that the whole point of inviting me here, Sire? Wasn't it?" Mist billowed off the demon as the glass thinned. Wind Rider took flight in the cramped space, squawking and hovering near the vaulted ceiling.

I had to agree with the King on this one; staying here with a killer demon about to be released was madness. Before I could utter my protest, Goldfeather cracked the gem across the demon's back and the glass splintered. I released the king and leaped at the demon. Before I could reach it, the glass exploded in a cloud of shards.

I shielded my eyes, catching dozens of jagged pieces in my forearms. Cursing, I stepped back as the demon rose up and stretched.

It was indeed some sort of fire creature as I could feel the heat radiating from it. It roared and barred its teeth, thumped its chest with powerful lava fists.

I answered with my own bellow and thumped my fists together. It coiled its glowing, gaseous body like a spring and launched at me, teeth and red-hot claws barred. But it snapped to a halt before me as Wind Rider seized the demon's shoulders with its claws. The demon howled and twisted towards the great bird.

"No, you don't," I roared and grabbed its hands in my fists and pulled. The heat of the demon burned my hands and pain shot through me. It shook and howled, pinioned between my hands as I strained to hold my arms apart. With a twist it looped its glowing body around my waist. My skin sizzled and smoked.

I heard a commotion behind me at the bed, and Goldfeather shouted,

"Godwyn!" I turned to find the Princess and her guardsman free. But now he had his hands wrapped around Madelina's neck. As the Princess gasped for breath, she put her hand under a pillow, produced a long thin knife, then drove it under his armpit and into his heart.

Her lover gaped and clawed at the blade, then rolled off the bed, dead as a duck. Rubbing her throat, Princess Madelina slid off the bed naked and stalked stiff-legged towards her father, glaring.

The beast pulled free from my grasp and shot toward the princess, its charge and duty now playing out behind its fiery eyes. The trail of smoke and flame cast behind it as its move shielded me from the princess. I could not see her, and my mistress was too far away, and frankly, too *human* despite her many strengths to do much about it. If it reached fair Madelina, she would be torn to shreds. It was up to me.

I accessed a deep sub-routine within my mind. It's an old, feral Shimfur algorithm that, if carefully activated, can increase my strength ten-fold. But it's deadly and inconstant, making me prone to servile rage and self-destruction. I've considered using it many times over the years to free myself from Goldfeather, but such an act would mean my death most likely and hers too. Her death I could live with; mine...

But such considerations were mute at this point. I had no genuine love or fondness for the princess, nor for her father, nor for the kingdom, but duty is paramount. And if I ever hoped to be free from Goldfeather to walk this earth independently, such events as the one before me had to be dispatched with skill and aplomb. A reputation preceded you, even in such a twisted, chaotic Earth as this. Word gets out: "Godwyn the beast killed the princess, the king, and his mistress. Kill Godwyn!" I could already hear the cries for my death ringing out across the world, and it would be a prison far worse than any Goldfeather had put me in.

I dove under the beast, leapt up and slammed into it. Its corporeal glowed like coals in a furnace. I was burned, badly, but I held my ground. The princess screamed behind me, holding up her arms to shield her face and naked breasts from a strike of fire that shot out of the beast's mouth like a long, hissing tongue. I drove my fist into the beast's maw and deflected the flame away from the fair maid.

The beast screamed and tried again, spitting out flames at the girl, all the while trying to slide by me to get at its prey as I blocked each attempt. And then I got lucky. Sometimes luck is better than skill. It was impossible to imagine that such a beast could cool, but it did, enough at least for me to grab hold of it. Perhaps its frustration at my ability to keep it at bay, or perhaps its inner heat fluctuated normally. Whatever the reason, I was able grab hold of its shoulders, use my increased strength to drive my claws into its roiling flesh, and with teeth clenched against the searing pain, I gasped, "That's enough of that," and jerked my hands apart. The demon tore down the middle, spilling glowing lava across the floor. It lost all coherence at that point, dropping into a smoky puddle at the feet of the princess. Bits of machinery and clockwork emerged as the lava spread thin. Its inner light dimmed, then went black.

It was dead.

The princess, her supple flesh seared a little but no worse for wear, rose gingerly to her feet, and stepped out of the death puddle. She seemed disoriented and shaken by what she had experienced. Her eyes were glassy, unfocused, and rheumy as she looked around the room, reconciling her situation with what had transpired. When she saw her father, her dazed look turned wrathful, enraged. She casually walked over to him and cupped his grotesque face with her soft hands.

"My *loving* father," she said. "I rejoice that you have blessed me with your presence at this moment. Otherwise, I would have had to chase you down!" She punched at him, and white dust shot out of a heavy gold ring on her finger, engulfing the king. The air around him crackled and shifted, and glowing glass solidified around his body. Within moments, the King was pinned to the wall, solid and wide-eyed, with mouth open in a scream and hands raised in defense.

Goldfeather walked over and regarded the frozen King with a feral grin. "Nicely done, dearest." She tucked the green gem into her robe. "And there he shall remain until you command otherwise." She frowned back at the dead, naked guardsman sprawled by the bed. "Pity about him. It was such a fine copulation, and he was so pretty."

Princess Madelina huffed. "I've had better."

Goldfeather nodded and took the Princess' arm and led her to the closet, now free of the glass. "I'm sure you have, dearest, but now let's get you dressed and out of all this nasty glass."

Funny how things end, but neither the princess nor Goldfeather, nor Wind Rider for that matter, seemed to notice me lying on the floor, in fetal position, as I tried to come down from my rage. They were playing dress-up while I suffered with an unquenchable desire to tear myself apart.

But who cares about little old Godwyn, eh?

***

In time, I did pull it together and end the algorithm. It was a near-run thing, but I did it, and with no help from Goldfeather, I might add.

I perched on a tiny hassock while a servant spooned ground meat and cooked oats into my mouth. I tried sitting on a chair for dignity's sake at first, but that put my mouth so far over the servant's head he dribbled half of it down my chest. My hands, hips, and chest were encased in thick swaths of cloth that smelled of mint and astringent. Needless to say, I did not like the smell. Goldfeather strolled in humming a cheery tune, face a-glow with joy. "How is my big patient today?"

"He would be better if these cursed servants would stop grinding my meat to mush. My hands were damaged, not my teeth." I gave the servant a teeth-barring grin to prove the point. "And some spices for flavor would be nice."

"Red pepper, eh?"

I nodded. "The hotter the better." I shooed the servant out and stood.

I held my bandaged hands out before me. "Now mistress, I've seen enough familial infighting to understand why the Princess sealed her father in glass. But where did she get that power? And where did the beast come from? King Carmelo was terrified of it."

She frowned and looked away. "King Carmelo is the same as any other ruler whose crown rests uneasy. He believed his daughter plotted against him. And I don't doubt she did, if for no other reason than for his suspicions. That is the way of Kings and their heirs."

"But the magic glass. And the demon. Whose were those?"

She laughed. "The demon was Carmelo's. That was clear from his fear of it. It was a killing machine, designed to slaughter any and all until it expired. Without a heat source, it would not have functioned long. He knew what the creature was capable of before we released it, so he knew he had to get out of the room.

"The glass trap was Madelina's. She used it twice, once to trap the demon when it attacked, and of course again to trap her father. Perhaps she learned that trick during her trip north to the Shimfur."

"What of the cavalryman? He went from lover to assassin in an instant."

"He was never anything else. Carmelo must have ordered him to woo the girl, so they would be found murdered in terribly compromising circumstances. Her reputation with the common folk would be ruined even as she was killed. I have no doubt the King had a scapegoat set up to take the blame for the killing, allowing Carmelo to play the grieving father, blameless of any wrongdoing."

"Gods above, you humans are heartless savages sometimes. And the green gem?"

She shrugged. "The Brotherhood of the Green Spire fights for the supremacy of humans. I assume Carmelo brought them into the fray as a counter to the Princess' plotting with the Shimfur, should things get ugly. And the Shimfur must have been very happy with their plotting to give her such a nasty weapon."

"But the gem broke the Shimfur magic!"

She shivered and pulled the cracked but glowing gem from under her robe. "Yes, it broke the Shimfur tech, but I'll be damned if I know why. I've seen this kind of magic only once before, when I was a young girl. It is not science, nor alien technology. It is something different altogether. And someday I will find out what it is." She tucked the gem away.

"So what happens to the Princess? And us?"

Goldfeather stroked Wind Rider's strong, soft back, fed him a nutrient globe, and said, "She rules, at least as long as she can hold it all together. As for us, the new queen will honor her father's agreement with me. I did what he asked of me, even if this was not the result he wanted. We can stay for as long as we like as an honored guest of the crown." She moved her hand to the nape of my neck and squeezed the hormone sacks which, unfortunately, survived the demon attack. "But you know us humans, don't you? Ever bored and restless, and never satisfied to stay in one place for long. We can stay or we can go. What do you think we should do, Godwyn?"

As the rush of love for Sarah Goldfeather washed through me, I said the only thing I could. "Whatever you wish, my lady. I'm yours to command."

On "Goldfeather and the Glass Princess," Robert writes...

I started this story on my own in the fall of 2009. About two months later, my son Jason suffered a terrible accident that left his leg broken above and below the knee. In the time needed to nurse him back to health, I set the story aside. When I returned to it, I had lost the narrative thread. So I asked Jim if he could help me finish it. He agreed, and quickly made revisions that fundamentally changed the narrative for the better. He turned our main character into a woman and gave her a vivacious attitude that brought her to life. Jim was also instrumental in defining the look and feel of the alien Aloo and Shimfur. All of these improvements helped to create a far future Earth filled with magic, science, and even a touch of clockwork. We hope, in time, to write more stories about the adventures of Goldfeather and Godwyn.

And Jim writes...

Truly, Robert did the heavy lifting here, imagining this world and the glass princess. However, the chamber pot scene was all mine, which may give you some insight into my sense of humor.

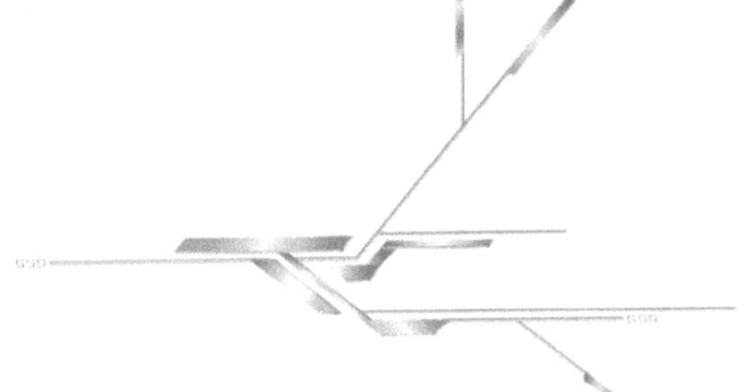

GOODBYE GREY SKY, HELLO BLUE!
KT PINTO

Mr. D came down the stairs, pausing at the landing to fix his tie in the mirror. He smiled when he saw his wife Mrs. D standing in the dining room, wearing a peach colored dress, conservatively cut and flared at the bottom, with a starched white apron wrapped around her waist and wearing matching peach pumps. Her hair was in a proper chignon, her make-up done perfectly, and her nails painted a subtle peach to match her outfit.

She smiled at him with peach tinted lips as she handed him the morning paper. "Good morning, dear!" She said as he sat at the head of the table. She gave him a chaste kiss on the forehead. "The kids will be down in a minute. Would you like some juice?"

"Thank you, honey. That would be perfect."

Mrs. D went into the kitchen and pulled the container of orange juice from the cool biopolymer gel, pouring a tall glass for her husband. She put the juice away and placed the glass on the table in front of Mr. D. He took a sip of it, nodding approvingly.

"Eggs?" she asked.

"I can't give you any," he replied with a smile. "I'm not a chicken."

Laughter from invisible people filled the air; Mrs. D touched her fingers to her chest as she giggled heartily.

"No honey, I meant would you *like* eggs for breakfast?"

"Scrambled?"

"Of course, dear."

"Perfect." He opened up the paper as she went into the kitchen and prepared to make some eggs and toast.

"Make sure they're made well done," he called as he turned to the sports page. "Last time they came out a little runny."

"They still taste good if you're quick to catch them!"

The invisible laughter filled the house again as Mr. D leaned back in his chair and had a good belly laugh. "Good one, honey. Good one."

As Mrs. D adjusted the settings on the replicator for her husband's eggs, their two teenage children came running down the stairs. Billy, the older child, was tall and lanky, with hair the same bright color as his mother's. Betty was dark haired, like her dad. She was, as usual, dressed in her JV cheerleader's uniform.

"Good morning, Daddy!" she said with an over-abundance of cheer, bouncing over to the table and giving him a kiss on the cheek. "Good morning, Mother!" she called into the kitchen.

"Good morning, Betty! Is your brother down yet?"

"Yeah, I'm here Ma!"

Mrs. D came out of the kitchen with three plates full of food. "Everyone sit! Breakfast is ready."

"Would you believe this?" Mr. D said as his wife piled his plate with eggs. He pointed to the paper. "The Packers lost again! You would think they would know how to make a pass in zero g by now! What do they get paid all that money for?"

"To get your blood pressure up?" Billy said, causing the invisible laughter to erupt.

His father put down the paper. "All right, all right... I get your hint." He put some salt on the eggs. "They look delicious, honey."

"Thank you, dear." She sat down next to Betty and frowned. "You aren't going to practice tonight, are you?"

"Ma, of *course* I am! The team is still playing this weekend."

Mrs. D made a face. "But after what happened at the stadium last week..."

Betty shrugged; the cheery expression never left her face. "Those boys were out after curfew. It's their own fault."

"Oh Betty," Mrs. D said, shaking her head, "sometimes you are so cold!"

She held up a red cardigan. "That's why I always bring a sweater!"

Laughter again from the invisible people.

"So what time are you going to be home?"

"Ma-aa!" Betty said, eating her breakfast. "I'll be home by curfew!"

"Well, it *is* a school night," Mrs. D replied. "Earlier than that would be better."

"That's silly Mother!" her daughter responded. "I never understood curfew. Day, night... it's not like it makes a difference."

"You can't see as well in the dark." Billy responded.

"Vehicles have headlights!" she countered.

"No matter," Mrs. D interrupted before they could continue. "There is a curfew and we must abide by it. But I would still like you home earlier than that."

"I can't promise," Betty said. "We might go to the malt shop after practice."

"I don't know..." Mrs. D turned to her husband. "What do you think, dear?"

He looked up from the paper. "I think it'll be alright," he answered, then looked at his daughter. "As long as you take the necessary precautions."

"Of course, Daddy!"

"There, you see?" Mr. D said to his wife. "She's a smart girl; she'll be fine."

"Well..." Mrs. D moved her eggs from one side of the plate to the other. "Alright. As long as you *promise* to be careful!"

Betty made an 'X' on her chest with her finger. "I promise!"

Her mother forced a smile. "Well then... does anyone want coffee?"

Billy took a bite of crispy bacon. "Me, Ma, please."

"Thanks honey," Mr. D said, then went back to the paper.

"Mother, can I..."

"You're too young, Betty."

She made a face. "You don't even know what I was going to ask."

"But did I give the answer you were expecting?"

Betty pouted as the invisible laugher began. "Yes."

The laughter got louder as Mrs. D came back in the room with the coffee pods and smiled at her daughter knowingly. "Then it doesn't matter what the question was, does it?"

Betty laughed. "Oh, Ma!"

"She got you there Betty!" Billy said with a smile.

Betty was about to reply when the sound of a really loud, un-muffled engine filled the house.

"Does he *have* to have it sound like that?" Mr. D grumbled.

"Oh honey, leave him be! He is actually proud that he got the bike to sound old fashioned like that."

"I don't know why," he said over the warning alarm. "Anyone else would *not* want his vehicle to sound like something from generations ago. Especially since it calls unwanted attention to you..."

The alarm shut off and the family visibly relaxed. A few minutes later the back door opened and Stephen Matriciani strode into the house, his heavy leather boots thumping on the linoleum in the kitchen. He looked through the counter window between the two rooms.

"Heeeeeeey! My favorite family! How are you all doing this morning?"

"Hello Stephen!" Mrs. D said cheerfully. "Would you like some breakfast? Coffee?"

"Whoa, don't get up, Mrs. D! I'll get a plate and pod and be right in!"

"You're up early Matris," Billy said, using Stephen's nickname.

Stephen shrugged. "Got to go into the garage early today; got a lot of customers waiting for their rides! So I went out this morning to pick up some stuff at the store for my date tonight."

"Oh?" Mr. D said. "Who is the lucky girl?"

"Girls, Mr. D," Stephen corrected. "Got me a date with the Tetrizini triplets."

"Triplets?" Mrs. D said, piling his plate with food. "My, my! Aren't you adventurous?" She walked around the table and put the plate in front of him, then patted his cheek. "Those are some lucky girls!"

Stephen blushed as Betty said, "Not so lucky. Aren't there only two of them now?"

"Are there?" Stephen shrugged as he drank some coffee. "They booked the date with me so long ago... oh well, I'm going to have to reconsider some of the entertainment then..."

"If you need any help handling them..."

Stephen shook his head at Billy. "My friend, even just one of those trip - twins - may be too much for you."

Mr. D cleared his throat loudly as the laughter died down. "How is it out there today, Matris?"

"It's a little busy down by the town square," he answered, shifting in his leather jacket. "Looks like the natives are getting restless."

Mr. D rubbed his chin. "I wonder why..."

"Because it's homecoming week!" Betty responded. "Everyone gets antsy during homecoming week!"

Billy smirked. "I think it's more that you get antsy enough for the whole town."

"Oh Billy!" she said as the family laughed along with the invisible people.

"And what about you, Billy?" Mrs. D asked. "Are you excited about homecoming?"

Billy shrugged. "Well, not really. I mean, what's the big deal over a stupid football game?"

Betty's face turned red with anger. "You take that back!"

"I will not," he answered. "Big, stupid guys running around after a ball..."

"It's not just about that," she countered. "It's about school spirit! And the dance that night!"

"I still say it's silly."

"Children..." Mr. D warned.

"Now Billy," Mrs. D said, "don't make fun of you sister just because you don't have a date yet for the party."

"Ma!"

"Heeeey, why didn't you tell me?" Stephen said, taking some more bacon. "Your friend the Matris can get you someone by Saturday!"

"You can?"

"Sure... but not the Tetrizini triplets."

"Twins," Betty corrected over the laughing.

Billy beamed. "Well then... go team!"

"There now!" Mrs. D said. "That was an easy problem to fix, wasn't it?" She stood and picked up her and her husband's empty plates. "Help me clean up, Betty. Will you?"

Betty rolled her eyes and sighed the sigh of the overburdened, but still stood and grabbed some dishes. Mrs. D took the plates from her and put them in the mural dishwasher above their heads. Betty gave her the rest of the dishes as the men went into the living room.

"You said the garage is busy today?" Mr. D asked Stephen.

He nodded. "Yeah! They must have heard what a master of machinery I am!"

"Then why are you here and not there?"

"Hey, the master has got to eat every once in a while!"

"What about you?" Mr. D said to his son. "Don't you have to go to school?"

"I'm waiting for Ralphy-boy and Wally to pick me up."

"When did we become the Intermodal Station?" Mr. D joked, spurring invisible laughter. "And those two can't seem to pick up a newspaper without causing problems! How they are still alive, I have no idea."

"Because they go after brains," Betty replied as she cleaned the table. "Ralphy-boy and Wally have nothing to offer."

The laughter became uproarious as the family joined in.

Mr. D shook his head ruefully. "Well, *some* of us have businesses to run."

"Hey, Mr. D!" Stephen said, standing. "I can give you a lift if you need it."

Mr. D chuckled. "Thank you, Matris, but I think pulling up to my store on the back of your bike may not be the best idea."

"Oh, honey! I think you'd look wonderful on a bike!" Mrs. D cooed as she sat properly on the couch with her legs crossed at the ankles.

"Really?"

She nodded. "Manly and rugged."

"I tell you, Mr. D," Stephen said. "The chicks love it."

Mr. D rubbed his chin. "As appealing as that sounds, I think I'll take my vehicle."

Stephen shrugged. "Your call, Mr. D!" He turned to the couch. "How about you, Mrs. D. Want a ride?"

She giggled like a girl. "Oh, Stephen! You're making me blush."

"How come you don't blush when *I* say nice things to you?" Mr. D asked his wife.

"Oh dear, I do! But *you* don't offer to take me riding on a bike."

Stephen shifted uncomfortably for a moment as the laughter died down. "Hey, Mr. and Mrs. D, you are the coolest people I know; you'd look good on a bike. One day, I'll get Mr. D to learn how to ride a bike and then he can take you for a spin. Whoa!"

"I'll make you a deal," Mr. D said. "If we make it through the end of the year, you can teach me to ride a bike."

"Hey, you've got a deal, Mr. D!" He was going to say more, but the warning alarms started wailing. "Looks like Rosencrantz and Guildenstern have arrived."

"Rosencrantz and Guildenstern?" Betty repeated.

Stephen nodded. "Yeah, Ralphy-boy and Wally."

"I didn't know those were their last names!"

There was a light chuckle heard as Billy said. "He means from Hamlet, sis."

"Isn't that a town near Shorewood?" she asked.

Billy rolled his eyes as the alarm stopped ringing and the invisible people laughed. "Good thing you're a good paper shaker, sis."

There was a lot of noise coming from the back door as Ralphy-boy and Wally ran in.

"Hey cats!" Wally said loudly once he was in the living room. "Sorry we're late. There was a stack up on Main. Some subterranean tore ass down the street, slamming into a rod and causing back up for miles!"

"Can someone translate what he said?" Mr. D asked.

"Car accident on Main," Billy answered as he grabbed his leather school jacket and books.

"Oh dear!" Mrs. D said. "Was anyone hurt?"

Ralphy-boy shrugged. "Dunno. We weren't in orbit. Just repeating what some squares told us."

"Any of *them* take advantage?" Mr. D asked.

Wally shook his head. "Nah, they didn't make the scene while we were there. We just made a patch because we knew we were late. I'll get on the horn later and see if we can find out the details."

"Speaking of being late," Mr. D said, standing. "We had better get going!"

Mrs. D rushed over to the coat closet by the rarely-used front door and started pulling out her family's outerwear. "Here you go dear," she said, handing her husband a long, black trench coat. "I fixed the pocket, good is new."

"Thank you, honey."

"Try not to get it caught again."

Mr. D made a face. "I would hardly call what happened 'getting it caught'."

"I am just saying that sewing leather is tough on the duplicator." She pulled out two maces. "On the chain or not?"

"I think chain this time," he responded with a nod.

She handed him the weapon and glanced down. "You are wearing the boots, aren't you?"

"Of course, honey." He lifted his pants leg to show her the heavy leather boot.

"Good, good. Billy?"

"War hammer, please."

Mrs. D frowned. "Try not to drop it on the school tiles this time."

Billy grinned sheepishly as the laughter started. "I'll try..."

"Aluminum bat for me!" Betty said.

Her mother sighed and shook her head. "I do wish you would take your weight training seriously so you can carry heavier weapons!"

"Oh, mother!" her daughter said as she put on her long denim coat."How could I be the top of the pyramid if I'm all heavy with muscles?"

"It won't be much easier if you're dead weight, dolly!" Wally quipped.

Betty snarled at him and held up the bat. "You're cruising for a bruising, daddy-o."

Wally held up his hands. "See me going ape here."

Mrs. D ignored them and said to Matris, "Do you need more ammo, Stephen?"

"Nah, Mrs. D! I'm stocked up to capacity."

"Excellent." She patted her hair to make sure not a strand had gone out of place. "Ralphy-boy? Wally?"

"No ma'am. We're good."

"Wonderful! Now all of you get going so I can clean up this house!"

She playfully herded them towards the back door, then watched as they piled into their vehicles in the garage. The warning alarm started to sound as the clamps came off of Wally's hovercar first. There was a moment of tension, and then the force field flashed green, saying all was clear. Wally only had 5 seconds to get through before the field became hot again.

Mrs. D watched as they each went through the routine to leave the garage. It was a slow process, but necessary. Ever since the Alteration happened all those decades ago, those that survived had to do whatever they could to protect themselves and stay alive until they could figure out a final solution to the problem.

She stayed by the back door, sledgehammer in hand, until they had all left the garage, the force field reestablished full power, and the garage door closed. She stepped into the kitchen, locking the back door behind her. She then walked into the living room and looked around the house.

It was time for her to get the food shopping done.

She strode to the front door of the house and cautiously opened it, posed to fight if needed. All that was there was the sliding door and force field of the aerevator. She stepped into the tube and felt her heartbeat go faster and faster the closer she got to the ground.

She straightened her shoulders as the door slid open again and waited those few seconds for the field to give the all clear. She then stepped out into the dark, dreary reality that they all tried to ignore as best they could with their kitschy lives, old school vocabulary and in-house laugh tracks.

But they couldn't ignore it for much longer. The killings were becoming more frequent; the hive mind of the Altered was eventually going to figure out a way to get past the security systems and...

There was no time to worry about that now. There was nothing she could do about what may come. What she had to worry about was keeping her family happy and healthy, and that meant having homemade food on the table at every meal.

It was a rather horrific trek to get to the supermarket these days. For some reason the city planners thought the safest place for the supermarket to be located was below-ground, using a network of aerotubes to carry shipments from the trucks, without the sky-tandems having to land on a platform where they'd be vulnerable.

Unfortunately, this meant that shoppers had to either fly at really low altitude—which meant weaving between buildings at high speed—or walk among the horrors to get to the guarded access doors of the market. It was a very dangerous trek for shoppers who didn't have incredible weapons and self-defense skills. If they weren't skilled, they usually didn't make it back from the store alive.

She gave that thought half a moment before she dove deeper into the stinking shadows. She supposed she should have stayed home, doing laundry and darning like the other wives in the neighborhood did all day long. But a proper housewife was supposed to make large sacrifices for her family, and personally choosing the food her family eats at the market, instead of having the store deliver it like others do, is one of those sacrifices she chose to make.

She was almost to the market when she saw one of the Altered skulk around the corner towards her. Its skin was a sickly blue with dark rotting patches sloughing off the body. The patches of hair left on its head were straw-like and filthy, and it's only eye was bulbous and rolling around in the rotting socket. Mrs. D stopped moving, stopped breathing, hoping that the creature would just pass her by. But the Altered was too new for a trick like that, its synapses firing just enough for it to notice something living nearby. It started towards her, its sagging breasts swinging on strips of rotting flesh. It was a horror their household laugh track would not be able to giggle away.

It has locked onto her, and she knew it would not stop following her until it had fed off of and killed her. Mrs. D could not let that happen; she had children to take care of! Without hesitation, she swung her *Mauser MG34* over her shoulder, took aim and fired. It wasn't until the creature fell to the ground with a bullet hole in its decayed forehead that she realized it was the missing Tetrizini triplet.

Poor Stephen!

It was simply undignified to take out the Altered that way, but there was no negotiating with them, and she knew what they could do if they were allowed to roam free.

Her first kill had been her son Chuck. The Altered had still been a new horror to their world and he had been taken by them right in front of her eyes. He had gotten out of his hovercar to help her with groceries, and they devoured him as she scurried into the car and made her escape. That attack was one of the reasons why she chose walking to the market instead of driving: there were too many variables on a hovercar that could go so very wrong...

Weeks later she saw her son again, a shambling lifeless mess heading slowly towards her, his letterman's jacket being the only thing holding his body together, and all she had was the heavy blacksmith hammer she had grabbed on the way out the door. She had to wait until he was close enough for her to see the vacant blue of his remaining eye, and then she bashed his head in.

After that, she went for gun lessons, and many times she found herself as the armed rear guard as her knitting club ran from the hungry Altered. Eventually, she became one of the best marksmen in town, and that was while running backwards and in heels. Her skills caught the eye of the Squad, who gave her even more powerful weapons and gear and taught her how to use them all. From that point on, she geared up daily and took out as many of the Altered as she could. She was always back in time before the family came home, wearing a proper matching outfit ready to tend to their needs.

It was a messy lot in life, and not one that a proper housewife should do, especially since she had to keep it a secret from her family, even – and especially – her husband. But she wanted her family happy and comfortable, and if that meant beheading and shooting and chopping the Altered into little pieces, she would do so.

In reality, she had no other choice. The world her children were growing up in was dreary and evil, and although they tried, they were not skilled enough to handle these monsters on their own. Going out and killing the Altered before they killed her was the only way she could ensure her children would have happy days in their future...

After all, it's what any good housewife and mother would do.

On "Goodbye Grey Sky, Hello Blue!" KT writes...

I've never written about zombies. No pun intended, but I tend to avoid them like a plague. I just never saw any beauty, sensuality or strength in them. It was a publishing weakness on my part, as zombies are going gangbusters in the media, and my precious vampyres are taking a back crypt, so to speak. This futuristic tale gave me a chance to delve a little into the zombie world, without getting too immersed in gangrene skin and rotting teeth.

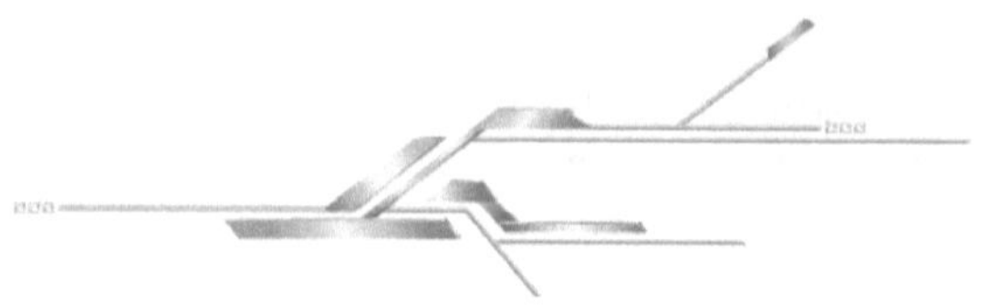

MAN IN THE WOODS
STUART JAFFE

"Please. Help me. A crazy naked man's trying to kill me," Jant had said. That's how the end of the world came for me.

People always predicted that the end of the world would be a bad thing. They envisioned a world in which those who survived would struggle like refugees from a war, would form roving bands of marauders who scoured the land for plunder, and who embraced anarchy like a license to indulge every deviant thought known to man. To be fair, it may have been like that at first. But only at first and only for a short, short time.

For me, the end of the world happened so long ago—centuries upon centuries—that I only know of what people thought and feared from the scraps of books I've uncovered in the ruined library nearby. For me, the end of the world was just the world. And none of those predictions existed in any significant way. For me, the *true* end of the world came when I met Jant, the man from the stars.

It happened when I turned sixty-three. I celebrated in good fashion. Of course, I tended the garden that morning—birthday or not, I had work to do and nobody else around to do it. The garden sat in a clearing in the forest. When I was a boy, Mother told me that the garden had fed our family for generations. Corn, carrots, onions, potatoes, broccoli, asparagus, lettuce, tomatoes, green beans, strawberries, raspberries, peas, and peppers—I grew and ate them all. Without the garden, I'd have been forced to become a predator, and as Mother reminded me so often, we have brains. We can be better than mere animals.

So, I took care of the garden. Even cleaned the old stone smoker we made long ago for when we caught fish or a rabbit that refused to leave the garden. Mother always said that though we're not predators, we don't waste what falls in our laps.

I pulled water from the river and cleaned out my one-room home constructed from a few trees and some scavenged bits. I've seen pictures in books of what homes had been like long ago, and I once found the remains of a chimney and a line of bricks in the ground that outlined where a house had stood. I had no need for such a place. All I ever required was a roof to keep me dry and comfortable while I slept. The rest of the time I spent outside.

So, on my birthday, I tended the garden, pulled the water, and cleaned my home. With all that done, I took the rest of the day off. I got out of my work clothes—a grimy T-shirt and muddy jeans—and I put on my favorite suit and tie. It had thin, pin stripes and though the cuffs were frayed, the suit had remained in decent condition. The cut fit me well, too. Mother said it belonged to my father and his father and his father. I never knew my father, so in a way, the suit connected me to him far more than the older generations.

I had made some apple wine earlier in the year, and that became my big birthday treat. I called it apple wine but really it was just fermented apples and strawberries—unrefined but potent. Very potent.

It had been a good day, and as I sat with my back against the log bench I had constructed when I was ten, as the world swooned around me with a pleasant warmth, I thought how lucky I had been to live such a rich life. Because in truth, I knew that there were people out in the world who did struggle, who did form marauding gangs, who did indulge their deviant sides.

But I had been born to this little paradise. With so few people left in the world, nobody ever bothered me. In my entire life, I had only met a handful of people. When I was forty-five, a nomadic family came by that I shared my food with and heard stories of their travels. At twenty-one, a young gal passing through stayed with me and possibly left with my child inside her. And at ten, a foul man sneaked into our home, attempted to steal what little we had, and wanted to have his way with Mother. She killed him with a knife into the neck but not before he had damaged her as well. She lasted a few weeks longer but no more.

On the day she died, she stroked my cheek and said, "Don't ever lose this little paradise. It's what keeps us human."

So, on my sixty-third birthday, I sat, I drank, and I celebrated my rich, peaceful life in paradise.

I had fallen asleep and probably would have stayed that way until the next morning, but I heard a falling body, a splash of leaves, and a quick curse. My eyes shot open as my ears sought more information. Certain sounds always woke me—wolves, bears, and other predators, of course, but the few times I've ever heard a human being always stood out. How could they not? The sound was so unique, so foreign. That was how we caught the intruder who killed Mother. I heard him in the night.

The human that startled me awake on my birthday had been clumsy and unsteady. Those were strange qualities. The humans I encountered were either sure-footed and confident or quiet and frightened. The loud and foolish tended to die young.

Without warning or greeting, a man bumbled toward me from the trees. He was oddly clean—clean shaven face, clean brown hair, clean brown skin. He looked odd, too—long jaw, smooth skin, and bone thin. Not like the rugged, filthy people I'd encountered in the past.

He wore the strangest clothes I had ever seen—pants, shirt, vest all bulging with filled pockets; rugged shoes (I wondered if I could trade some food for those); and bits of metal attached at various spots, each one with little colored lights. I had never seen little colored lights at night except for the stars but I had read about them. Mother, too, had told me stories about the world as it once had been. Still, there is a big difference between stories of electricity and seeing it in action.

I considered the possibility that this was no more than a drunken hallucination. I almost believed it until the man saw me, waved, and said, "Please. Help me. A crazy naked man's trying to kill me."

"Go away," I said, still clinging to the hope that I was dreaming.

The man looked toward the woods and then back at me. With less panic and more reason, he stepped closer and said, "My name is Jant. Many centuries ago—"

"And you can call me Old Man. Now go away."

"Pleased to meet you, Old Man. Many centuries ago, the people of Earth built a generation ship and sent a few hundred men and women toward the star Alpha Centauri with the mission of finding a viable planet to live on and to colonize. We have returned to report our success. We are reaching out to reconnect with our motherworld. I'm supposed to find your cities, your governments, but I seem to have landed in the wrong place. Please. Can you help me?"

I stared at Jant as he made his speech. I would have laughed in his face and assumed this was either the most fanciful drunkenness I'd ever enjoyed or an elaborate joke (though I had no clue who would do such a thing), but one thing stopped me—his voice. Each word came out with a shake, with a fear, and with a tinge of hope. That fear, though, was too real for my imagination, and there was no joke waiting behind it.

I climbed to my feet and the world swayed around me. "A naked man attacked you?"

"He was covered in painted stripes and he carried a spear. His hair was wild, all over the place, and his eyes...he seemed insane."

This sobered me up quick. "That's Ol' Billy. What did you do to him?"

"Nothing. I landed my shuttle and started looking for people. I got a little lost in the woods," Jant said and pointed to the metal patch on his wrist. "My tracker went down, so I couldn't home in on my ship. And then I saw this man standing as still as a tree. I wasn't even sure he was real—thought he might be a statue. So I walked up and introduced myself. He didn't respond. I thought for sure he was a statue but he looked so real. So I poked him."

I didn't understand much of what Jant said, but I caught the basic idea.

Besides, I only needed to hear the last sentence. "You don't touch Ol' Billy," I said. "Especially when he's hunting."

"I didn't know."

"Obviously." I turned in a small circle, scanning the trees as I moved. I saw no sign of Billy but that didn't mean he wasn't there. "We've got to get you out of here. Back to where you came from."

"But I have to meet with your government."

"I'm my own government. Billy's his own, too. And right now, the only reason he hasn't killed you, is that he respects the boundaries of my government. But that won't last for long. So, come inside my little home, let me get a few things we'll need, and we'll leave here."

"I don't understand. Where are the cities?"

"All gone. Long ago."

"All?"

"Every last one," I said and swerved a path towards my front door.

"When we left, things were good. Most countries were at peace and we had worked together to make projects like ours possible. We were explorers, bravely striking out into the frontiers of space. What happened?"

I shrugged. "The little I've read talks about wars and famines and wasted resources. Long before my time."

The two of us squeezed into my home but it wasn't a comfortable fit. I had a small bed, a tiny table at the side, as many books as I could stack against the walls, and a rusting box for my important things. As I opened the box, a loud howl echoed across the forest.

"Is that him?" Jant asked.

I nodded. I hadn't heard Billy howl in nine years. Though I did my best not to show it, that howl frightened me. Billy was more than just angry. Hearing him howl, I understood that Jant had not been exaggerating—Billy had lost his mind.

"I'm too old to fight that fool," I muttered.

"What?" Jant asked, his voice shivering.

"You had to come bother me, bring your problems here." I looked at my hovel. Not much but it had been mine.

From the box I pulled out my hunting knife—always sharp, always ready—and a pouch that contained little paper sleeves. In each sleeve, I carried seeds from the best harvests. Last, I grabbed Mother's gold necklace. The only thing she ever kept from my father besides the suit I wore.

"Let's go," I said and Jant had the brains to keep quiet.

I walked fast. I didn't bother searching for Billy. I knew he watched us from nearby. He would either attack or wait. I couldn't control that. I could only keep to my plan and hope I would react fast enough when the time came.

I led Jant back toward the garden. He tagged along, his breathing ragged as his eyes darted from shadow to shadow. When we passed the tomatoes, I pick off two and handed one to Jant. "Eat now," I said. "We may not get the chance for a while."

As we crossed through the garden, we finished our tomatoes. I snapped off some green beans and a sweet red pepper. We ate those as well.

Halfway across, Billy stepped to the garden's edge back where we had entered. He always struck me as an impressive figure. Tall, muscular, lean—his naked body covered in white, black, and red painted stripes. He had leaves and feathers in his unkempt hair. Arching back, he let loose another long howl. With his eyes wide open—wild, frantic eyes—he stared right at me as he straightened.

"Billy," I said with parental tones I hoped would sink into his head. "This man made a mistake. He didn't know what he was doing. Forgive him this error. I don't want you to kill him."

Billy raised his spear in the air and barked. My hands tightened around the hunting knife. I hadn't used it in a long time. Gardening was not good training for this. It occurred to me that I might not be able to defend myself, let alone protect Jant, should Billy do more than threaten. And I could see in his madness that he intended to do more.

"I'm too old to play this game with you, Billy," I said. "Go home. I promise we'll find a way to make this right for you."

Billy hopped from one foot to the other a few times, swung his spear over his head, let out another howl, and dashed back into the forest.

"W-What does that mean?" Jant asked. "Is it over?"

"Far from it."

"He's crazy. You can see that, right?"

"Doesn't matter what he is. He wants to kill you and probably me too."

"This is not how this was supposed to happen."

I picked a few strawberries and headed off. "Sorry about that. Nobody told us you were coming."

I didn't look back, but I heard Jant let out a huff before he scurried to follow me. We reached the opposite end of the garden and cut straight into the woods. Having spent my entire life around here, I knew the area well. That seemed to be our major advantage. Except Billy knew the area too.

Entering the woods, I now had a decision to make - go for the boulder or the river. All other options would have put us in either the open where Billy had the advantage or in the position of running beyond my scope of knowledge which, again, gave Billy the advantage. The boulder, if we could reach it and climb it would afford us a full view in every direction. Billy couldn't approach us without being seen. But, of course, it also meant we'd be stuck atop a huge rock. The river, on the other hand, would not protect us the same way; however, it acted like a moving road. We could build a basic raft and float on down, traveling faster than Billy could run in a day, and we'd most likely end up finding other people.

The decision lay out before me in a flash and I made my choice quickly. "We head for the river," I said. I didn't like it—I had no desire to meet anybody else in the world—but it was the safest way to get distance from Billy, and I figured if we met another human, I could get rid of Jant. Billy might prowl my garden for a while, but he was a hunter. He'd eventually move on and I could reclaim my home. He'd let me, too. He didn't like growing food, but he liked eating it. Eventually, when his madness subsided a bit, he'd realize he needed me.

But I was wrong.

When we hit the river—a wide swath of churning brown water—Billy waited for us. Though he had to have sprinted to beat us there, he hardly struggled for breath. Madness scoured his face. I had never seen him like that before.

"Billy," I said, raising my hands and opening my palms, "I'm an old man and I'm tired. Let this fool go on his way. You and I can go back to my house, I'll make you something to eat, and we'll see if there's any more to drink. Doesn't that sound good?"

I didn't expect him to agree, but I had to try. It was true, too. Though I was strong from years of working the soil, I had never built the muscles for all this chasing. That was a hunter's way.

"I saw him come down from the sky," Billy said, and Jant gasped at the sound of Billy's hard, rather sane, voice. "If he lives, more will come. We will lose all we have."

"We have an entire world," I said, making a little turn with my hands upright.

"You're the fool if you think that."

Billy charged up from the river bank, his spear leading the way. Jant jumped behind a tree, but I stood my ground. Not out of bravery. I simply knew he wasn't attacking me.

I was wrong again.

When he reached me, he spun his spear around and jabbed me in the gut with the dull end. I crumpled to the ground, spewing out my birthday drink, and worried he had cracked a rib. I rolled on my back in time to see him twirl the spear overhead and slam it at Jant. Jant ducked and the spear smacked into the side of a tree. Billy reversed his motions, catching Jant on the back of the head and knocking the poor boy unconscious.

He turned to me. "Sorry, Old Man, but this one will destroy us all."

"Don't kill him. Please."

"I have to. More will come, if I don't."

"They will come anyway. And if you kill him, they'll be angry."

Billy frowned as he tried to process this possibility. He lifted his spear, and I cringed at the expectation of hearing Jant's life stabbed out of him. Instead, Billy hit me in the side of the head, knocking me out.

***

When my eyes fluttered open, my head ached far worse than a night of binge drinking had ever caused. I went to touch the lump growing on my head, but my arms wouldn't move.

Billy had tied me to an oak tree. Jant had been tied to a maple only a few feet away. Made from braiding strands of plant fiber, the rope would not break easily. Billy made the stuff all the time—I assumed for animal traps, but I never ventured far enough into his territory to know for sure.

Jant stared off toward the river flowing somewhere behind me. His face bore the dried paths of tears and his mouth had turned down. Billy had taken the man's shirt, leaving him bare-chested. He had a no hair, looking young and naive.

"Where is he?" I asked.

Jant startled. "Why are you doing this to me? We came to be reacquainted with you, our parents. We came as friends."

"Where's Billy?"

"I don't know," he snapped.

The far-off look in Jant's eyes worried me. Bad enough dealing with Billy, but if Jant succumbed to madness as well, I'd have no chance of surviving this.

"I'm sorry our world isn't what you were expecting," I said. Anything to get him talking and thinking in an orderly, rational way. "It makes me wonder what kind of world you came from."

"Me?" Jant said from far away. "My world is wonderful. It's a thriving place where you can live out your dreams. There are cities and farms and all the marks of civilization. We've overcome the technological problems that faced it and found a balance with nature so we wouldn't pollute the planet to death. We wanted to share all of that with you. I gave it all up to bring it here for you. And now look at me. I'm going to be killed by a lunatic running naked in the woods."

"I'm no lunatic," Billy said as he climbed down from a nearby tree. He glanced at me and shook his head. "I know you want to believe in this man. But that's because you're so lonely."

"I'm no lonelier than anyone else," I said.

"That's a lie. But then you often like to lie to yourself."

I looked up at Billy and what I saw chilled my skin—sanity. "I'm no threat to you," I said, but I didn't expect my words to matter. I just wanted to keep him talking. As long as Billy was talking, he wasn't killing. I had to do one more thing as well—get free.

With what little motion I could make, I felt around the tree. It didn't take long to pick out a sharp edge on the bark—probably where a branch had started but never survived. I rubbed the rope back and forth on this edge. I could hear Mother as clear as if she were alive and helping me: *Keep him talking.* She was right, of course. I needed time, maybe more than he would ever give me, but I had to try.

"This is silly," I said. "I'm just an old man. Let me go."

Billy chuckled and turned to Jant. "How many of you came down here?"

Jant stared at the ground. When Billy nudged him with the side of the spear, he said, "Forty-three. We've spread all across the planet. Killing me will do you no good. The others will report in."

"I'm sure they will. And before you start dreaming that this is all just my insanity, that the 'real' world is actually a fully-running society and you just had the misfortune to drop into this wild area, I assure you that this is what it is like everywhere. Probably less violent then some areas but the idea of towns and cities and an organized populace are long forgotten."

"You speak quite well for a madman," Jant said.

I had been thinking the same thing. I had never heard this many words come from Billy's mouth, and it shocked me that he seemed to be quite intelligent. He also had a knowledge of history that could only have come from books. "You've read my library," I said, not realizing I had spoken aloud.

Billy nodded, and when he looked at me, I had to stop cutting the rope. "Some days while you worked your garden, I'd slip in to read a chapter or two of a book. Frankly, that library of yours is worth far more than your garden."

"What do *you* know? Running around the woods like an animal. Killing and destroying to survive. I nurture the land. I grow the food. I don't kill."

"Of course not. You're the civilized one."

"Don't mock me," I said, my teeth grinding.

Jant's red face turned to me. "Be quiet. Stop trying to provoke him."

Provoke him? I was the one tied up. I was the one being made a fool of. And for what? To help this idiot who didn't know enough not to go poking a man on the hunt? Jant didn't understand anything going on around him. If he did, he'd help me engage Billy in any way that prevented us from getting killed.

I worked on the rope faster.

To Billy, Jant said, "I don't know what I can say to convince you that we don't want to hurt your people. We truly came here as friends."

Billy rubbed his back against the bark of a tree. "I have no doubt that's why you chose to come here, but that's not why you're here."

"Don't listen to him," I said, for if Billy had read my books, then I knew a lot of what he knew. I knew some of how he thought, and I didn't like where he wanted to take this. I also knew that if I argued enough, he would debate me, and that meant more time. I couldn't be sure, but it felt like Billy's homemade rope had started to give way.

"Let me ask you something, friend," he said, adding such a heavy sneer to the last word that Jant flinched. "A trip like this one you've taken, all the way across a vast amount of space, using a special ship that can get you here in just a few years when the original ship took generations to get out there, a trip like that must cost a lot of money. Am I right?"

Jant squinted and his mouth tightened. "What do you know about money out here?"

"Oh, we have no money. No need for it. Money is for when people don't want to provide for themselves. They'd rather pay another person to do the jobs that need doing." Billy paced a circle in front of us. If not for being painted and naked, if not for us being tied up, Billy would have seemed like one of the rational intellectuals who wrote many of the books I owned. "It may surprise you, friend, but while we don't have money, I do understand the concepts. Not just from Old Man's books, either. We barter when necessary. And barter is really the foundation of economics." Billy paused long enough to lean towards me with a wink. "That is the right word, no? *Economics?*"

I looked away.

Back to Jant, Billy went on, "You're smart enough—I don't think they'd send an idiot on this mission—so tell me, since this trip had to have cost a lot of money, who paid for it?"

Jant shook his head, but it seemed more for himself than Billy. "You don't understand. We don't think that way."

"Then how do you know what I'm implying? You know because whether you like to act on it or not, you still have those thoughts. You know like I do, like Old Man knows, only two sources would have enough money to fund your ship—either a government or a business. If it's a government, then once they know we don't have a formal way of life here, they'll want to colonize here, get more land and cut it up amongst themselves. If it's a business, they'll want to rob us of anything they think is valuable. Only individuals like you want to be friends. The rest just want to cut us up."

"And what's wrong with that?" I said. I hadn't meant to speak, but the words just popped out. Jant stared at me, just as surprised. Again, I had to stop cutting the rope while Billy listened to me. But since I had spoken, I couldn't stop myself. Mother would have said that it was because I so rarely had the chance to speak with others. Maybe she was right. I went on, "We could use a little control around here, a little organization. You say I'm lonely? Maybe I am. Maybe it would be nice to have other men to talk with and women to love. If that means we have to give up some land, live by a few rules so we all get along, what's the harm?"

"Exactly," Jant said. "I don't like the idea, Mr. Billy, but if you're right, then what is the harm? We can offer so much to you."

With a patronizing shake of his head, Billy gestured to the forest. "Look around you. Over here, there was once buildings that touched the sky. Over here, machines on wheels that moved on black pathways carved into the land. Everywhere, people. Ask the Old Man; he knows I'm right. I've seen the pictures in his books. I've read the words. We had all of it, and what happened?"

"You can learn from that," Jant said. "Technology is not good or bad. It just is."

"But *we* are bad. It doesn't matter how great the technology. We will pervert it. We always have. And in the end, we destroyed ourselves."

The rope snapped.

I kept my hands still. I didn't want him knowing I was free until I could take advantage of the fact. But I wanted to jump up and scream at him. I wanted to race off for Jant's ship, to let his whole planet know that there were humans still alive on Earth and that some of us at least craved contact with them.

All of Billy's arguments might be true, but what good is all this freedom if we don't have anyone to share it with? He boasted as if he lived in a network of hunters, but that had to be a lie. Why would anybody prefer a crazy naked fool running through the woods killing animals over a kind, old man who had plenty of delicious, grown food to share?

Even Jant, someone who knew nothing of the real Earth, even he ran from Billy and sought friendship from me. And that's what this really had come down to—did we want to share Earth with our new friends, or did we want to pretend we could hold on to it? For that matter, it also came down to how we wanted this other world to see us. We could show them how kind, gentle, and nurturing we could be, or we could show them that we've learned nothing from the violence of our past, that deep inside, we are still animals trying to survive.

I heard Jant whimper and realized I had missed part of the conversation. I looked up at the sky—the sun had lowered toward dusk. How had I lost so much of the day?

Billy sat against a tree with his legs straight out and crossed. He perked up when he caught my eye. "You're back," he said. "Jant thought you'd lost your mind under the stress. I told him you did this now and then, but he didn't believe me."

"What? What did I do?"

"The way you drift off somewhere in your head for a few hours. Haven't seen you do it in a while though." Billy nodded to Jant. "The last time he did that, he was working in the garden. He stood there with a tomato plant in his hand, just stood still, for at least half the day."

Jant sniffled and tried to brush away his tears with his shoulder. He couldn't quite reach. "Why are you torturing us? If you want me dead, then kill me already."

"I'm not going to kill you. I let you think that because you were scared, and that made you easier to control. But in a few hours, I'm going to let you go."

"Huh?"

"If I understand the way an organized group like yours works, and I admit, I'm going on some old, old texts, but I'm guessing that you've already missed reporting in to your group several times. I also know that you are lost here and will have a slim chance of finding your way back to your ship. I know exactly where it is, though."

Jant's eyes widened. "You're going to let me starve out here? Lost in the woods?"

"You'll be fine. There's plenty of food to be had. We all live well out here. You can even stay with the Old Man. I'm sure he'll love the company, and he grows lots of good stuff to eat."

"If I keep missing reports, my people will search for me."

"And they'll find your ship smashed up. They'll figure that you crashed and died."

"How are you going to make it look like the ship crashed?"

Billy shrugged. "I'll figure out something. At least, I'll try. And if it doesn't work, I'll do the same thing I did to you to those who come looking."

"But why? They'll keep coming."

"Eventually. For a while, though, they'll stop. They'll guess that this is a dangerous land filled with vicious animals. They'll have found other, more hospitable areas of the planet to colonize first. And that's another thing about governments and companies, they like the easiest path. I think I can make this forest dangerous enough that we can live out the rest of our lives in peace without any more contact from your people."

Jant's face screwed up tight but he still gasped out a little cry.

"Don't worry," Billy said, getting to his feet. "You'll learn to love the wild. Now, this day has made me hungry, and lucky for you, I've already caught some fish for dinner. See that? You didn't even have to work for your food today. A good start, right?"

With a soft laugh, Billy headed back toward the river to get his fish. This was it. With night coming on and Billy gone for less than a minute, I had to move.

I brought my arms around and rubbed my shoulders. My old body struggled to find the strength to stand but once I did, I could feel the blood flowing through me, reawakening me. Jant watched me in astonished silence—

at first, that is.

"Quick. Help me," he said in a harsh whisper that, no doubt, traveled clear down to the river.

"Be quiet," I said. I didn't have much time, and Jant's alarming noise would only bring Billy back faster. I stood motionless and listened. Good ears often meant the difference between life and death in the forest. As I grew older, my ears no longer behaved like they should. I had good days and bad. I couldn't tell, however, which kind of day I was experiencing—I heard nothing to indicate that Billy approached, but I couldn't be sure if that was the truth or a result of bad hearing.

And then I remembered what I wanted from all of this. My mouth lifted at the corners. Who cared about my hearing? Billy would be coming back. He had to come back. And that worked fine for me.

"I'm going to save you," I said, and Jant's head bobbed vigorously. "He'll be back any second. So, trust me, and don't let him know where I am."

"What?" Jant said, the hope draining from his face.

I ignored his pitiful look and walked off into the woods. I crouched low which sent a sharp biting along my back, but I kept all my groaning inside. Billy approached, and as long as Jant didn't betray me, Billy would think I ran off for my home. That's what I would have done on most days. He would kill Jant and come visit me later with a peace offering of some sort. He'd make his excuses knowing that I didn't care about anybody else. I just wanted to survive in peace on my own.

But that was all wrong.

I've always wanted to be with other people. Ever since Mother died, I wanted to find another person to share my days. The best I got was Billy, and I've only encountered him a handful of times in my entire life.

I've been alone all these years. We all have been.

I settled behind a wide-trunk tree, stayed low to the ground, and peered out from the base. Billy walked in carrying a string of three fish. When he saw that I had gone, he dropped the fish and dashed toward Jant. Once he insured that Jant could not leave, he looked off toward my home.

"He left you here?" Billy asked.

"Um, sure he did. Just ran off." Jant tried to look upset, but his pathetic attempt at lying could be seen through even by the densest mind.

"Doesn't matter," Billy said. "Once I'm done with you and your ship, I'll get him a rabbit or a fox, and he'll forgive me. He always does." *Not this time.* "I do feel sorry for you, you know. This was the last place you should've landed in. Not with a crazy mind like his around here."

"He's saner than you."

"Old Man?" Billy laughed hard and took time to regain his composure enough to speak. "Let me tell you something—Old Man lost his mind when he was a boy. Watched his mother get killed not too far from here. He tries to grow food and he collects books, but he's not sane. A few of the hunters around here and myself, we bring him meat. Without us, he'd have starved long ago. I don't know how he survived before we came along."

None of that was true. I never ate meat. Not often. Just when the winter hit so bad and my stores emptied up. I wasn't going to die like that. I had to eat their food. But he said it as if they were being so generous. If they were so generous, how come they never stopped to talk? How come they always slipped in and out while I slept? I'd go to sleep hungry and wake up to a slab of venison at my door.

Jant didn't know any of the details, but he picked up on something I had missed. "The other hunters?" he said. "Then there are more people around here?"

"Not really," Billy said. "Not anymore. They've all moved on because of Old Man."

"What did he do?"

"We wanted to befriend him, but he attacked anybody who tried." *That's not true. They threatened me. They wanted to steal my food, rape me, kill me.* "Twice he succeeded in killing hunters. After the second time, nobody went back."

"You did."

"I can't let him die out there. It's not his fault what happened when he was a kid."

I don't need pity. I lived fine long before you and I'll outlive you still.

Jant leaned out against his ropes. "Please. If you let me go, if you let me contact my people, we could help him."

As if I needed their help.

Billy shook his head. "I won't destroy all that we have here to save a crazy man who'll probably be dead soon enough on his own."

And there it was. His true plan. I knew he coveted my wonderful garden. He stuck around after the others had left because of the garden. Oh, he said that he wanted to look after me, to help me with a little food here and there, but I knew better, and here he had finally uttered the truth. I didn't matter enough to save in his feeble mind because he would love nothing more than for me to die so he could swoop in and take my home, my food, and most of all—my garden.

Just like the rest of those bastards.

I walked up behind him, slow enough that he wouldn't hear my approach. Night had come on, and from the angle I walked in, even Jant couldn't see me. Billy crouched before Jant, and when I stood over him, Jant's face paled.

I don't recall how the rock got into my hand, but it served me well. I smashed it down on Billy's head. The first strike disoriented him long enough for me to strike again. The second time, I hit him on the temple and he fell over. Then I pummeled his head with the rock, splashing blood and skin into the air, spraying my face, hands, and arms with bits of Billy.

The world ceased around me. I struck him again. His skull cracked open and when I brought the rock down a final time, it slipped into the mush of his brain. Jant screamed. Or he had been screaming. I looked up and saw a man horrified, crying and yelling, and kicking out as if he could push through the tree he was bound to. He spoke to me, but I heard only gibberish.

I stood, my back unhappy with my exertions, and I felt Billy's blood dripping off my fingers. For a moment, I considered leaving Jant tied to the tree. I thought of finding his ship and playing things out just as Billy had planned. But I didn't think it would work with Billy, and I knew I didn't have the strength anymore to pull it off myself. Besides, I did want Jant's people to come. Except I didn't, too.

I wanted them to stop by, drop off a gift of food now and then, maybe even talk with me for a little bit. After that, I would want them to leave. Because Billy was right—the peaceful, free world we lived in would be destroyed when these other people started to arrive. Just like in the books, they would come and take over and in a few hundred years, they'd outgrow the planet. They'd start in-fighting. They'd kill themselves, and we'd be right back to me standing over Billy's corpse knowing that I'd be alone for the remainder of my life.

In the back of my mind, I could still hear Jant blubbering away. It was an annoying sound. Scratched inside me, scraped on my bones.

"Jant," I said, and the fear that shut him up filled me with a youthful sensation. "You came to help me, right?"

Jant managed a nod.

"Then that's what you'll do. Without Billy, I have nobody to provide food for the winter. Except you."

"I-I'm s-sorry. I don't know h-how to hunt."

"Not what I meant," I said and smashed the rock over Jant's head. Just twice. Just enough to kill the man. "See, Billy," I said. "You wanted to know how I lived all those years before you and your friends showed up. Simple. Smoked meats last a long time. And Mother provided."

On "Man in the Woods," Stuart writes...

When Robert and Jim asked me to write for this anthology, their timing couldn't have been better. On the one hand, I had been thinking about the impact of post-apocalyptic isolation on humans in relation to being social animals, and on the other hand, I wanted to attempt writing an unreliable narrator. And when I smashed these elements together, my narrator proved unreliable to me as well. Even after the rough draft, when I knew where it all ended up, he still tricked me in many little details. This was certainly one of my stranger writing experiences.

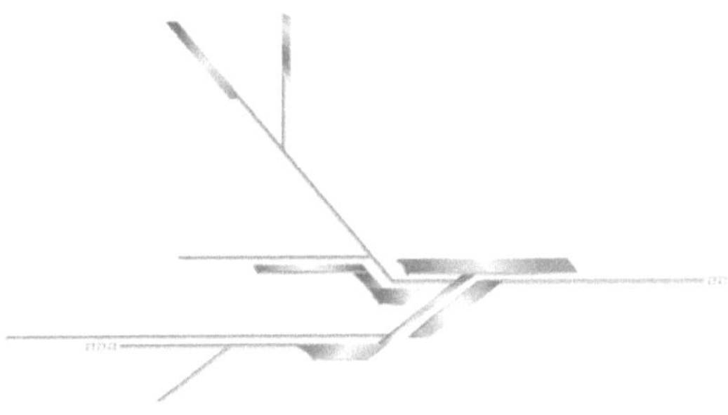

A TALENT BEYOND MY TALENTS
JEFF YOUNG

Avalem came to the Pillar of Night, when his art failed him for what he determined was the last time. Looking upwards at the vast cylinder where it blotted out the sun and cast its shadow across the lands to east, he forced himself to admit his ability had not always failed him. Second thoughts gnawed at him as he tried to make a case for all of the things that he was good at: painting, illuminating, drawing, writing. But on the whole he was just *good* at these. He would never excel at any of them and no one wanted to pay for just good when it came to art. Might as well paint a barn, do accounting or drafting, Avalem thought. *I know I was meant for more.* So when the latest commission failed to live up to his patron's expectation, Avalem left. He turned toward the east and walked across the lands until he came to the Pillar of Night.

The stories said much about the Pillar: how it was the result of when the Long-Chain-Makers fled Earth, how it was hollow, how it went up so high that there was no air at its peak and that it was inhabited. But those were not the stories that brought Avalem here. The story that moved him inexorably to the Pillar of Night was that of the greal, a strange thing that given to a man would imbue with him a talent beyond his current abilities. He'd seen some of the art made by the greal-touched and it was amazing. There was a depth to every piece that seemed to transcend what a mere man could make. Also there was the fact that such pieces were priceless and collectors of fine works fought like feral dogs over them. So Avalem was here for the greal, here to step beyond what he was no matter the price.

Avalem found that the closer he approached, the less of the sky he could see until the Pillar was a vast silvery wall covered in dark gray veins. He shook his head in amazement. It was said that in the last days of their leaving, the Long-Chain-Makers grew the Pillar and launched themselves from its peak. They built the tesseract that floated overhead at night out of the moon, went out amongst the other worlds and rearranged things to their liking and jumped from the edge of the solar system like divers to swim for the other stars. One of these days soon others would tell stories just as fantastic about him.

A well-worn path led him onward into the valley. At the lowest point was the entrance to a tunnel. Just inside the tunnel as the light began to fade, someone stepped forwards and laid a hand on his chest, bringing him to a halt. "How you planning on seeing, boy?" came a rough voice. A tiny light appeared beside the face of a gray-haired man.

Avalem started and stepped backwards. It hadn't occurred to him that the Pillar of Night would be completely dark. There was an opening at the top and some light had to get in. Of course he also hadn't planned on the tunnel either. The man looked at him with a bit of a grin and offered, "Could sell you this here light, if you need it." He handed the strange lamp to Avalem. It was a loop of glass tube containing one small bright point of light. The light bobbed about as Avalem tilted the tube.

"Gonna' play with it or buy it?" barked the seller, his arms crossed over his chest.

"A fiscum," Avalem offered, turning the light about again.

"Two, that's final."

"Done." The man grabbed the coins from Avalem's palm and turned to go into the darkness.

Without thinking, Avalem asked, "Don't you need a lamp?" Looking at the lamp merchant, Avalem realized there were a number of the tubes tied together on the man's back; all of which were glowing. The merchant's eyes flashed in the half-light, glowing like an animal's outside of a fire circle.

"Do I look like I need a lamp?" The merchant's footsteps faded into the darkness. Then Avalem heard him exclaim in the distance, "Don't forget to tell it you love it!"

Crazy old man, Avalem thought, starting down the path once more. When he held the lamp out to the side he could barely see anything in the darkness. There were no walls nearby and the ceiling was invisible overhead. Occasional drops of water fell on him and the ground was rough and uneven. Avalem kept on walking.

At first he thought that he must be tiring enough that it felt like the light was fading; then he realized the lamp was going out. The bright point was fading away. Shaking the tube of glass produced nothing. The lamp seller had tricked him. The darkness was closing in around him and his breathing grew hoarse. He would be trapped here in the darkness at the mercy of the strange inhabitants of the foothills that could see in the dark. With some trepidation, he cleared his throat and said, "I love you." The spark grew to a globe the size of a grape and gave off a soft, lambent light. It made no sense, but looking at the light source again he said, "I love you, I love you." In his own mind he realized that he loved the fact that it was no longer dark and he was no longer afraid. But the spark of light before him grew into a white hot sphere that pushed at the confines of the glass tube. Avalem had to grasp the tube using the edges of his cloak to keep his hands from burning. Then he turned back to the path.

The point at which he entered the Pillar of Night itself was undeterminable. A small amount of ambient light caught his attention. As his eyes grew used to having something to lock onto, Avalem thrust the lamp under the edge of his cloak. The land around him glowed in an unexpected reddish radiance. He could see a body of water ahead that shone with a crimson aura illuminating its depths. There was grass under his feet that was black with a single stripe of glowing incarnadine down the spine of its shaft. Trees were dark forms that loomed upward. The country of Night was nothing like he expected.

He took several steps and then pitched forward, tripping over a rock he had not seen. Avalem pulled out the lamp once more. It would mark him as a stranger here, but the alternative was to stumble through the darkness and hope his eyes would adapt. He made good time walking a game trial along the edges of a wood. Several deer, their eyes blazing golden reflections bounded out ahead of him and crashed through the underbrush. He stole another look at the heavens. Was the pinpoint of light he could see overhead growing dimmer? A few steps further and he was certain. *Night in this country would mean absolute darkness*, he thought as he made his way into the woods. Finding a fir tree, Avalem cut down several low limbs and made himself a bower. Wrapping his cloak about him, he did his best to get comfortable. Perhaps it was the darkness, but despite his strange surroundings he dropped off to sleep without any hesitation.

When he awoke, the lamp was flickering until he renewed his vow to it and just as he said the word "love" it brightened once again. Gathering his belongings, Avalem left his sleeping place and resumed his quest. He continued onward as the land dipped downward. The Pillar of Night was forty miles from one side to the other and his goal was the sinking well at its center. When he stepped into a stream, it occurred to Avalem that now he had a guide. All he had to do was follow the water down to the center of the country of Night. Walking along, he lost any concept of time. He could see better now. Perhaps his eyes were adapting. There were no homes or buildings along the side of the stream as he trudged on. Silvery white fish with huge bulbous eyes swam upstream against the current. Their motion was disturbing and odd. Avalem hoped his food would hold out long enough until he could leave the Pillar once again.

The land continued to slope downward. Down and down he went, scrambling over half-seen rocks following the water. The sound of it running and gurgling filled his ears. It kept his mind away from what might be wandering the forest unseen about him. After a time, he could see a glow of red below him as the forest pulled back away from the stream.

When he scrambled over the last rock, Avalem set the lamp down for a moment. The stream flowed across a plain until it came to a lake that glowed with red light. There were copses of trees here and there and large rocks that dotted the flat land. Glancing up, he could see what looked like a slender thread that hung down from the darkness overhead. White at its center, the light from the outside faded to red and then to darkness. Underneath lay the lake and it glowed with reflected luminance. *This is my destination*, he told himself. He picked up the lamp and started eagerly out onto the plain.

Standing on the shore of the lake, his hands and cloak painted red with the reflected light, Avalem breathed a sigh of satisfaction. *I am here, at last I am here.* He shrugged off the cloak and dropped his satchel on the shoreline. Now that he was here at the source of the greal, he wasn't certain what to do next.

Hearing a footfall, he turned to discover a group of men had come up behind him.

"You have no idea what to do next, do you boy?" The group's largest member strode forwards. He held a stout walking staff tucked up under his arm. Turning back to the others he continued, "They spend all this time trying to get here and then never have a clue what's next." This brought a chuckle from the other dozen men. The staff bearer turned back to Avalem, "Well if you have no idea, I have a suggestion." The staff came out from under his arm, its end swinging around in an arc that ended against Avalem's head.

Staggering backwards into the lake, Avalem threw up his hands in an attempt to ward off another attack. Swinging the weapon over his head, Avalem's attacker ducked in for another jab, knocking Avalem onto his back and into the water.

Feeling his feet give out from underneath him, Avalem kicked feebly in the water and then slid under the surface. Flailing about, in the red darkness of the lake, he hit bottom and pushed himself back up again. Taking shuddering breaths, Avalem lurched forward out of the lake. His attacker looked up from the contents of Avalem's satchel. "Still haven't figured it out have you?" the man growled, hands tightening on the staff once more. Avalem crouched down in the reeds and balled his fists, anticipating another strike. The leader of the band feinted once toward Avalem's head and then swung the end of the staff around hard into his victim's stomach. The air burst from Avalem. He teetered on his heels for a moment, his belly lurching in pain. The red light wheeled overhead and there was a rushing sound in his ears. He wasn't breathing. Knees buckling, Avalem pitched forward. Just before he hit the water, he pulled in a ragged breath and heard from his assailant, "You've gotta drink it boy, drink it deep." Then Avalem was plunging into the lake, its cold water cascading down his throat.

Reddish light exploded behind his eyes and in the water about him. He felt himself strike bottom. The water he'd breathed in came choking out and more water slid into his mouth and up his nose. His feet slipped and his hands sank into the mud. *I'm going to die here*, he thought. Flailing his arms about, he pushed himself away from the mud. For a moment, he lost the surface. There was so little light and it was diffused throughout the lake. In his confusion, Avalem pushed out his legs and arms, seeking any contact. He felt a grip settle around his ankle and then he was drawn from the lake. As soon as his head broke the water, Avalem spit up the remaining water. Soaking wet and shivering, he clung to the shoreline. Something blocked out the red light, and he drew back, still gasping in air.

"Welcome to Night, boy. Hope you found what you were looking for. Thanks for all the goods. Won't be seeing you again." The owner of the voice strode off into the dark, his footfalls diminishing. Avalem felt his awareness start to fade. The light before his eyes wavered. He pulled at the reeds before him, trying to draw himself from the water before losing consciousness. He dragged his feet over the rocks of the shoreline and then curled into a ball, shivering with reaction.

***

Warmth was the last thing that he expected upon awakening. Clean blankets covered his nakedness. Avalem pulled himself up to a sitting position, memories of almost drowning making him twitch. He was inside a room with minimal light. Fibers dropped from the ceiling like fishing nets. Thick strands of material draped over everything in the room covering chair, a loom, a spinning wheel and a wardrobe. There was a small window but it too was shrouded over as if wrapped in cobwebs. He was on the floor, he realized, wrapped in a nest of blankets. Pulling one around his hips, he stumbled to his feet. Ducking lower to avoid the hanging strands, he walked through the small dim room to the doorway. The next room was larger and the ceiling was once again lost in fibrous netting. But he estimated that this room, which looked to be the main one of the house, was at least two stories tall.

He held his hand in front of his face for a moment. Even in the dimness of the room he could see the lines on his palms. Blinking he looked again. He knew his hands. He used them all the time in his work. Why did they look different now? Did the fingers look longer? He was certain the lines were not where he remembered. Even his arms felt awkward, as though his forearms were too long and didn't fit. A rustling sound from overhead pulled him away from his observations. Looking up, he saw a graceful pair of legs push through the overhanging strands. The rest of the woman who followed was lithe and slim. She smiled at him for a moment and then coming to touch down on the floor, turned away to the other side of the room. Stopping, she looked over her shoulder and said, "I am very glad to find you better. Please come and break your fast with me."

Avalem found himself following her into yet another chamber that was lit by several of the strange lights similar to his erstwhile lamp. His hostess touched each in passing and the illuminations within all grew brighter. In the increased light, Avalem noticed her strange garment. From some angles it appeared a short dress, but as she turned, he could see that more of her legs were covered than he remembered. Stumbling a bit over the sheet wrapped about his hips, he then noticed that her one shoulder was bare and the dress was gathered up at one thigh. Looking away and back he found that her clothing had altered yet again. The fabric was constantly in motion, individual strands sliding to and fro in an unsettling manner.

So instead, he settled on her face, its slim lines set into a knowing smile. She pushed her long red hair over one shoulder and he saw something for a moment in the line of her shoulder that made him want to look twice, but already she was pulling fruit from a cabinet and setting it on the low table that sat along one wall. She drew a chair from the other side of the room and placed it next to the other one at the table. "Please," she said urging him to sit down. Avalem managed the feat without falling over but with little grace. He caught a quick smile trace its way across her face as she joined him at the table.

There was bread, apples and other fruit, and despite the soreness of his throat, Avalem found himself quite hungry. She pushed the woven baskets across the top of the table in front of him and settled back to watch, hands clutching a small cup of tea. Breaking off bread, he dipped it in a small dish of honey and paused after the first bite, eyes closed in enjoyment. Her short laugh caught him by surprise.

"It is so good to see someone enjoy something so simple," she said, hiding her smile behind the teacup.

"I am quite in your debt for, well, for everything. Thank you for rescuing me." Avalem bowed his head briefly to his host.

She made a vague gesture with one hand and the curtains on the nearby window parted. Ignoring the view for a moment, Avalem was fascinated by the fact that the material seemed to almost unravel and then reform on either side of the view. His host's house sat just up from the shore of the lake.

"All sorts of things wash up here and occasionally I take an interest." Her eyebrow flicked upwards briefly as her smile grew more mischievous.

Avalem was suddenly very aware of his lack of dress. He covered the awkward moment by reaching for the tea in front of him. The woman turned to gaze out the window and once again, he caught a glimpse of something on her shoulder, close to the nape of her neck. Now if he looked he could see that her hair did not just fall in waves, but was lifted by something that rose from her back.

"I am sorry to be rude. My name is Avalem. I should have told you that before."

"Interesting, but unnecessary. Out there, I am sure that you have a use for names so that you can tie things down to your definitions. Inside, we don't care much about what one calls anything. We care about what it really is and what it's potential is to be."

Taken a bit aback by that statement, Avalem paused with his tea half way to his lips. "What do I call you?"

Her laugh was sweet and brief as her gaze returned to the lake. "You can call me the Lady of the Lake, the Sorceress of the Night, the Greal Witch. You decide, I will know no matter what, when you choose to call me." Her head shot round, and she met his gaze as every thread in the entire house leapt through the air to connect with her. For an instant, she was a glorious spider lying at the heart of a web that encompassed every portion of her house. Just as quickly, a ripple in the curtains by the window caught his attention and the all-pervasive threads had vanished.

Avalem sat there for a moment, overwhelmed. Then cautiously, he said, "I think I shall just call you Lady."

Her red eyebrow shot up as well as the corners of her mouth, "Oh, foundling, you and I shall get along well."

When they were done with the meal, she found him trousers and a shirt of the ever-present material that filled her home. When she led him out into the light, Avalem started to ask her why he could suddenly see, but she silenced him with a finger across his lips and pulled him down to the lake. They spent the afternoon walking along the incarnadine sands of its shore. Reaching down she cupped a handful of the lake's waters. Like a liquid ruby, the surface rippled with each of her breaths. "Do you know the story of the Long-Chain Makers?" she asked.

"I know they remade the world and left."

"There is a great deal more. Years and years ago men were trying to make intelligences other than their own. They used the tiny machines to weave great nets of logic, but it never occurred to them that the small ones would learn as they worked. Each one of the Chains is forged of links of makers, communers and unmakers. They were made to be more than the sum of their parts, and they came together, becoming more than the whole."

Avalem looked up at the immensity of the interior of the Pillar of Night, "And they built this."

"Yes, and they also changed us. They left humanity with an extended lifespan, the ability to heal most injuries and to consume nearly anything. But the Long Chain-Makers also built us a cage, taking away our ability to undo their alterations. They changed us so we can't survive anywhere but Earth. Then they took away all of our toys, leaving us with just enough to get by. They founded a world where the works of one's hands and mind and the flavors we could enjoy became a new currency. The world became temperate and plentiful everywhere under their touch. Lastly, they also made the greal. But even that is fading." With that she flicked her hair aside and Avalem could clearly see the series of growths which looked like shelf fungus that ran up the back of her shapely neck.

"In the beginning, merely a touch from the lake would have transformed you. Now those ruffians practically had to drown you before you had taken enough in."

"Do you mean..."

The Lady let her hair fall back once more with a laugh. "Don't be foolish; how could you see as well as you do if you haven't changed?"

Avalem stepped away from her side and ran his fingers over the back of his neck. Then he stared intently at his hands.

"There's nothing yet, it's too early."

"What," he took a deep breath, shaking with relief and astonishment that he was at last different from everyone else, "what can I do now?"

She threw her hands up in the air, a shower of scarlet water raining down. "Who knows? Each ability is unique."

Then she led him back to the house and between the rows of sculptured shrubs that extended on either side and back into the woods. They walked the corridors of the maze until she brought them to the center and the rose garden concealed there. A copper orrey whirled about from nothing but the air of their passing. Scattered about were works of art clearly fashioned by the greal touched. A tree was shaped into a mermaid leaping from the spray and yet overhead its foliage gave them shade. A granite rock was braided like hair. Each nook and alcove hid another treasure. When the Lady led them to a marble bench, Avalem was still bemused at the variety of the wonders.

"They are presents from those who have found their aspect of the gift the greal bestows on them."

"Finally," Avalem sighed, convinced that at last his life was changing for the better.

The Lady reached out and laid her hand against his cheek. "What you will do, will be amazing no matter where your talent lies. But there are some who cannot learn to master their abilities and others who fall under the influence of the unscrupulous. I do my best to teach them, but you've seen how others react to what the greal touched make."

Indeed, thought Avalem and briefly found himself unable to meet her gaze.

The Lady continued, "What you have is just like a hammer. It can be used to build an edifice of towering beauty, or it can be swung with murderous intent. We'll find out together."

"Then I'll give you a gift that will make all of these other gifts pale in comparison."

Her smile took him by surprise, so too the warm twining fingers among his own. Together they walked hand and hand back to the house. There she stroked the closest lamp into light.

"Why does that work?" Avalem asked.

"It's a talent, a greal given talent."

"You mean the man in the tunnel...." It did explain the other's ability to see in the dark. "But the 'I love you'?"

The Lady ran her fingers across the top of the glass and the light within chased after their tips. "It's a maker, a maker of light. It works because we want it to and it can actually sense intent. Therefore we need to prove we need its light."

"But-"

Her smile stopped him, "Love is a word we don't say often." There was a brief awkward silence that the Lady finally broke. "Hungry?"

Dinner was full of the Lady casting him glances through the curtain of her hair that kept falling forward in a fetching way. As the light faded in the window across the table, Avalem found no surprise that once again she reached for his hand and drew him further into the house after the incidental touches throughout their meal. She pulled him onward, the webbing of her home growing deeper, the fabric of his clothes rustling on its own. Her clothing was unweaving before his eyes, revealing more and more of her milk white skin. When she drew her hands to him, he felt his own shirt and pants slough away and rejoin the mass of threads about them. Threads swept under their feet and buoyed them up; threads that wove them into a vast cocoon sealing out the world. Then like the giant web that it was, all of the strands in the house began to sway with the gentle motion their joining imparted.

When he awoke in the darkness due to nature's need, Avalem wondered briefly how he might find his way down to the floor. The nest reacted to his turning and unknitted itself in such a way that he was able to exit their bower without disturbing the Lady. He looked back and found himself bemused by her splayed form, the fall of her breasts and way that her tresses merged with the strands of the net.

She turned and her shoulder came into view, the design that broke its alabaster skin drawing his attention back. There was a rose raised above the surface of her skin. A filigree of woven skin lay across its stem and petals, holding it in place. The stem grew from the Lady's skin at the base, and several of the petals on the underside of the flower were also joined to her. Shock filled him and for a moment only, she breathed. Staring at his hands, the inevitable revelation came: *I have done this.*

Avalem fled.

Whipping strands from his path, he found his way back to the room where he first awoke and threw open the closets there until he discovered most of his clothes. Beneath them also lay his satchel and the lamp. For an instant he was drawn further into shock. Why would the Lady have these things? Could she have recovered them from the pack of ruffians - or rather, had she actually ordered them to cast him into the lake?

No matter how hard he looked he could not find his shirt, but in another closet was one made of the Lady's material. His hands were shaking as he drew on her shirt. He gathered up his belongings, sliding once more through the webbing, fearing to signal the spider at the heart of his departure. He was caught between the elation of discovery and the fear of how she might react to what he had done to her. In this state of mind, he could only think to run. When he finally cleared the doorway, Avalem breathed a sigh of relief.

Walking through the forest, returning to the entry tunnel, he once again considered the surface of his hands. Was there more detail to the lines that traced his palms? How could these ordinary parts of him that he had known and used all of these years have accomplished what he'd discovered? The more he thought about the entire strange occurrence, the less sense it made. He'd had a dream the night they shared together where roses grew throughout the web while he and the Lady lay there in each other's arms. Their sickly sweet odor clung to his sense of smell. When he'd turned away from her, the thorns had dug into him. The pain jolted him from sleep. They had dug into his hands! How foolish of him. All artists used their hands; where else could he have imagined the greal coming from to work such a transformation? But what could he do with a talent like this? It was almost worse than before he come. Avalem's head sank forward as he continued to trudge along. Changed forever, but who was to say if such a change was for the best. He passed into the tunnel and left the Land of Night.

***

It was a week later when he came upon the girl drawing in the dirt, her left arm hanging limply by her side.

Something is wrong with me. Avalem couldn't understand it. He wasn't able to explain why he'd come here. Once the Pillar of Night became a smudge in the distance, he'd deliberately avoided villages. Going out of his way to stay away from others became the norm. His hands itched incessantly. At night, he forced them into his satchel, drawing the string tight with his teeth. Several times, he'd blanked out and discovered himself with his arm plunged into the ice-cold streams of the area. The back of his neck was full of strange bumps that grew day by day.

Now Avalem was stumbling up to her, reaching for her dragging limb. Some part of his awareness was bemused by the fact that her arm was so damaged. The gifts of the Long Chain Makers altered human physiology so that such a break should easily heal, but something must have gone wrong. In the instant his fingers touched her arm, all of the confusion and the irritation in his fingers passed away.

She had a moment to look up at him confused before the greal acted and then its insidious strength was pouring into her, reworking the very nature and stuff of her limb. Some portion of him was aware of the greal as it flicked through possibilities until it settled on an answer. Then a wave of heat cascaded from his reworked digits, both making and unmaking at the same time. The end result gave him a brief sense of satisfaction that he later attributed to the greal, and then a growing sense of horror at what he'd done. This stranger, whom he'd never met nor spoken to, now had a new arm. This limb was a helical weaving filled with spiraling filigrees whose bones and joints were refashioned into not only an efficient but also elegant form. The skin was woven over the entire construct but not so densely as to hide the new architecture within. Avalem had never seen anything like it. He'd taken her broken arm and made it into a work of art. Maybe, just maybe, his talent did have value. That was when the other man grasped his shoulder and threw him to the ground.

While Avalem lay there staring at the hulking figure that reached for the long curving threshing blade that hung at his waist, he felt the need rising from the greal once more. It wanted. It wanted him to lay hands on this other, to remake him, to string the sinew differently, reorganize the skin and weave bone into something amazing. The sensation overwhelmed him, and he did not move quickly enough to stop the stranger from lopping the arm from the girl.

Shock overwhelmed Avalem. Instinctively, he knew that the arm would grow back, that it should be straight and whole once more. It was like the beating he'd received at the side of the lake in the Pillar of Night. Mankind's bodies were designed to take so much more punishment now that it was very difficult to truly hurt one another. However, the greal influenced part of him also wondered just in what state the limb would return. The natural repair systems of her body must have failed before leaving her with a useless limb. Avalem had just enough time to observe that her bleeding had stopped immediately and the skin of her back was stretching to cover the missing area before her assailant turned on him.

"Whatever you did to my daughter, I won't stand for it. She'll have a perfectly good arm now, not that abomination you created. We were only waiting until she was ready to accept what had to be done until you stepped in."

The blade turned towards him, and Avalem caught the other man's wrist with both hands, once again feeling the slippery hot sensation of the greal at work. The makers inside of him evaluated the wrist and remade it even as he turned the blow away. The metal of the scythe was raw material, reappearing as part of the architecture that resulted. It was a well-intentioned mistake, for now the farmer turned his wrist in a way that should have been impossible and captured both of Avalem's. The rewoven mesh of metal and flesh's grip was inexorable. Her father gave a long wail of frustration and cried out, "Help me!"

Then Avalem felt the first blow strike his head and others fell about his shoulders as the villagers came to their comrade's rescue using the handles of their farming implements as weapons. Avalem's body desperately tried to keep him conscious, and he could feel the greal at work here and there when another came within his grasp. Finally, as he curled in upon himself on the ground, he felt his awareness slipping away.

***

When he awoke, Avalem found himself inside a small conical granary. The door was blocked and light only came in through chinks in the gaps between the masonry. When he stood up, his shoulders brushed the sides of the enclosure. The heat and the grain dust were stifling. Worse still the itching in his hands had begun again. The greal was anxious once again to alter flesh after he'd finally used his talent. Sitting down, he wrapped his hands in his shirt. He wasn't sure when he started, but Avalem began to rock back and forth. The heat surrounding him grew as the sun rose farther into the sky. Emanations from the greal grew more and more intense. The walls wavered in his vision. The granary was a forge, and he felt as if he was being cast anew.

***

The Lady followed Avalem. Once again she touched the rose that was now forever a part of her. Something had drawn her forth from the safety of Night-the material of his shirt calling to her. But its song was growing weaker when she arose in the morning and rapidly faded away. Still she suspected she would not have to look any farther than the village that lay in the valley below her. When she walked down its central road, a small crowd of children flowed about her on either side, noisily playing with strange toys. There were mechanical birds who sang sweetly, flying creations that spun of their own accord lifting into the air, musical instruments and more. From each, the Lady felt the vague echo of her work. When she looked carefully, the parts seemed to be carved from ivory or bone and bound with tanned thongs. Beyond the children the men and women of the village picked through a bounty of knives, tools and baskets all strewn about the remains of the last of three granary towers.

Possibilities flashed through her mind. The Lady knew that Avalem was here, all about her now. The greal had remade him entirely; frustrated at its inability to act when the villagers had locked him away. Unconsciously, she rubbed at the back of her neck. But why, she wondered. Then it came to her, a truth she had not expected. Avalem's greal was a tool too valuable to be wasted. For the first time in untold years something was at last loose in the world that could undo the very chains that bound humanity to Earth. Because it could alter human physiology, Avalem's greal could reverse the changes made by the Long Chain Makers. She felt a fair certainty that each and every piece that resulted from his transubstantiation bore the greal to its new owner. More than likely a new version of the greal, better tempered and less likely to consume its host. The ability would spread from person to person, a plague of possibility where before there had been none.

The Lady's hand came to rest on the rose again as she remembered waking last night and staring up at the stars. In the Pillar of Night she'd long since forgotten the simple joy of considering their multitudes. What wonders awaited them now out there? At last they could walk the path that the Long Chain Makers had laid so long ago. There was still, however, a long way to go before humanity could leave Earth, but each journey began with a single step. She knelt down and reached out for the nearest toy. The puzzle box slowly unfolded under her inquisitive fingers, and she was not surprised to find the rose hidden at its heart.

On "A Talent Beyond My Talents," Jeff Writes...

This post-singularity cautionary tale is the result of a line from Monty Python... but I'll explain that later. Most folks will probably get the Arthurian references with the Lady and the similarity of greal and grail. But there's also the theme of Pandora's Box with Avalem's greal being the last remaining element - hope. Finally, from Monty Python's Holy Grail, *the Witch scene, while the participants are discussing the flotation of the practitioners of magic and the possibility of their being made of wood comes these lines: "How do you know she is a witch?" ... "Build a bridge out of her!" Those off kilter thoughts encouraged me to write a story about a character who is built into something else. The whole story cooked in my head for a long time before reaching completion and was also definitely influenced in style by Roger Zelzany's* Jack of Shadows *and Jack Vance's* The Dying Earth.

FREETHINKER
C. L. WERNER

He could hear the loathsome reptile's claws scratching across the cement floor as it crawled through the shadows. Its purple tongue would be flicking from its scaly jaws, dancing before its snout as it tasted the air and picked his scent from the thousand stenches in the protein production plant. The creature didn't need to see him, didn't need to hear him. It would find him by his smell, the smell that had betrayed him to Omega-Four's omnipresent sentinel drones, had announced that he was no longer a drug-dulled cog in the machinery of the Dome. He was an Aberrant, aware and awake. Perhaps alone among ten million inhabitants, he *knew*.

Javier Nine-three-six pressed himself still closer to the cold porcelain casing of the algae vat, clinging to the hope that the pungent stink of slime and water would conceal his presence. The red glow of an emergency lamp served to illuminate the narrow pathway between the vats employed by cultivation autoums to nurture the crop through its gestation until it was ready to be harvested by human farmers.

The robots were silent now, frozen in place when Section Security had pursued Javier into the facility. From his position, Javier could see them standing upon the observation deck, intimidating in their black coveralls, heavy neuro-tasers clenched in their gloved hands. They were waiting for the synzards to ferret out his hiding place. Then the officers would move in, converge upon his position and use their electrified batons to subdue him.

Re-education. Javier shuddered as he thought about what that meant. He would no longer be awake and aware. He would no longer *know*. He would be like the other ten million denizens of the Dome, an oblivious and obedient mechanism in the machine. The worst thing was he wouldn't even understand what had been done to him.

As the scratch of reptilian claws drew nearer, Javier's hand tightened about the piece of alloy he had pried from one of the deactivated autoums. Even now, he felt the urge to submit meekly, to give himself up to the dictates burned into his brain by a life of genetic, cultural and chemical conditioning. It took every ounce of his newfound will to resist the urge. He would not surrender! *They* would not take him back; smother his identity with medications and psychotherapy. Seeing, he would not be led back into the darkness.

The stink of the synzard's musk was close now. Javier could hear the rasp of its flickering tongue against its scaly jaws. He felt doubt gnaw at the very core of his being. Could he really do this? It was one thing to run away, but it was another thing entirely to descend into violence! Certainly the synzard was just a lab-grown gene-organism, but even so it had life. Did he have any right to strike out at that life?

Javier trembled at the awfulness of such a thought. If he allowed himself to strike at the reptile, might he not do violence to the Section Security officers? What justified him in such a terrible course of action? Was his new sense of identity and freedom worth descending into the barbarism of tribals?

What had set him upon this course; what had turned him from a docile cog to an Aberrant? The answer to that came easier to Javier than the morality of the path he had followed since.

***

There was a musty, unkempt odour about the tiny habitation unit, the smell of old things kept well beyond their usefulness, the stink of reclusive decay. It was an odour that was, perhaps, sensed more by the brain than the nose, making its ugliness felt despite the thick layers of rubber and plastic that smothered the faces of the men working amid the hoarded clutter which filled the little room.

Javier Nine-three-six shook his head as he pulled down a pile of dust and neglect, watching as it smacked against a similar pile and sent both of them crashing against the wall. He felt a confused medley of pity and disgust as he watched the detritus collapse into the narrow little walkway. It was such a wasteful, primitive sight, all those sheets of organic material smashed and pressed into thin little pages. A barbaric reminder from a less-enlightened age when men abused their world with reckless abandon. They had butchered entire forests to feed into their printing presses, churning out tons of disposable text in the name of consumerism and short-sighted greed.

The world had suffered for such greed, driven to the brink of destruction by the excesses of a society governed by materialism and selfishness. The men of the Plastic Age had poisoned the earth with toxins, turned the oceans filthy with rubbish, filled the skies with pollutants. It was not to be wondered that their society had crumbled in the furnace of the Conflagration, an ecological catastrophe that had driven three quarters of the planet's species to extinction before its violence had been expended.

It was depressing to think of all that had been lost in the holocaust of the Conflagration, yet from that climatic upheaval had come human enlightenment, a new wisdom that stripped away the base impulses and petty desires of tribal man. The men of the Reborn Era were unified, governed by reason and logic, sharing a sense of common purpose and motivated to serve society rather than warp it towards their own selfish demands. The invisible tyranny of tradition and culture had been cast away, replaced with a true liberation of mind and body that could be bestowed only by the unbiased principles of science.

Javier smiled sadly as he looked about the little habitation unit with its clutter. There were always those who couldn't function in society. The loners who existed on the fringes, unable to adapt to the modern world. Doctors spoke of mental aberrations and chemical imbalances, genetic atavisms that would, one day, be overcome through the development of new drugs. Until then, however, such people would persist, pitiable recluses clinging to the bones of the past.

Javier brought the scoop of his shovel under the heap of fallen books, lifting them from the floor and casting them into the churning jaws of the mobile recycler. The mouldy old rubbish would be ground down into its constituent elements, treated with chemical baths that would render it into viable protein for the Dome's algae ponds. From useless clutter, the old junk would be transformed into sustenance for Omega-Four's ten million inhabitants.

As he watched the recycler grind down the hard edges of the clapboard spines, Javier reflected on his vocation in Reclamations. It was a curious job, one that perhaps wasn't as fulfilling as most, being dependent upon antisocial eccentricities. Instead of helping to advance mankind, Javier thought of himself as a bulwark against a slow slide back into the materialism that had nearly eradicated civilization. It might be a grandiose conception of what amounted to being a garbage collector, but it gave him a feeling of purpose.

His shovel dipped into the musty heap, but as he raised it towards the jaws of the recycler, Javier noticed the lettering on one of the spines. A flicker of curiosity flared up inside his brain and, after a moment of indecision, he lowered the shovel. Javier wiped the dust from the book as he held it up. He hadn't been mistaken; the book's spine did identify it as *The Hound of the Baskervilles*. A smile flashed across his face as he leafed through the book, enjoying the old illustrations scattered among the text. Sherlock Holmes was his favourite fictional subject. He'd referenced the stories and films many times when he was linked to the Interface, enough so that he could conjure the stories almost from memory.

Javier looked around the habitation unit, a new feeling of pity rising within him. The book was a relic from a time when there was no Interface, when people had been compelled to accumulate material units in order to reference information and entertainment. Wood-pulp books, crystal discs, petrol and plastic tapes, silicate drives, there had been so many ways people had been forced to gather primitive data assemblies. It was so much more efficient now, a single Interface maintained for the edification of all people rather than individual hoardings that could be consulted only by physical proximity.

The discovery of a Sherlock Holmes book gave Javier an inkling of sympathy for the reclusive Aberrant who had once lived here. He felt sad that they had descended into such a state, shunning the conventions and advances of modern society to indulge atavistic attachments to physical possessions. It was a sobering thought to consider that the Aberrant had enjoyed some of the same things Javier enjoyed. It injected a human quality, a sense of kinship to what had been moments before nothing more than a faceless pariah.

The insistent beep of the idle recycler dragged Javier from his ruminations. Who the Aberrant had been wasn't any concern to him. He had a job to do and if he didn't want to fall behind, then he had to hurry. Machines might be allowed to labor around the clock but men were permitted only six hours of labor in a cycle. If his work wasn't done within his shift, then another Reclamations officer would have to be detached to complete it for him. Javier had too much pride to allow that kind of embarrassment to afflict his performance.

On a whim, instead of dropping the book back into the shovel's scoop, Javier stuck it in the pocket of his coverall. He knew it was juvenile of him – and he would certainly be laughed at by his co-workers should they learn of it – but somehow the idea of consigning Sherlock Holmes to the churning maw of the recycler was offensive. He would take the book with him at the end of his shift, a keepsake of sorts. After all, one souvenir would hardly make him an atavistic hoarder.

***

At end of shift, Javier Nine-three-six strolled through the simulation at the centre of his neighbourhood, dialing the sequence of his neural feed so that his mind would interpret the simulation's transmissions as an urban park complete with singing birds and a cool breeze. The smell of fresh cut grass and blooming flowers filled his lungs as his feet crunched against the grit of simulated gravel. He could see other people walking through the zone and idly he wondered whether any of them were dialled into the same simulation as himself. Short of intruding upon their experience and asking them directly there was no way to know, so Javier restrained his curiosity. Inquisitiveness was never an excuse to disrupt privacy and especially in a place like the simulation.

Javier stepped away from the gravel path to stare up at a hoary old oak tree, its branches leaning out over the path, its trunk painted white as a preventative against insects. The simulation was very exacting in its details, even guarding the images against non-existent parasites. Javier's heart went cold as he considered how appropriate the term non-existent was. There were no termites anymore, not real ones. Neither was the great and mighty oak still to be found outside a few horticultural preservation reserves. Once there had been great forests of the trees, but those had been gutted by the greed of Smoke Age industry and what little had been left had been squandered during the excesses of the Plastic Age. It was a wonder any seeds had endured through the Conflagration to be nurtured by botanists of the Enlightenment. One small triumph against the vast extinctions ushered in by the collapse of the Plastic Age.

The simulated oak was more impressive than the seedlings in the reserves. It might be only a sensory impression, an apparition fabricated by an information feed, but it was real enough for Javier. Some of the Domes, the first to rise after the Conflagration, didn't have simulations like Omega-Four's zone. They had archaic gardens filled with botanical gene-orgs, synthetically engineered plant replicants that in the Plastic Age would have been branded and patented as GMO products. In the Reborn Era, such organisms belonged to all mankind, not the selfish interests of a tyrannical elite.

A wave of depression rushed through Javier as he thought about those long-dead despots, the shadowy cabal of men who had aggrandized themselves with titles like Banker, Lawyer, Entrepreneur, Politician, Industrialist and Globalist. Those titles were strange to Javier and to the inhabitants of the Dome, as meaningless and esoteric as an ancient fable told in a foreign tongue. No one could say what those men had been like, what sort of thoughts had governed them. That they had been illogical and sociopathic was evident from the legacy they had left behind. Their greed had ushered in the Conflagration and the climatic upheaval that had nearly annihilated civilization and cast man back into a new Stone Age. To sate their own lust for prestige and position, they had been willing to destroy the world – just as long as the consequences of their greed fell onto the shoulders of their descendents long after their own time was past.

It was a mindset Javier couldn't understand, so alien to him that he could only pity the unbalanced men who had been afflicted by such madness. In the Plastic Age, there had been no structure to differentiate between balance and aberrancy, even less had there been any way to correct the Aberrant and make them productive contributors to society. The Enlightenment had brought the wisdom and knowledge to do both. The Aberrant could be discovered before their defects could corrupt the individual or become detrimental to society. Those chemical and genetic imbalances could be corrected through medication, healing the imperfections to make the person whole and clean.

The world had suffered enough from the greed of Aberrants.

Javier felt tears growing in his eyes, his emotional state becoming moribund as he considered how greatly the planet had suffered. Depression was a condition that was counter-productive and contributed to inefficiency. At the earliest age, children were instructed in how to fend off such debilitating moods, a knowledge that continued to serve them into maturity. As he felt the emotion settling more firmly about him, Javier reached into the breast pouch of his coverall to remove the little capsule of blue pills. Blue Twenty was a fast-acting restorative, prescribed for those whose disposition lent to depressions and melancholy. From his sixth year, his first away from the juvenile dormitory and his first attending the internment-school, Javier had been prescribed Blue Twenty to amend the weakness in his emotional constitution. He still carried a balance with the Health and Welfare Bureau which had subsidized his medications in his pre-employment stages, a payroll deduction at the end of each month slowly eating away at that debt.

In reaching for his pills, Javier's hand brushed against the stiff spine of the book he had removed from the habitation unit. A sudden impulse made him draw it from his pocket, forgetting for the moment the blue pills. He felt a twinge of amusement tug at his face as he stared down at the familiar illustration on the cover, the black image of a hound. How many times had his mind registered that impression when he accessed the Interface? After so many years, it was like looking into the face of an old friend.

Glancing about, watching the other citizens strolling through the simulation, Javier experienced a moment of self-consciousness. There was nothing illegal about possessing physical text, but it did carry a social stigma, regarded as both improper and immoral. Sometimes, motivated by a perverse impulse to shock their associates, someone might seek out the grey dealers who sold such materials, but it was done more from a sense of being naughty than any real affection for the object itself.

Despite his appreciation for how ridiculous the very concept of physical text was in a society that could access the Interface at any time, Javier couldn't shake a genuine attachment to the book he held. More than an adolescent thrill of naughtiness, he appreciated the book for what it was. He knew none of his associates would appreciate that feeling, certainly his partner Alexander Two-six-five would think him peculiar for such an impulse. Alexander already thought Javier a bit off-kilter for being satisfied with a position in Reclamations rather than aspiring towards a career in Engineering or Design. Devoting serious thought to a bit of physical text salvaged from an Aberrant hoarder would only bolster that opinion of him.

Javier had half made up his mind to sell the book to a grey dealer he knew in the Third District when he flipped the volume open. It was a page chosen utterly at random, and at first Javier didn't notice what was wrong. There was an illustration, one of the Sidney Paget pictures he remembered so well. Or at least thought he remembered. The picture was that moment when Sir Henry Baskerville, driven by crude biological impulses, made his assault upon Miss

Stapleton's person. The image was quite striking, representing as it did the baser instincts of the tribals and how those instincts would denigrate and oppress the female sex. As he remembered it, the picture displayed Sir Henry reduced to an almost semi-human brute by the disruptive impulse, Miss Stapleton trying to drive him away with a desperate vitality born from the anguished offense stamped upon her face.

Here, however, it was a quite different image. There was no atavistic devolution of Sir Henry's bearing and countenance. Miss Stapleton was almost genteel in her effort to hold back his advance, her face not contorted with fear and injured pride, but rather presenting a downcast expression of remorseful resignation. If not for the small image of Mr Stapleton running along with his butterfly net in the background, Javier might have doubted this was indeed the same moment in the story or the same illustration. How could he have so dramatically misremembered it? If there was one aspect of his person that Javier considered a strength, it was his exacting memory for detail.

A moment of consideration brought an easy answer to Javier's mind. The "book" was in fact nothing but some crude attempt by a grey dealer to make a quick credit by preying on the gullibility of an atavism desperate to gather more objects for their hoard. It wasn't uncommon for dealers to manufacture their own specimens of physical text, and rarely with the exacting consultation of the Interface that would be required to produce an accurate representation. What he had here was nothing more than some cheap simulacra.

Only the understanding that the book would be more useful processed and recycled kept Javier from tossing it into the nearest rubbish bin. Disgusted, he looked at it again, flipping it open to that point where Holmes and Watson discover the body of the outcast Selden on the moor. Here he was in for another surprise, for in discussing Selden, the detective and his partner spoke of the man as a criminal and murderer. Javier was certain such was not the case. Selden, he remembered, was a fugitive forced into hiding because of his defiance of the oppressive Tribalist regime which dominated Britannia in the Smoke Age. Holmes had spoken of him as a heroic and tragic personage, not as a mentally unbalanced sociopath!

Javier nearly dropped the book in disgust. How could any dealer no matter how slipshod make such an error? What exactly was this noxious bit of physical text he had preserved from the recycler?

Again, he was on the verge of casting the book from him, a tremor of unaccountable fear slithering through his veins. Curiosity, nagging and compelling, restrained him. Javier wondered what else was wrong with the book. Yes, he decided, he would keep the thing and consult the Interface. He'd compare the two versions and see for himself how grossly this shabby copy had strayed from the story proper.

As he extracted himself from the simulation and made his way along the conveyor-walk to his habitation unit, Javier couldn't shake that impression of danger, that little chill of fear that gnawed at his gut. It was his first intimation that something was wrong and that by merest chance he had stumbled upon a discovery that would change him forever.

***

The Hound of the Baskervilles was the beginning. Javier read the curious physical text edition from cover to cover, restraining his revulsion at the outrageous alterations only through a supreme effort of will. He was alarmed to find the story so changed and altered. To be certain, the basic thrust of the narrative was the same; murder wrapped under the cloak of superstition, but virtually all the small details had been changed. Holmes and Watson were merely friends, not partners. Barrymore the butler was married – that peculiar old concept of female suppression by a male keeper – to the sister of Selden and their actions in providing for the fugitive stemmed not from respect and sympathy for his fight against Tribalist tyranny but rather from what amounted to tribal affiliations of shared lineage and emotional connections at odds with their feelings of social duty. The murderous Stapleton proved to be a more scientifically minded personage, driven to commit his deeds solely for material gain rather than out of some Religist effort to contaminate the region with superstition and curb any doubts among the populace about their Tribalist rulers and the Religist dogma that empowered them. Indeed, in this version Stapleton was exploiting the Tribalist concepts of lineage and heritage in an effort to secure Baskerville Hall for himself.

The more Javier read, the more impressed he became with the degree to which the story had been adjusted. The core was still there, the characters were still there, but around everything there had been fabricated a very different context. The societal and cultural mores were alien to those of the Enlightenment.

Javier resisted where that train of thought must lead him. Deep inside him, he felt a consuming horror for the monstrous idea that had blossomed in his mind. He expended every effort to deny its poisonous reasoning, fighting it with such despair that he soon became physically ill and had to be convalesced from his duties with Reclamations.

It was while he was convalescing, dutifully taking the medicines prescribed to help him recover – and at the same time avoiding the blue pills which might interfere with the other prescription – that Javier reached the conclusion that he had tried so desperately to deny. The physical text wasn't a crude forgery. The truth was far more monstrous. The book represented the *real* words of Conan Doyle – heralded by the Tribalist title of Sir Arthur in the physical text – and what could be accessed by billions of citizens through the Interface was the fake.

As he lay upon his bed, Alexander having relocated to other quarters during his illness, Javier considered how such a monstrous thing could be perpetrated. Was the book he had encountered simply an isolated example or was it but a sampling of a much wider pandemic? Was it possible that the whole of the Interface had been corrupted, all the literature of the past amended and adjusted, expanded and contracted until it conformed to the mores and values of the programmers who maintained the Interface?

The prospect was as hideous as anything Javier could contemplate, all the more because such a conspiracy on so vast a scale could only be conducted with the collusion of the governing councils, those men of progressive logic who had lifted mankind from the rubble of the Conflagration into the Enlightenment. The idea that these great men might lend their sanction to the deliberate adjustment of literature, the excision of anything that did not reflect the values and morals of the Enlightenment, the designed insertion of passages to conform to the modern view...

Or was it more than that? Perhaps through the manipulation of literature the Progressors had done more than just make the works of the past conform to their vision of the future. Through their manipulation, hadn't they killed the very ideas that might threaten that vision? The Reborn was a time of limitless freedom, unfettered by the thousands of prejudices and judgements of past eras, yet if no ideas were permitted to be expounded beyond what would conform to the Enlightenment, then wasn't that freedom simply an illusion?

It was tempting for Javier to dismiss the frightening prospect. After all, why would the Progressors bother about literature at all? The written word was a commodity only a very small percentage within the Dome cared about. The domains of the Interface devoted to music and film, game and simulation, enjoyed far more consultations than that devoted simply to text. It was, in a very real sense, nothing but an antiquated style of communication that had been superseded by far more immersive formats. Why would anyone bother with text when there were so many other forms of communication that influenced a far greater number of the population?

As he tried to dismiss the conspiracy, a new thought rose to send a chill through Javier's body. What was there to say that whoever had manipulated the text domain hadn't also manipulated the areas for music and film? If there was a deliberate effort to eradicate all dissenting ideas, it would be essential that the effort be utterly thorough. How could he know if a Plastic Age movie hadn't been altered, dialog amended and adjusted to reflect the changing attitudes of the Enlightenment? How could he know if an actor hadn't been digitally replaced, new scenes added or old ones stripped away? The lyrics in a song might be distorted, their original meaning perverted into an echo of the Progressors' design.

Javier tried to tell himself these thoughts were nothing but feverish imaginings. Yet deep inside himself, a chord had been struck. The longer he went without the blue pills, the more certain he felt his growing fear was justified.

***

After his recovery, Javier carried a terrible secret inside him, one that he knew he couldn't confide to anyone, not even Alexander. At best, he would be thought an atavism, but more likely he would be viewed as a full Aberrant and removed from society for treatment and re-education. That didn't sound as helpful and beneficent as it once had, because bit by bit he was losing the naivety, the blind trust in government that had been imprinted upon him almost from his first steps at the incubation dorm.

He continued his vocation in Reclamations, but now he did so with a new awareness of what he was doing. He wasn't recycling out-dated clutter; he was destroying ideas that were inconvenient to the Enlightenment. When he could, Javier would steal a book from the recyclers, bearing it away with him to his habitation unit for consultation. Invariably, he found the physical text didn't match the purported version that could be consulted through the Interface.

Bit by bit, Javier began to understand that the Interface wasn't a convenient instrument of entertainment and education. It was a tool to help perpetrate a tyranny more monstrous than anything from the Plastic Age, a despotism all the more terrible because it went unnoticed and unseen by the populace. An invisible tyranny that controlled its subjects not through force and martial domination, but through the very thoughts inside the brains of its slaves. By eliminating exposure to any idea that didn't conform to their vision for mankind, the Progressors could reshape society into their own image. By stigmatizing physical copies of text and film as wasteful atavism, using Reclamations to acquire and dispose of them as opportunity presented itself, they could conceal the true nature of the Interface. There was no need for force, not when they had already engineered a society that would castigate and marginalize those who would seriously pursue antiquated forms of media. They could simply sit back and allow Reclamations to slowly whittle away at the dwindling supply of physical media.

Logically, the Interface had been corrupted in the same way. A single passage changed here, a line of dialog there, a shift in motivation to a character in still another place. All subtle, all gradual. Nothing too alarming. Nothing that would immediately draw attention – just slight changes that the Interface consultant might put down to mistaken memories. How gradual it must have been, year by year chipping away at the originals until they became mirrors for the Enlightenment. How inhumanly patient the Progressors must have been!

***

As he acquired more and more books, Javier's habitation unit began to resemble that of an atavistic hoarder. Alexander departed after an unsuccessful effort to get Javier to abandon his curious obsession. His partner even went so far as to take his symptoms to a doctor and acquire a new prescription for Javier, but Alexander's efforts were futile. Javier had stopped taking the blue pills; taking the new purple ones wasn't an option. After a final row, Alexander had left.

Strangely, the departure of his partner made little impact on Javier. Perhaps as a consequence of what he was coming to view as a new mental awakening, he had felt his emotions towards Alexander growing detached. As he'd been exposed to the morals and beliefs of the past, Javier had started to doubt everything about the present. Past society had been founded upon marriage, something that the Enlightenment vilified as an instrument of sexual oppression and inequality as well as a key contributory to biological confusion and tribal perpetuation. The overpopulation that had been the leading cause of the Conflagration was blamed upon these primitive and animalistic concepts.

Yet to what degree had the Enlightenment gone to engineer the root of overpopulation from society? As much as anything else, had they gone and tried to manipulate the heart against the natural desires of the individual? Through what extremes had they employed to ensure there was no unsanctioned procreation among the subjects of the Dome? What measures had they taken to remove the distinct characteristics of the old tribal nations, eliminated the old physiognomy that had made different breeds of men? The old tribal concept of family had been replaced with harvest farms where seed and egg were collected as needed from pre-selected citizens, fertilized within machines by an automated process. Viable infants were reared in incubators then sent along to dormitories before education in the schools. At every level, the only parent a citizen possessed was the state itself.

In the face of such monstrosity, how could Javier trust his own feelings? Were they even his own or had they been implanted in him by the Progressors, nurtured in his mind by the information they allowed him to access, by the environment they allowed him to experience, by the genetically-modified foods they allowed him to ingest and by the medications they employed to adjust his biology. Was any of it real? Did any of it belong to him or was it all only the lie they expected him to conform to?

Huddled in the protein production plant, Javier realized the mistake he had made. It hadn't been his slow accumulation of physical text or his increased use of the Interface that had brought him to the attention of Section Security. Those hadn't marked him as an Aberrant and a potential threat to the invisible tyranny of the Dome.

No, he had given himself away when he had stopped taking the blue pills and the dozens of other medications prescribed for him, drugs designed to maintain him as docile and compliant. He had continued to fill his prescriptions, stowing the pills away in his habitation unit. According to the data stream, he was still adhering to his physician minders. However, he hadn't taken into account what physiological changes absence of the drugs might cause. To be certain there were uncomfortable withdrawal symptoms, but these he had been careful to suppress when out in public, succeeding to such a degree that he doubted anyone could detect when he experienced them.

His self-control, however, wasn't enough to deceive a machine. The hovering sentinel drones which patrolled the avenues of the Dome and kept it safe for its inhabitants weren't deceived. Javier knew that the first time he suffered a sudden fit of itching on his way out of the simulation. A sleek grey sentinel had descended from an altitude of some hundred metres to hover a dozen or so above him. He could see the optic package slung underneath its stubby nose rotating about, fixing him with its dark lenses. The drone dropped another six metres and a panel opened in its side, displaying a triangular filtration system and the rotating blades of a fan. As the blades began to whirl, Javier knew that the sentinel drone had detected something wrong with him and was now making an effort to draw his chemical signature into its filtration system.

Staring up at the drone, Javier had done the worst thing he could. He had run. Almost immediately, the drone had started emitting a high-pitched wail, shifting about on its rotors and pursuing him across the simulation. A human pursuer might have been distracted by the transmissions of the zone, but the machine wasn't attuned to such frequencies. Straight as an arrow, it sped after Javier, chasing him down the next avenue and through the intersection beyond.

It wasn't long before other drones began to join the chase, blaring their alarm sirens, clearing the streets of citizens to better expose the Aberrant they had detected. Javier's faculties, his reasoning, crumbled beneath the primal impulse of a hunted animal. He had to flee, had to escape. The drones kept on his trail, giving him no respite, no opportunity to stop and think and plan. Had the machines been so equipped, Javier could have been captured right there in the street, but the drones were designed only to detect. Apprehension was left to the men of Section Security.

With three drones hovering about him, trying to herd him like a Smoke

Age steer, Javier saw the armored transport come trundling down the street, the gold emblem of Section Security emblazoned across its face and sides. The tank growled to a stop, the doors in its sides opening like steel irises, disgorging its occupants.

Javier's pulse was like thunder in his ears as he saw the black-uniformed troopers emerge from the transport, their gloves wrapped about the aluminoid stocks of their neuro-tasers. Three of the officers carried the control rods for a half-dozen synzards, immense five-foot long reptiles, their bodies encased in the blocky constraints of thermo-vests. Genetically engineered for their function, the synzards were controlled by the vests; when speed and action were demanded the vests could be made to generate heat, when the reptiles were required to be docile the vests would turn cold and put the synzards into a sluggish stupor.

There was nothing sluggish about the hulking two-metre long reptiles as they turned towards him, their tongues flicking from between their jaws. Javier hadn't considered until that moment how eliminating the drugs from his system might have affected his scent. Just as the drones had noticed the alteration in his chemical signature, now the synzards were picking up his changed scent. They would be able to use it to pursue him, just as pre-Conflagration man had employed extinct canids to hunt.

One of the troopers called for Javier to surrender himself, promising that he wouldn't be harmed. The officer claimed that Javier was sick and needed help, that Section Security was only there to prevent him from hurting anyone. There was no threat, no attempt at coercion. Just an appeal to his sense of community and society, an effort to make him understand that he needed to be adjusted so he was no longer Aberrant. It occurred to Javier that even the troopers were blind to the invisible shackles they wore, that they truly believed the words they called out to him.

Better to be Aberrant than blind! Before the thermo-vests could grow warm enough to rouse the synzards to their full awareness, before the troopers could get close enough to turn their neuro-tasers against him, Javier was dashing down the avenue again, darting beneath the hull of a hovering drone, the draft from its rotors plucking at his clothes as he rushed beneath the machine.

Escape was foremost in his thoughts, but to do that he needed to elude the synzards. Javier wracked his brain for a way to deceive the reptiles' sense of smell. Sighting the protein processing plant had given him the idea that the pungent stench of the facility would confound the animals while the sound of the autoprocessors inside would conceal him from the detectors of the hovering drones.

***

The rasp of the synzard's tongue as it crept closer drove Javier Nine-three-six into action. Sweat dripping down his brow, his heart hammering in his chest, sickness boiling up in the pit of his belly, Javier reared up from his place of concealment and brought the heavy strip of alloy smashing down into the reptile's flat head. The weapon smacked into the brute's skull with a meaty impact, tearing the layer of scales and sending a thin trickle of blood dripping across the floor. The synzard stared up at him with dull black eyes, its tongue still flickering from between its jaws, its tiny brain trying to understand that it had been struck.

Javier tightened his grip on the piece of scrap and brought it crashing down once more. This time the synzard made a low *umph* and sagged to the floor, its tail lashing about furiously behind it. The brute's attacker stared down in disgust at what he had done, horrified at the blood coating his weapon, the gore spattering his coveralls. With a moan of anguish, he dropped the strip of alloy and set off running.

To either side of him, Javier could hear the other synzards chasing after him. Not the slow, almost lethargic plod they had exhibited when stalking him among the vats. This was different, almost like a spastic scramble. He could hear their tails slapping against the vats, their bodies blundering and crashing against the deactivated automs. They did not bark or howl the way extinct canids would have done, there was only a rasping hiss as the reptiles drew breath past their sharp fangs.

More than the noises the synzards made, it was the frantic shouts from the catwalks and gantries that sent fear pulsing through Javier's veins. The troopers were alarmed, he could hear the control officers shouting among themselves, trying to dial down the thermo-vests and put the synzards into a stupor. Something had happened and the brutes were out of control.

Javier stared down at his hand, coated in the blood of the synzard he had attacked. Blood! It was the smell of the blood! The other synzards had picked up the scent and it had thrown them into a frenzy. Like himself, the conditioning and manipulation of their controllers had fallen away, opening the reptiles to their true nature. They had become atavistic Aberrants driven by the base instincts that every attempt had been made to suppress and breed away.

A synzard struck Javier from the side, leaping at him from the narrow space between two vats, its long claws raking across his chest and opening his leg almost to the bone. Its jaws snapped only a few centimetres from his face, the flicking tongue brushing across his nose. Javier pushed the brute away, stumbling back and collapsing against the side of a protein vat. The reptile glared at him hungrily with its black eyes, lashing its body viciously from side to side in an effort to reach him. Its bulk was too great to pass between the vats, however and try as it might, the reptile couldn't reach him.

"Quick! Give me your hand!"

The shout came down to Javier from above. Lifting his eyes, Javier saw a Section Security trooper leaning across the railing of a gantry, his gloved hand stretched towards him. There was an expression of fright and concern on the officer's face. Looking into the man's eyes, Javier knew that some awful danger threatened. The racket of the pinned synzard was so loud he couldn't hear the other reptiles, but from the officer's expression he knew they were close.

Section Security wouldn't harm him. They would get him to a surgeon and have his wounds attended, then he would be taken to some doctors and a regimen of drugs would be prescribed to address the chemical imbalances that afflicted him. Re-education would undo the pernicious influences that had brought about his descent into Aberrancy. In a few short months he would be a healthy, productive member of society once more.

He would be just the way the Enlightened wanted him to be.

Javier turned away from the officer above him, ignoring the trooper's cries of warning. Smiling, he welcomed the jaws and claws that came for him. He felt like Selden, the brave crusader for social justice, standing defiant against the ferocious Hound, refusing to the last to be cowed by superstition and fear. Then he remembered that Selden wasn't a brave crusader, but a murderous sociopath.

How, Javier wondered as the fangs sank into his flesh and tore him apart, would his own life be rewritten. *Will I be remembered as a hero or a villain? Will I be remembered at all?*

I wonder...

On "Freethinker," CL writes...

In writing this story, I explored the nightmarish potential within a world that is being steered towards digital mediums. It isn't hard to cite examples of films being tinkered with and "revised" by film studios and directors, sometimes for mere cosmetic reasons at others through more mercenary inclinations. The original versions, for whatever reason, almost always become withdrawn and obscure. If this sort of deliberate revision of art could be perpetrated for such comparatively innocuous purposes as appearance and monetary gain, is it any stretch to envision the same methodology being employed for purposes of indoctrination and social engineering? There are some perfect examples of this in the last century with the actions taken by various regimes. How much more complete might their efforts to kill ideas have been if, instead of simply trying to burn them they could go in and rewrite them, alter them to conform to their own ideology? It is, I think, a question well worth speculating on as our world casts aside books and CDs in favour of non-physical files, intangible as phantoms. And perhaps one day to prove just as elusive should their contents be deemed "undesirable".

ABOUT THE AUTHORS

Award-winning author **DANIELLE ACKLEY-MCPHAIL** has worked both sides of the publishing industry for over seventeen years. Her works include the urban fantasies, *Yesterday's Dreams*, *Tomorrow's Memories*, *Today's Promise*, and *The Halfling's Court*, and the writers guide, *The Literary Handyman*. She edits the *Bad-Ass Faeries* anthologies and *Dragon's Lure*, and has contributed to numerous other anthologies, including *Mermaid 13*, *New Blood*, and *Barbarians at the Jumpgate*, all by Padwolf Publishing. She is a member of the New Jersey Authors Network and Broad Universe, a writer's organization focusing on promoting the works of women authors in the speculative genres. She can be found on LiveJournal (damcphail, lit_handyman), Facebook (Danielle Ackley-McPhail), and Twitter (DMcPhail). Learn more at: www.sidhenadaire.com.

JAMES CHAMBERS' tales of horror, crime, fantasy, and science fiction have been published in numerous anthologies and magazines. In 2011 Dark Regions Press published his collection of four Lovecraftian-inspired novellas, *The Engines of Sacrifice*. *Publisher's Weekly* described it as "chillingly evocative." Most recently, Dark Quest Books has published his zombie novellas, *The Dead Bear Witness* and *Tears of Blood*, the first two volumes in the Corpse Fauna novella series. Chambers is also the author of the short story collections *Resurrection House*, published in 2009 by Dark Regions Press, and *The Midnight Hour: Saint Lawn Hill and Other Tales* with illustrator Jason Whitley. His stories have appeared in the award-winning anthology series *Bad-Ass Faeries* and *Defending the Future*, and he has also written numerous comic books including *Leonard Nimoy's Primortals*, the critically acclaimed "The Revenant" in *Shadow House*, and *The Midnight Hour*. His work has also appeared in *Bad Cop No Donut*, *Dark Furies*, *The Dead Walk*, *The Dead Walk Again*, *The Domino Lady: Sex as a Weapon*, *Dragon's Lure*, *The Green Hornet Chronicles*, *Hardboiled Cthulhu*, *In An Iron Cage*, *Mermaids 13*, *New Blood*, *Warfear*, *Weird Trails*, and the magazines *Bare Bone*, *Cthulhu Sex*, and *Allen K's Inhuman*. He is a member of the Horror Writers Association and the chairman of its membership committee. His website is: www.jameschambersonline.com.

KEVIN DIVICO is a Gentleman Adventurer who has been a writer, game publisher, member of Military Intelligence, Business & Social entrepreneur, futurist and aspiring raconteur. He tries to play a positive sum game - always looking for the Win/Win. Currently his passion is to preserve civilization past extinction level events & finding the perfect coconut cream pie.

JOHN L. FRENCH has worked for over thirty years for the Baltimore Police Department as a crime scene investigator and has seen more than his share of murders, shootings and serious assaults. As a break from the realities of his job, he writes science fiction, pulp, horror, fantasy, and, of course, crime fiction. Since 1992 John has been writing stories partly based on his experiences on the streets of what some have called one of the most dangerous cities in the country. His books include *The Devil of Harbor City*, *Past Sins*, *Souls on Fire*, *Here There Be Monsters* and *Paradise Denied*. He is the editor of *Bad Cop, No Donut*, *Mermaids 13: Tales of the Sea* and *To Hell in a Fast Car: On the Road to Death and Disaster.*

CJ HENDERSON, creator of both the Teddy London occult detective series and the Piers Knight supernatural investigator series, among so many others, is a legendary figure amidst the struggling writers of our great land. Defiant of punctuation and grammar rules, scornful of outlines, contemptuous of the writing found in "real" outlets such as *The New Yorker,* favoring genre fiction and pulp formats, and other means of expression which actually attempt to entertain people, he has somehow managed to get nearly 80 books into print, despite the fact he is hated and despised by the literary intelligentsia of almost every nation. For more information on this truly brilliant/sad/mediocre (take your pick) talent, please feel free to drop in at www.cjhenderson.com. The hideously lonely author welcomes all to his electronic doorstep.

STUART JAFFE is the author of *The Malja Chronicles*, a post-apocalyptic fantasy series, *The Max Porter Paranormal-Mysteries*, *The Bluesman* pulp series, and *After The Crash* as well as the short story collection, *10 Bits of My Brain*. Numerous other short stories have appeared in magazines and anthologies. He is the co-host of *The Eclectic Review* — a podcast about science, art, and well, everything. For those who keep count, the latest animal listing is as follows: one dog, five cats, one albino corn snake, one Brazilian black tarantula, three aquatic turtles, assorted fish, one lop-eared rabbit, twenty chickens, and a horse. Thankfully, the chickens and the horse do not live inside the house.

EDWARD J. MCFADDEN III juggles a full-time career as a university administrator and teacher, with his writing aspirations. His first novel, a mysterious-dark-thriller called *The Black Death of Babylon,* is now available from Post Mortem Press. His steampunk fantasy novelette, *Starwisps*, was recently published in the anthology *Fantastic Stories of the Imagination* and his novella *Anywhere But Here* is scheduled for publication in 2013 by Padwolf Publishing. He is the author/editor of six published books: *Jigsaw Nation, Deconstructing*

Tolkien: A Fundamental Analysis of The Lord of the Rings (eBook format released Fall 2012), *Time Capsule, The Second Coming, Thoughts of Christmas,* and *The Best of Pirate Writings.* He has had more than 50 short stories published in places like *Hear Them Roar, CrimeSpree Magazine, Apocalypse 13, Terminal Fright, Cyber-Psycho's AOD, The And,* and *The Arizona Literary Review.* Over the last seven years he has written six novels, all of which are at various stages of rewriting and submission for publication. He lives on Long Island with his wife Dawn, their daughter Samantha, and their mutt Oli. See www.EdwardMcfadden.com for all things Ed.

KT PINTO - awarded 2012's Best Author on Staten Island - writes about vampyres, mutants, witches, merfolk, werebeasts, deities, courtesans, criminals, zombies and pop stars... sometimes all in the same story. For more information, go to www.ktpinto.com.

PAUL POPIEL is a writer, photographer and gamer who lives outside of Philadelphia. He's currently shopping his novels set in Philopolis to publishers and agents. When not shooting faeries, trolls, superheroes and stranger things with a camera, he can be found at conventions or haunting coffee shops working on a novel or short story. He writes video game and movie reviews for www.Leviathyn.com, with a focus on horror, sf and fantasy.

BUD SPARHAWK is a short story writer who has sold numerous science fiction stories to *Analog, Asimov's,* and other widely circulated magazines. He has been a three-time Nebula novella finalist. His work has appeared in several anthologies as well as print, audio, and on-line media both in the United States and overseas. His stories appear most frequently in *Analog,* less so in *Asimov's* and annually in the *Defending the Future* series of anthologies. He has two print collections (*Sam Boone: Front to Back* and *Dancing with Dragons*) one mass-market paperback (*VIXEN*), and several eBook collections and novels. Bud is currently the Treasurer of SFWA and a member of SIGMA. He maintains a weekly blog on the writing life at budsparhawk.blogspot.com. A complete bibliography of stories, articles, and other material can be found at his web site: www.budsparhawk.com.

With over a million words in print, **PATRICK THOMAS** keeps busy writing the popular fantasy humor series Murphy's Lore (*Tales From Bulfinche's Pub, Fools' Day, Through The Drinking Glass, Shadow Of The Wolf, Redemption Road, Bartender Of The Gods, Nightcaps and Empty Graves*) as well as the After Hours spin offs *Fairy With A Gun, Fairy Rides The Lightning, Dead To Rites* and *Lore & Dysorder.* His Mystic Investigators series has grown to include the books *Bullets & Brimstone* and *From the Shadows,* both with John L. French and *Once*

More Upon A Time and the upcoming *Partners In Crime*, both with Diane Raetz. He co-edited *Hear Them Roar* and *New Blood*. Patrick's humorous advice column Dear Cthulhu has been collected in *Have A Dark Day, Good Advice For Bad People* and *Cthulhu Knows Best*. A number of his books are part of the set and props department at the CSI television show. He was voted Preditors & Editors favorite author of 2010 and first runner up in 2011. Laurence Fishburne's production company Cinema Gypsy Productions has taken a film and television option on Patrick Thomas' urban fantasy *Fairy With A Gun*. As an artist his work has graced covers for Dark Quest, Padwolf and Marietta, interiors and a cover for Space & Time magazine, a cover for Cemetery Moon magazine and comic covers for Ghostman. A mockumentary about him has recently surfaced on Youtube. To learn more, drop by www.patthomas.net.

JEFF YOUNG is a bookseller first and a writer second – although he wouldn't mind a reversal of fortune. He received a *Writers of the Future* award for "Written in Light" which appears in the 26th *L. Ron Hubbard's Writers of the Future* Anthology. He's been published in: *Realms, Neuronet, Trail of Indiscretion, Cemetery Moon, Realms Beyond,* and *Carbon14*. Jeff has contributed to the anthologies *By Other Means, Best Laid Plans, In an Iron Cage: The Magic of Steampunk* and has stories in the forthcoming *Clockwork Chaos, Ministry of Extraordinary Weapons, TV Gods* and *Gaslight and Grimm*. He also serves as an editor for Fortress Publishing on their Drunken Comic Book Monkeys line. Jeff has led the Watch the Skies SF&F Discussion Group for more than twelve years.

C. L. WERNER was a diseased servant of the Horned Rat long before his first story in *Inferno!* magazine. His Black Library (Games Workshop's publishing arm) credits include the Warhammer Hero books *Wulfrik* and *The Red Duke, Mathias Thulmann: Witch Hunter*, the ongoing saga of Grey Seer Thanquol and the *Brunner the Bounty Hunter* trilogy. His first full-fledged foray into the gothic sci-fi universe of Warhammer 40K occurred in 2012 with *The Siege of Castellax*. He has also written several fantasy stories about the wandering samurai Shintaro Oba for Rogue Blades Enterprises. Currently he is laboring upon further installments of the Black Plague series for Warhammer's Time of Legends line, as well as other projects far too insidious to name. An inveterate bibliophile, he squanders the proceeds from his writing on hoary old volumes - or at least reasonably affordable reprints of same - to further his library of fantasy fiction, horror stories and occult tomes. Visit the author's website at www.vermintime.com.

ABOUT THE EDITORS

JAMES R. STRATTON is a chameleon. By day, he is a mild-mannered government lawyer, and lives with his wife and children in southern Delaware. But he's been an avid fan of speculative fiction all his life, and began writing genre fiction 20+ years ago. In recent years he's been forging his dark alter ego of genre fiction author through publication of his tales in venues like *Big Pulp*, *Ennea* (published in Athens, Greece) & *Nth Degree Magazine*. The appearance of his first foray into the world of poetry in *The Broadkill Review* is but another step in his master plan. Soon he will step into the light with his story in this anthology and in the "Paper Blossoms, Sharpened Steel" Anthology of Oriental fantasy from *Fantasist Enterprises*. His final reveal, the novel "Loki's Gambit", is under review for possible publication in 2013, when he will finally step into the brilliant light of day, triumphant.

ROBERT E. WATERS has been publishing fiction professionally since 2003, with his first sale to *Weird Tales*, "The Assassin's Retirement Party." Since then, he has sold over 20 stories to various online and print magazines and anthologies, including stories to *Padwolf Publishing, The Black Library, Dragon Moon Press, Marietta Publishing, Dark Quest Books, Mundania Press, Nth Degree/Nth Zine*, and the online magazine *The Grantville Gazette*, which publishes stories set in Baen Book's best-selling alternate history series, *1632/Ring of Fire*. From time to time, he also writes short fiction reviews for *Tangent Online*. He also served for seven years as an assistant editor for *Weird Tales*. Robert is currently living in Baltimore, Maryland with his wife Beth, their son Jason, their cat Buzz, and a plethora of tropical fish who like to play among the ruins of a sunken Spanish Galleon. His website is: www.roberternestwaters.com.

It's the end of the world as we know it....

Now available from

PADWOLF
PUBLISHING

v i s i t   p a d w o l f . c o m

More GREAT Science Fiction!

THE STARSCAPE PROJECT

As his quest begins, an artificial intelligence life form enters the galaxy and launches a series of covert attacks against the Empire. The Teconeans assume that the Federation is responsible, and galactic peace is about to unravel. As Stryker chases his nemesis into Teconean space, he finds himself thrown into the middle of the battle. Knowing that Earth will be the aliens' next target, Stryker must decide whether to let them destroy the Empire, or to join forces with his Teconean enemies against the invaders. The key to the mysterious aliens lies buried on the moon of Kennedy Prime, and it's up to Stryker to solve the puzzle before war begins. The fate of the galaxy is at stake.

ZONE OF THE TENTH DGREE

In 1912, an alien ship crash lands in the Atlantic ocean, setting up a secret colony that remains undetected for centuries, allowing them to manipulate some of the most important events in human history -- from the sinking of the Titanic to the Bermuda triangle to global warming. Now, the technology of the 26th century has discovered the aliens' distress beacon, and it's a race against time as the Navy tries to stop a terrorist armed with a nuclear weapon from destroying the colony and triggering an all-out war as the mother-ship approaches

Now available from

PADWOLF® PUBLISHING

v i s i t   p a d w o l f . c o m

IT'S A CRIME TO MISS THESE GREAT STORIES!

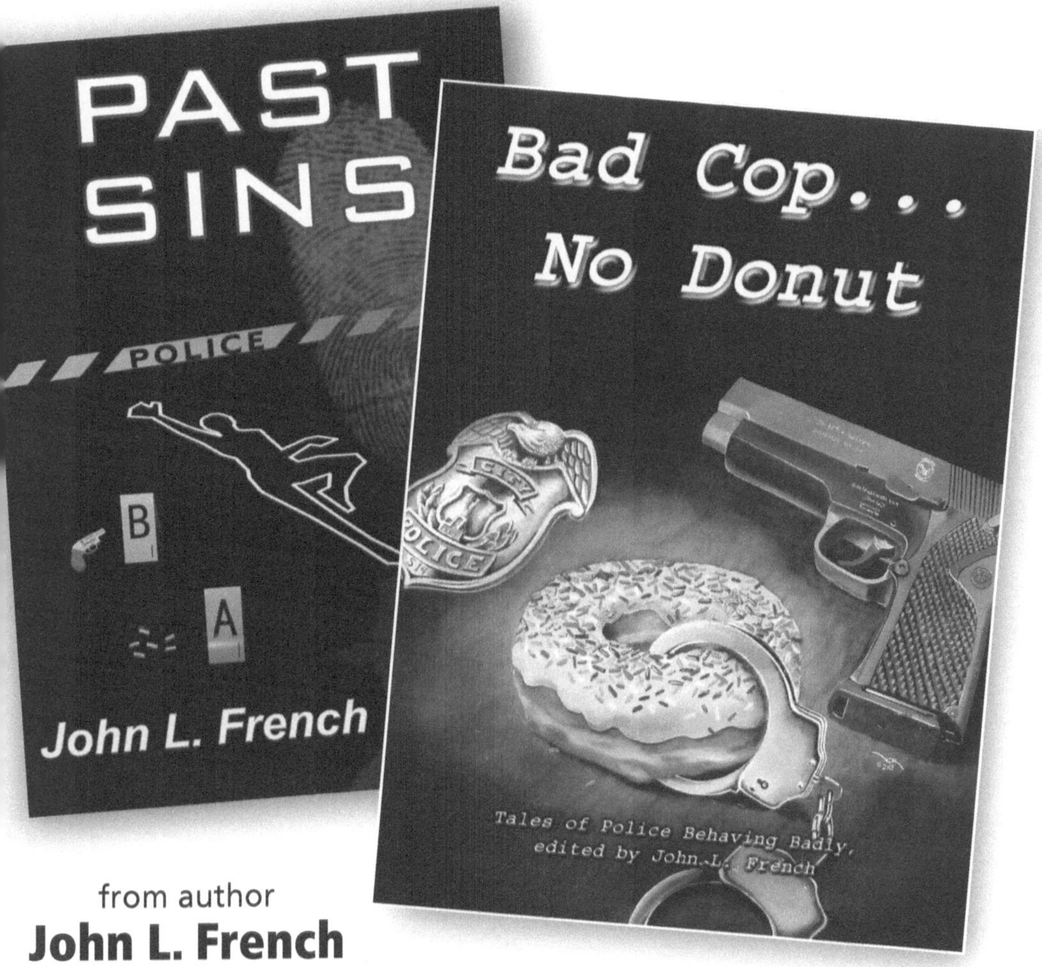

from author
John L. French

PADWOLF PUBLISHING